THREE BONE ANTHOLOGY 3

THREE BONE
ANTHOLOGY 3

T.K. WRATHBONE

☠ Royal Star Publishing ☠

Skull & Bone is an imprint of Royal Star Publishing
www.royalstarpublishing.com.au

First edition paperback published in 2018
All Rights Reserved, Copyright ©T.K. Wrathbone 2018

Trade Paperback ISBN: 978-1-925683-82-0
Large Print Paperback ISBN: 978-1-922307-06-4
Case Laminate Hardcover ISBN: 978-1-922307-07-1
Dust Jacket Hardcover ISBN: 978-1-922307-08-8
The Howler e-book ISBN: 978-1-925683-00-4
Shadow Walkers e-book ISBN: 978-1-925683-37-0
Faded e-book ISBN: 978-1-925683-99-8
The Bones of Wrath: Ghosts e-book ISBN: 978-1-925683-69-1
A catalogue record for this book is available from the National
Library of Australia.

Cover design: Royal Star Publishing and Odyssey Books
Cover photos: istock.com/Koya79
Typesetting in Minion Pro by Royal Star Publishing

CONTENTS

THE HOWLER

CHAPTER ONE

"Hey Ben, you comin' to the Halloween party next week?" Sam Almaw asked his schoolmate. "Nathan said you were." The boys were in the school yard, yelling back and forth across the quad during lunch.

"Yeah, I'm comin'," Ben Kingston yelled back. At thirteen and six feet tall, he was the tallest in their grade, having begun a growth spurt the year before. "Mum changed her mind and said I could come, so I am." He bounced the basketball hard enough for it to bounce up and into the basket. "Score," he yelled and ran around his group of friends with both arms in the air. They yelled, cheered and whistled back. Ben came to a stop in front of Sam. "What *you* wearin'?"

"Dunno," Sam replied, throwing his sandwich wrapper into the bin. "Whatever it is, it's gonna be somethin' *you've* never seen."

"Yeah, I bet." Ben rolled his eyes. "You'll come up with somethin' we've all seen before. Last year you dressed as a spaceman, and so did three other kids. The year before you were SpongeBob, and so were five other kids. And the year before that you came as an alien, and so did *ten* other kids. Ideas are hard to come by round here. Ain't no costume you can come up with that no one else will be doin'." He went back to playing basketball.

Sam cast a sideways glance at his best friend, Elliot Gunfield. At twelve years of age, Elliot wouldn't be having his thirteenth birthday until December first. Sam's would come before that at the end of October. Meanwhile, all their friends had turned thirteen. The dreaded thirteen. The teen number that finally made them *teen*agers. Except for him and Elliot. "Hey El, what ya wearin'?" He studied Elliot's dark brown hair and matching eyes, but in some light, you could swear both were black.

Elliot shrugged. "Dunno. I'm trying to come up with something different too. I don't want to look like all the other kids. I want to win the prize for best dressed."

"Don't we all." Sam packed up his bag ready for the last class of the day. "But it always seems to be Gretchen that wins it."

Gretchen Merryweather was a girl from their class who always wore the most elaborate costumes. She always won year after year, as their school consisted of both primary and high schools and they simply moved up as a class each year, so it annoyed *everyone* else.

"And this year, I want to beat Gretchen at her own game," Elliot said. "I don't know what she's wearing, or what she's doing, or how she does it, but

I want to beat her." Elliot clenched his hand around his soda can and crushed it. His eyes had narrowed and his lips pursed because he was dead serious about beating the self-absorbed, self-appointed queen of the school.

Sam stared at his friend's face. He figured Elliot had a crush on Gretchen, but didn't want to admit it. Everyone suspected, but no one said anything, and Elliot certainly didn't say anything. But it simmered below the surface, like now. "So…" Sam pouted and raised a brow. "What are you comin' as then?"

"Dunno. But I'm gonna beat Gretchen." Elliot slammed his can into the bin as the bell rang.

The boys grabbed their bags and met up with Ben and their schoolmates, jostling and laughing their way into the science lab for the afternoon double class where they took their seats behind the benches.

"Afternoon, class," Mr Appleby said as he walked in. "Everyone in their seats? We're going to be talking DNA and genetics this afternoon."

They quickly settled down and listened to Mr Appleby explain in simple terms DNA, genetics, and diseases that could be passed down from parent to child throughout generations.

"Can being a show off be passed down?" Elliot asked, waving his hand in the air. His pointed look was at Gretchen, but she had her back to him so he couldn't see her face from two rows behind her.

"No, Elliot." Appleby smiled. "Show-off-ness is a learned trait, not a genetic one." At thirty-five he had studied to be a teacher of high school science and was happily ensconced at Betton High.

"What about being a general pain in the bum and acting like you're better than everyone else," Elliot went on, his eyes still pointed at Gretchen.

Appleby noticed. "Elliot, all of that is learned and acting like that is a choice. *None* of it is genetic."

"You sure?" Elliot asked, his eyes not leaving Gretchen as they burned through her back.

She finally turned around and saw him staring. "You're just jealous, Elliot Gunfield. You can't stand that someone is better than you and that person is a girl." She flipped her long light brown braid over her shoulder before turning to the front.

"Jealous!" Elliot spat as everyone in class sniggered behind their hands, but he didn't notice because he was so focussed on Gretchen two rows ahead of him. "Of *you*?"

She swung her head back to look over her shoulder at him. "Yes."

Elliot seethed. "Of all the low down—"

"That's enough!" Appleby stepped between them so they couldn't see one another. "Enough," he warned. "We are here to study DNA, not snipe and bite at each other. So, stop it now." He raised a brow in defiance at Elliot. "No more."

Elliot finally looked him in the eye. "Yes, sir."

"Good." Appleby got on with the class, but Elliot and Gretchen kept glaring at each other with daggers flying back and forth.

"In some cultures," Appleby was saying, "there are stories of DNA being passed down from fathers to sons where they're vampires, werewolves, zombies, and moths even. Personally," he waved a hand, "I think it's all a load of hooey and don't believe it. But many cultures do, and you should respect a culture whether *you* believe it or not."

"So, they're folklore?" Sam asked. "Made up stories to scare people?"

"You might think that," Appleby paused and stared thoughtfully at Sam, "and you'd be more than entitled to. Stories are passed down from family to family, and people swear they see the beasts or animals or things themselves. The story gets wilder and wilder, and soon you don't know who or what to believe; whether it's real, or whether it's just a tale they're telling to scare you."

"Have these things ever been reported by scientists or cops?" Sam went on, fascinated by the topic.

"Well," Appleby moved on. "Some claim to have reported them. There are some stories that have been "documented"," he made quote marks with his fingers, "cases from scientists who have written an account of things that happened, but they are long dead, and we don't know what they *actually* saw *if* they saw it at all." Appleby stopped at the front of the classroom. "Folklore, fantasy, rumours, family stories, doesn't mean that these were actual things that happened."

"But we don't know that they don't happen either," Sam interrupted. "You told us diseases were genetic. So, then those diseases or things can be too.

If cancer cells or diabetes can be inherited, then why can't things like being vampires, werewolves, monsters," he shrugged, "be inherited too? If it's a disease and can be inherited, then it's possible. Just coz we don't understand it, doesn't mean it doesn't exist in some far away country or race of people. Who knows, maybe there's some tiny little island in the middle of nowhere that we don't know about, where giant apes or dinosaurs still exist or live. How do we know? How do we *not* know? Because the world is a very complex creature that still holds many secrets that none of us have discovered. Just because *you've* never seen it, doesn't mean it doesn't exist."

Appleby's eyes were twinkling, his head moving up and down. "You're absolutely right, Sam. Just because we haven't seen it, doesn't mean it doesn't exist, and there are many small islands and cultures we are yet to discover. On that point, you are correct. We do not know everything on this planet," he told the class. "We assume we know everything, but we actually don't. We are still surprised by science. The clues we find can lead to a big breakthrough in research. We're finding diseases all the time and coming up with vaccines and cures. The world and science is still a huge mystery that we will never truly solve." He glanced back at Sam and smiled. "You saw that fright night movie run at the theatre last weekend, didn't you?"

In the lead-up to Halloween at the end of the month, the local movie theatre had been running scary creature movies on the weekends.

Sam grinned. "Haven't missed one."

"Well, your imagination is what science is after. If you can think outside the box and ask *why* a lot, and add that to a very active imagination, who knows how far you could go." The bell rang and Appleby looked up at the clock. "Time for home. Don't forget to read chapter four of your textbooks by next class," he called as the kids rushed out the door. He thought about Sam as he packed up his books and the wild imagination the kid had. *The irony is, Sam's right,* he thought as he walked to the staff room. *We don't know what's on some tiny island somewhere. What mutated gorillas scientists have come up with. For all we know, there really is an island with giant dinosaurs roaming across it, or huge apes the size of fifty-storey buildings. We just don't know.*

*****

In the queue for the bus, the kids all elbowed each other to push in.

"*So,* what was that about?" Sam asked Elliot. "You got angry at Gretchen."

"She makes my blood boil, the snot-nosed little princess," Elliot spat. "I hate her." He crossed his arms and scowled so deeply his eyebrows met in the middle.

Sam noticed how his friend's eyes looked like his cat's eyes when he was angry. Feline, flashing, fiery. He shuddered slightly as a chill flew down his spine.

"Besides, don't worry about me," Elliot ranted. "What was all that about creatures really existing?" He had been going to the movie theatre with Sam on the weekends for the creature marathons, but hadn't put a second thought into it.

Sam shrugged. "Why not? If diseases like cancer and diabetes exist to be passed down, why can't other things? I find it fascinating."

"Yeah, well," Elliot huffed as the bus pulled up. "I don't. I just want to sit and watch a movie and get scared, that's all I want." They checked their tickets and took their seats. "I have no interest whatsoever in whether that stuff actually exists."

"Well, I do." Sam swayed gently as the bus pulled onto the road. "I find it really interesting, especially the voodoo hoodoo that goes on in some countries. You know what you're wearin' to the party?"

"Nuh! I'm hoping to get some inspiration from the movies this weekend. You still going?" Elliot settled back in his seat and calmed down a little as Gretchen had taken a different bus.

"Absolutely!" Sam said. "I don't get to watch this stuff at home. Mum and Dad won't let me. Say I'm too young and I'll have nightmares."

"Like last weekend?" Elliot chuckled. "You woke up *how many times* during the night?" Sam had stayed at Elliot's for the weekend and bunked in with him. "I heard you moaning and groaning all night."

Sam scowled. "I was not. I was just digesting the information in my brain."

Elliot rolled his eyes. "Yeah…sure you were."

CHAPTER TWO

The boys went to the movie theatre on Saturday for a five-movie run. *The Blob, Invasion of the Body Snatchers, The Thing, Dracula,* and *Werewolves in London.* They were going to be there for all five movies, and were glad that food was cheap.

Settling in with popcorn and drinks at ten a.m., they laughed through *The Blob* and threw popcorn at the screen with everyone else. *The Body Snatchers* had them shaking their heads at the corny storyline. *The Thing* had them jumping out of their seats and lifting their feet off the floor, scared something was going to reach out and pull them under. *Dracula* had them wrapping their hands around their necks, and *Werewolves* freaked them out even though they laughed at the fake wolves. When it was all over they walked outside into the chilly late afternoon air and heaved huge sighs of relief.

"I am *so glad* that's over." Sam exhaled. "I was actually starting to feel a little freaked out in there."

"A little!" Elliot scoffed as they pulled their bikes from the racks. "You were *plenty* freaked out."

Mounting, he waited for Sam to sort out the chain on his bike.

"I was," Sam admitted. "Some of those freaked me out big time." He shuddered against the cold air finding its way down the back of his coat. "Let's get out of here." With a glance around, he got on his bike and they rode off for Elliot's house.

Making their way out of town, they had to ride past the wooded area that shielded the road from the river. The woods went on forever along the river bank, but there was only about a kilometre of it to go past. Elliot lived out of town on the outskirts, and while there were houses and suburbs to the right, the woodlands to their left made them scared and eager to get home in the fading dusk.

A scathing howl tore through the woods and they skidded to a halt.

"What was that?" Elliot stammered, his knuckles white from gripping his handlebars.

The howl repeated, making the hairs on the back of his neck stand up. Elliot peered into the dark woods, unable to see much in the fading light. His heart hammered in his chest as the howl came a third time.

Closer. Louder. Angrier.

"Elliot." Sam stiffened. "Let's get out of here." He started pedalling madly down the road only to realise Elliot wasn't with him. Looking over his shoulder, he saw Elliot still rooted to the spot and did a skidding turn. Racing back to his friend, he yelled, "What are you doing? Come on." He pushed

Elliot into gear and they raced down the road to the turn that took them to Elliot's home.

They sped into the yard, dumped their bikes around the back and slammed through the back door, shutting and locking it behind them.

"You kids hungry?" Mrs Gunfield yelled from the kitchen. "I got fried chicken and wedges."

Breathing heavily, the boys looked at each other, unable to shake off the fear they had just felt. Their eyes were wide and their mouths open to gulp in air.

Mr Gunfield walked from the lounge room, down the hall, and into the kitchen, seeing the boys huffing. "Must have made good time coming home. Must've been hungry for Sharon's fried chicken." He grinned and kept on moving.

Finally, breathing normally, they removed their coats and hung them on the wall rack and sat down to dinner. They made small talk with Elliot's parents and washed the dishes. Afterward, they huddled in Elliot's room, talking about the sound they'd heard.

"What do you think it was?" Sam was sitting on the floor with his back against Elliot's bed. His knees were under his chin, and his arms were wrapped around them tightly. "Have you ever heard it before?"

"No." Elliot stared at the window from his spot on his bed. He couldn't see out as his curtains were drawn tightly over it. "Never heard anything like it."

"Do you know of anything lurking in the woods? A stray dog, a cat, an animal that may have wandered in from the river?" Sam asked.

"No, nothing." Elliot shook his head. "I've lived here for all my life and I've never heard it before. No stories, no howls, no nothing."

"I wonder what it was," Sam mused. "It was definitely loud. I wonder how big it would be."

"Dude! I don't care. There cannot be *anything* in there that makes that sound." Elliot's head kept shaking. "That *cannot* be real."

"So…some*one* howled to scare people off?" Sam thought about it. "I doubt it. What could be worth scaring people away from?"

Elliot shrugged. "Dunno. But that was scary shit. Did you hear it crashing through the woods?"

"No. I must have missed that part," Sam murmured, frowning as he thought about Elliot's words. "It was crashing through the woods? Are you sure?"

"I heard branches breaking and stuff." Elliot remembered the sound. "Someone or something was definitely smashing through the woods towards us." He blinked and looked at the back of Sam's head as he sat behind him with the wall behind *him* so he couldn't be grabbed from behind.

"Did it sound big or small?" Sam tilted his head.

Elliot thought. "Big."

"I definitely know those howls were creeping *me* out. Unless someone has taken some sort of cat or dog howl and run it through a computer program to make it louder."

"Dunno, dude. But I know I won't be able to go to sleep tonight," Elliot said, clutching his pillow to his chest. He was glad his parents had locked up the house after dinner.

Sam sighed. Maybe the movie marathons weren't such a good idea after all. They were giving him the heebie-jeebies and he didn't like it. Not one bit.

*****

After a fitful night, the boys decided it was just some prankster playing jokes on people and rode into town to watch the final set of movies. Halloween was a week away, and the theatre was planning the last Halloween movie run, so this was the last time to watch on a weekend. They sat through *Godzilla, Frankenstein, Creature from the Black Lagoon, The Fly,* and *The Mummy.* It was five-thirty when they got out to part ways. Elliot heading for his house, and Sam for his on the other side of town.

"Why don't you get your dad to pick you up?" Sam asked as they unhooked their bikes from the racks.

"I'll be okay," Elliot said. "It's still early and light. I'll ride on the other side of the road so I'm not near the woods."

"Sure?" Sam hefted his backpack on his back and clicked the strap into place to keep it on while he rode.

"I'm sure. See you tomorrow at school." Elliot waved as he rode away.

Sam frowned, but didn't follow. Instead, he rode for his own home and his own family, and his own warm bed for the night. Plus, he had work to do.

*****

The next day Sam met Elliot for lunch. "How'd you sleep last night?"

Elliot blinked. His eyes were wide, his ears unhearing. He'd been mute all day, unable to hear his teachers, his friends, unable to see anything, but somehow managed to still make it through. He said nothing.

"Elliot?" Sam studied his friend's face and knew something had happened. "What the hell did you do? What happened? Did something happen on the way home?" He poked Elliot's arm, then his face. "Elliot? You in there?"

Elliot blinked. Elliot swallowed. Elliot turned toward his friend. But he still said nothing.

"You stopped at the woods," Sam said. "You said you wouldn't!" Rolling his eyes, he threw his hands up in disbelief. "You said you wouldn't. *Why* did you stop at the woods?"

Elliot blinked. Elliot swallowed. Elliot opened his mouth. "It howled."

"Then you ride harder and faster until you get home," Sam said. "Hang on, you left the movie theatre at five-thirty, plenty of time to get home before dark. Why did it howl?"

"Dunno," Elliot managed. "But…" The faraway look came into his eyes. "It came crashing through the brush."

"Why did you stop then? Why didn't you go home?" Sam asked, exasperated.

"Dunno," Elliot murmured. "I was racing past, but something made me slow down. Like I was being drawn to it, like a magnet. I stopped and listened then heard it howl. Then I heard it come crashing through the woods. I couldn't move. I couldn't breathe. I just stared at the woods and heard it come crashing towards me and then it stopped. It all just stopped." His eyes were glassy, scared. "All was quiet. There was no howling, no crashing, no nothing. But I couldn't move. I just stayed there looking at the woods. And then..."

"Then?" Sam asked, intrigued and scared at the same time.

"Then I heard a low throaty sound and saw..." Shudders went through his body and he fell to the ground, jerking.

"Elliot?" Sam just stared down at his friend. "Elliot?"

"He's having a seizure," Ben yelled as he ran over. "Get a teacher, get the nurse. He's having a fit." He held Elliot while the fit continued.

A couple of kids raced away and returned with teachers who waited while Elliot calmed down. Others raced away for the nurse.

"Fit?" Sam stared dumbfounded down at his friend as he lay on his side. "But he's not epileptic."

"Is he diabetic?" Mrs Stewan asked from her spot beside Elliot.

"No." Sam stared at the scene before him. He'd

known Elliot all his life and had never seen him fit, never heard of fits, and never been told by his parents of fits. So why was Elliot having a fit?

The nurse rushed over and took charge until the ambulance came. The paramedics bundled Elliot up and took him to the hospital. The school bell rang, and most of the kids disappeared.

Except for Sam. He had no idea what was going on, but he knew it had to do with the howling in the woods. Elliot had been about to say something before the fit, but what? What had he done? What had he seen? What had he heard? *What isn't he telling me?* Sam frowned. *What isn't Elliot telling me about?* He looked up at the teacher as he was led to the nurse's room and given some water to revive his flagging spirits.

A half hour later, after talking to the counsellor, he was allowed to go to class for the rest of the afternoon. He couldn't concentrate. Maths was not important when his best friend had fitted right in front of him. Fitted from something, not epilepsy, not diabetes. Because Elliot didn't have those things, so what had caused it?

He leaned his head in one hand and flicked his pencil back and forth with the other. *What did Elliot do last night? Why did he stop? Why did he stay there to hear it? Wait, he said it had crashed through the woods and then stopped. Then he heard a throaty growl and saw... That was the last word he'd said before collapsing. Saw... Saw what? Saw the thing? Saw what it was? Did it scare him? Hurt him? What? What had happened to Elliot in the half hour from when I left him to when he should have gotten home? Why didn't he go straight home like he promised? Why did he stop to listen? Stop and hear? Stop and see? What did he see? What was it that made him so scared out of his brain? What was it that made him have a fit?*

CHAPTER THREE

After school, Sam rang his parents for permission to go and see Elliot and took the bus to the hospital. He found him in the kids' ward watching TV. "Well, you look all right. What's wrong with you?"

Elliot glanced from the TV to his friend. "Nothing. They couldn't find any reason why I fitted, but want me to stay in for the rest of the week or something."

"So you get a week off school. Cool." Sam dumped his bag on the floor and sat next to Elliot on the bed. "What *is* wrong with you? Do you have epilepsy?"

"Nope," Elliot replied, scrolling through the channels. "They have absolutely no idea why it happened. That's why they want to keep me in. For more tests."

"But if you aren't epileptic..." Sam thought about it. "Tell me what you were going to say before you jerked like a weirdo. You said you heard it and saw... Saw what? What did you see?"

Elliot blinked. "I *really* don't want to talk about it." He went quiet and looked away with a frown.

"Because you don't remember, or you crapped your pants?" Sam joked.

A brief smile lit up Elliot's face. "I didn't crap my pants. You do that."

"So…spit it out. Maybe it will help you," Sam said, wanting to hear the rest of the story.

Elliot sighed and relented. "I heard thrashing in the underbrush and couldn't move. I was frozen in place. Then it stopped, but I couldn't see anything. Then the threatening growl came from just metres in front of me. It was like really…" He tried to think of the words. "Deep and angry and throaty and then…" His voice wandered off.

"Then?" Sam urged. "What?"

"Then…" Elliot blinked. Elliot swallowed. Elliot opened his mouth. "I saw…its eyes…" A shudder racked his body and he started jerking.

Alarms on the machines sounded and nurses came running in. "Out of the way," they told Sam who almost fell off the bed.

He stood back and watched them work on Elliot's body, trying to revive him, trying to bring him back to normal.

Scared, Sam collected his bag and stood in the hallway until it was done, and they brought Elliot back and settled him comfortably into his bed. Clutching his bag to his chest, Sam waited for the doctor. "What's wrong with him? He's not epileptic, so why is he fitting all of a sudden?"

The doctor scribbled notes on a clipboard and turned to Sam. "We don't know. He was fine by the time they brought him in. But now he's had another fit. We don't know what's causing it."

Sam pondered his next question before asking it. "Will he die?"

The doctor smiled sympathetically. "We don't think so, but we don't know."

"Can he still come to the Halloween party at school this weekend?"

"If he's okay I don't see why not," the doctor replied. "Why don't you say goodbye and he can get some rest."

"Okay." Sam walked silently back to Elliot's bed. "El, I'm gonna go. Not much point me being here when you're sick."

Dazedly, Elliot reached out and grabbed Sam's arm. His lips moved but no sound came out. His eyes were hooded and sick.

Sam leaned closer. "You say something?"

Elliot tried to speak, but nothing came out.

Sam hoisted himself up so he could lean over Elliot and put his ear to his friend's mouth. "Repeat it."

"The...Howl...er..." Elliot rasped.

Sam looked into Elliot's feverish eyes. "Did you say The Howler?"

Elliot's head barely nodded as his eyes closed. He was asleep.

Moving back from the bed, Sam studied his face. Pale, tired, sickly. And he knew regardless of what was going on, he was going to find out what Elliot saw in the woods.

After getting the bus home, Sam finished off some homework before and after dinner, then spent a couple of hours googling The Howler. He found a whole bunch of horror movies like *The Howling,* but couldn't find anything straight out on The Howler. After coming up with different phrases, Sam finally found a page on an old folklore and fables blog. It didn't have much information, just the basics. Cat face with dog-like snout, black fur, red eyes, growls a lot. Only eats people who do wrong, like a rights fighter.

"He's Robin Hood in fur," Sam read aloud. "Saves the good people from the bad people by taking down the bad. But most folks think it's just an old fable made to scare people into being good. There are plenty of sightings, but all in Egypt where the fable originates from. The DNA is passed down from father to son, and on the son's thirteenth birthday he turns into The Howler as part of his initiation into teen years. It is said it only happens to those born on Halloween and you should never say 'The Howler' three times. That is only for conjuring the snarling beast to do your bidding, and even then you may not be able to control it. Three times, huh. Like Beetlejuice and Candyman," Sam mused. "Never say it three times unless you want to bring death and destruction."

Staring at the screen, he sighed. "If it's not real that is. These are just stories. There's no proof, no nothing. Just fables and myths. Besides…*who'd even know* about The Howler to say its name three times? There's no movie, no song, no nothing telling us about it. We know Beetlejuice and Candyman, but we don't know about The Howler." He read back over the description. A cat face with dog-like snout. Well, that would explain the howl. He remembered back to when he had heard it on the way home to Elliot's. It had been horrible. Loud and scary. Seriously, why would you even know how to conjure up such a beast, and who did?

"Yes," he hissed, the thought popping into his head. "If The Howler is in the woods and it can only be conjured by saying its name three times, then who summoned it?" He sat up straighter, his brain working a thousand miles a minute.

Someone had to have summoned it. It had to be in the woods, Elliot had to have seen something for him to think there was something there, and how did he know its name unless he was the one who conjured it? How did he know its name? Did he go looking for it like I did? Did someone tell him? Or did something more sinister happen? What did Elliot see in those woods? He mentioned eyes. Could the eyes have hypnotised him? Whatever those eyes were, could they have done something to his brain? Affected it, made him fit? Dunno, but something happened, and the fits both happened when he started talking about its eyes. So it has something to do with that.

After printing out the website information, he continued looking, but couldn't find anything more, so went in search of fables, TV shows, movies, anything that contained a creature or being that is brought into life by saying it three times or more. He found a wide assortment of varied Candymans from different countries, and a few other references to saying the name three times.

"So, basically the same theme, but different characters, and nothing about The Howler." While printing off the synopses of the movies, he found a manila folder in his desk drawer to put them in. He was going to show Elliot the next time he went to the hospital and try and get to the bottom of it.

By the time he got back to see Elliot, it was Thursday and the Halloween party was Saturday night. "El?" Sam stopped at the doorway, watching his friend who *looked* normal.

Elliot blinked. "Hey Sam, come on in." He waited while Sam pulled a manila folder from his bag before speaking again. "Don't tell me that's homework," he groaned.

"Nope. Something much more interesting," Sam replied and laid the folder on Elliot's lap. "Take a look and tell me if any of it's familiar."

Elliot opened the folder and read through the printouts about the Candyman movies and Beetlejuice before coming to The Howler. "Wow." His eyes widened. "It exists."

"Well," Sam said critically. "It's an old folklore. Has never been proved."

"Yeah, but it's all the…" Elliot looked from the paper to Sam. "I saw this. I heard this. And I…" He blinked. "I don't think I should talk too much about it because I seem to fit when I do."

"Why is that?" Sam was dying of curiosity.

"Dunno. It's like it put some spell on me." Elliot quickly re-read the Candyman synopsis. "Let's just say…The Candyman came crashing through the brush and stopped. He growled and breathed, then Candyman opened his eyes and they were blood-red. Candyman looked inside my brain, he knew what I was thinking, what I was feeling, and he spoke to me…"

Sam leaned forward excitedly. "What did he say?"

"He…" Elliot blinked. Elliot swallowed. "The Candyman told me his name and what he was there for, and not to breathe a word to anyone."

"He did something to your brain?" Sam asked, wondering what his friend had been through.

"I guess, because I've never been epileptic or diabetic or any kind of tic to fit like that, and the doctors can't figure it out. They say I'm not all of that, but that's what it looks like. And if it…did anything to my brain, I dunno what it was."

"Maybe it made you fit. Every time you start talking about it you fit. Except for now because of Candyman. Maybe it did do something to your brain." Sam gathered the papers and stowed them back into his bag. "Did any of the Candyman series seem familiar?"

"No. Just the concept of the…Candyman itself," Elliot finished slowly. "Call multiple times to avenge and destroy, but never really have control over it. It will destroy all who gets in its way."

"Just don't get in its way," Sam said softly. "I

wonder who conjured it up and why it's in the woods."

"Dunno. But all the times I've ridden past them I've never heard or seen anything," Elliot said, rubbing his neck where it met his skull. "I've never heard of any of it until Saturday."

"Someone conjured it up before that. Maybe for Halloween, but lost control of it," Sam mused and bit his lip. "Maybe it's roaming free from its shackles and the person who conjured it up lost control of it."

Elliot shrugged. "I don't want to talk about it, so you can do all of the talking for me. I don't want to see it, hear it, nothing it."

"Well, someone had to summon it forward into this time, this place. The dates on the website said before B.C. to 1779, and they're only the ones people knew about. Nothing has happened in the last two hundred plus years or so, so either everyone forgot about it, or it didn't exist in the first place."

"Then what the hell did I see?" Elliot asked him. "Are you saying I made it all up?"

"No," Sam quickly butted in. "I think you saw *something*; I don't know if it was *that* particular thing and if it was, who knows about it to conjure it into 2002. Who knows enough about these things, this in particular, to bring it forth?"

Elliot yawned. "Dunno, but I'm tired and you need to go home before dark."

"All right. I'll keep digging and you get some rest." Sam squeezed Elliot's arm and left.

CHAPTER FOUR

Curiosity got the better of Sam, and after dinner he went through the phone book looking for someone or something that might help. When that didn't work, he went and asked his parents. "Do you guys know anyone I could talk to about fables and folklore? You know, someone really old."

"And how old is *really* old?" His dad, Geoff Almaw grinned. "To you, really old could be twenty or thirty or forty." He glanced at his wife who was smiling.

"Ha ha." Sam rolled his eyes. "I'm talking like, been here *forever*."

"That *would* make them *really* old," Geoff said. "The only person I know of is Sadie down by the river bank."

"The old kook with the long grey hair who has a hundred cats?" Milly Almaw asked, laughing. "She's crazy, why would you pick her?"

"Because she's the only one I know who's *really* old." Geoff's grin got bigger.

"I suppose, but she is a bit of a whack job and

I'm not sure I want you going near her, Sam. What's it for anyway?" his mother asked.

"Science," he lied. Well, sort of. "Genetics, DNA, kinda turned into folklore and fables." He wasn't sure what else to say so kept it to that. The simple basic truth. Sort of.

"Well…" Milly stared thoughtfully at her son. "You clearly can't go tonight or tomorrow, so you'll have to leave it for Saturday."

"But that's the Halloween party." Sam frowned, wondering if he could fit it all in.

"If you go in the morning then you'll have plenty of time to get home to change into your costume," Milly told him. "Otherwise, wait until Sunday."

"Mmm," he grumbled. "Guess I'll have to go Saturday. Where is she exactly?"

His parents showed him on a map. The old lady didn't live that far from them, just before the edge of town and near the river.

*****

On Saturday at ten, he biked his way to Sadie's house and left the bike outside, leaning against the wall. After wiping his sweaty palms on his jeans, he knocked on the door and waited.

A few cats screeched and a voice called out, "Who is it, what do you want?"

"Um," Sam murmured, suddenly feeling nervous. "My name is Sam…Sam Almaw. I want to talk to you."

The door was flung open and a withered old woman stood in the space. "About what?" She eyed him up and down, taking in his boyish shape and charm.

"Um." He eyed her back. She was short, like him, in old third-hand hand-me-downs full of holes and cat fur. She wore layer upon layer, fingerless gloves on her withered hands, old army boots on her feet. Her face was wrinkled and teeth were missing. "Some folklores and fables and things."

"About *what*?" She cupped her hand behind her ear. "Speak up. I can't hear you."

"Um." Sam gulped. "About folklores and fables," he all but shouted.

"Which ones? I know a few, so which ones in particular are you after?"

"The Howler."

Her face froze, her body stood still, and she stared at him as if he was the devil himself. Then she slammed the door in his face.

"Oi!" He jumped back. "Okay then, kook," he muttered. Blinking, he walked over to his bike and climbed on.

"What do you want to know for?"

He stumbled off and turned around. She was in the doorway watching him intently.

"Well?"

He leaned his bike back against the house and rushed over to the door. "My friend Elliot said he saw it on the way home the other night. He's been in the hospital all week having seizures."

"Mmm," she croaked, rubbing her chin thoughtfully. "You'd better come in." Letting him past, she bolted the door behind him.

The cottage had a lovely view of the river, but the stench of cat urine got in the way. Every surface had a cat on it, and Sam lost count after thirty because they kept moving.

"Sit, sit, and tell me what you know." Sadie ushered him into the lounge. "How does your friend know about The Howler?"

Sam sat awkwardly on the sofa, surrounded by about ten cats, and quickly told Sadie what had happened over the last week.

She nodded here, nervously bit a fingernail there, and finally asked him what *he* knew about The Howler.

"Only what I read on the website I found. That no one else has ever heard of it."

"Just because that electric box doo-daddy thing can't find anything doesn't mean it doesn't exist." Sadie pointed a finger at him. "That's why books were invented, to keep a record of everything that happened in history, so future generations knew about those left behind in the past. Mmm." She rocked back and forth mumbling to herself, and then she shot up out of her chair and into another room.

Sam rolled his eyes and glanced around while she was gone. He heard stuff being moved and thrown, but what interested him most was the way all the cats in the room were staring at him. It was eerie. As though they were possessed, their ears flattened as the anger came to them. He thought they were going to attack, especially when the one right beside him growled in its throat. His eyes slowly lowered to his right to see it ready to attack, but for some reason whatever fear he had went away. And from nowhere he growled in his throat too, scaring the cat and all the others into running away. He cleared his throat as Sadie came back into the room.

"Oh, where are all my kitty cats?" She looked around, but saw only Sam sitting on her couch.

He shrugged. "They just got up and left."

"Mmm." Sadie sat opposite him and fumbled through the heavy, thick book in her hands. "Now, let me see. The Howler, The Howler…" She flicked through the pages.

"Don't say it three times," Sam cried out in alarm, putting his hand out to stop her. "If you say it three times you'll conjure it."

Sadie stared at him and laughed. "Where did you hear such pish posh?" She went back to looking for the pages she was after.

"On the website," Sam said. "It says, if you say its name three times, you'll conjure it up to do your bidding."

"What a load of codswallop." Sadie found the page and ran her finger down it. "It says no such thing here. It's in the blood, so it's all genetic anyway. Nothin' you can say or do to stop it. You can't conjure it up like some crass TV movie. This isn't Candyman." She went back to reading and left

Sam smiling at her reference.

"It reveals itself in boys on their thirteenth birthdays, when born on Halloween, at the exact time they were born. They will turn into the beast and begin the initiation. Once it has been completed, it will occur once a year upon the same night and time until the boy turns twenty. Then once every tenth birthday, thirty, forty, fifty etc. It can last longer each time and occurs in the lead-up to the birthday, to end at the exact time of birth on Halloween."

"Why was it in the woodlands, and how did it make Elliot read its mind?" Sam glanced at his watch, impatient for answers, and impatient to leave for the Halloween party later.

"I'm getting to that," she grumbled, reading on. "The Howler is a cat with a part dog face, mainly the longer snout. It can act like a dog, howling and snarling, its eyes are blood-red, its fangs a foot long. It is a huge beast, on all fours he is as tall as any man, on hind legs as tall as any house, its paws are bigger than a man's head, and one swipe will knock that head right off the man's shoulders for its claws are razor sharp. It is fast and silent and will attack in all manner of speed. It will howl until dark and play in the underbrush and forestry and if you, a human being, are ever faced with such a creature, its eyes will captivate you, hold you, brainwash you, get inside your head and make you do what *it* wants you to. And after, you will remain in its enigmatic grasp. If you ever speak of it, it will know and shock you, making you fit and jerk on the floor. Doctors will find nothing, for there is nothing to find. No lesions, no injury, no reason for the fits. That is why humans must never mention its name."

"That's what happened to Elliot," Sam interrupted excitedly. "But how can we be sure he really saw one and isn't making it up?"

"You heard it howl." Sadie looked at him knowingly.

Sam blinked. Sam swallowed. Sam opened his mouth. "I heard *something* that sounded like howling. But it could have been a wild dog, or someone playing tricks. I didn't *see* anything."

"That doesn't mean your friend didn't." She pointed a finger. "He clearly saw something, and it could very well have been an adult Howler."

"Why an adult?"

"Because you heard the howl, and then your friend saw it the next night. That's two nights it was out. Unless it was two males, but then it isn't Halloween until today. A week ago, it would have been the lead-up to some man's rounded birthday. Know anyone who celebrated a birthday today?"

Sam shook his head. "No."

"What about your friend?"

"Elliot's birthday is December 1st."

"And his father's?"

Sam shrugged. "I don't know."

"Mmm." Sadie finished reading the book. "Well, it is Halloween tonight, and if there *is* a Howler, a Howler is alive. Which will mean carnage."

Sam blinked. "What? What carnage?"

Sadie blinked back. "On the boy's thirteenth Halloween he must feed once he's turned. That is a part of the initiation. It must feed on humans once he's turned into The Howler."

"Oh, my God…" Sam felt sick to his stomach. "There's some kid somewhere turning thirteen tonight who's going to turn into one of those beasts and eat people?"

"Well," she cackled. "It's not to say he lives here in Belmont. He could live in another suburb or town. Just because there was a Howler here in our woods doesn't mean he's *from* here. He could be on the prowl and travelling."

"So what do we do?" Sam's panic was rising. "We have our Halloween party tonight. What if that thing turns up and eats people?"

"If it's a full-grown man it won't, if it's a thirteen-year-old, bad luck, you're dead." She raised a brow.

"Well, gee, thanks for nothing," Sam muttered and stood up to go. "Anything else I need to know before I party to my death?"

"Cats will either bow to it or run from it. Dogs don't care either way, but will never attack. Amulets will not work unless it is an old family symbol signifying safety and protection."

"For The Howler or us?" Sam stared down at her as she curiously stared back.

"The Howler. If he is wearing an amulet, he cannot be harmed. If *you* are wearing it, it will not save you from harm, but it will save you from death."

CHAPTER FIVE

Sam had no idea what his costume was going to be. He'd left it up to his mother, who said she had the most awesome idea of all, and had begged him to let her handle it. He called Elliot after lunch and found his friend home from the hospital and resting. "Are you coming tonight?"

"Yeah. Mum wants me resting until the last minute, then they'll drive me over. They're chaperones anyway, so that's the only way they'll let me go."

"So, what are you coming as?"

"Not telling. Keeping it until the big reveal. You?"

"Dunno, still haven't made up my mind," Sam replied, having no idea what his costume was.

"Okay. I'll see you later. I need to rest before the party," Elliot said.

"See you later." Sam went back to trolling the internet for anything on The Howler until it was dinnertime and time to get ready.

"What the hell is this?" he asked his mother when she presented his costume. It was a mass of black fur.

"Your costume," Milly said. "You wanted something

no one else would be wearing…well, they won't be wearing this." She held it out.

"What is it?" Sam took it and saw it had arms and legs.

"You'll see." His mother's eyes twinkled and she helped him into the costume and zipped up the back.

Sam looked down at the huge paws he had for hands and feet. "Is this a dog or something?"

"Or something." Milly slid the face mask-slash-hood over his head and adjusted it so he could see out of the eyes. "Can you see? Can you breathe?"

"Yes." Sam shifted the mask a bit. "So, what is it?"

"Take a look." She escorted him to the floor-to-ceiling mirror in her bedroom. "All we need to do is put this on." She attached a black collar around his neck with a pendant hanging from it, then turned him around. "What do you think?"

Sam peered through the eyeholes to the mirror and saw a black cat like animal with a part dog face, mainly in the longer snout, terrifying red eyes and snarling fangs. He ripped the mask off and stared in alarm at his mother. "Why would you make this? Why would you make me this costume?"

She looked back, startled. "Because it's a cat. You said you wanted something different that your friends didn't have."

"But this…" He stared at the mask and saw how blood-red the eyes were.

"Well, it's a cat. The ancient Egyptians worshipped them. That's why I put the amulet on the collar, to signify the culture."

Sam frowned. How was he going to turn up to the school Halloween party dressed like The Howler? Not that anyone knew of The Howler except him and Elliot, and he couldn't scare his best friend.

"If you don't want to scare anyone, you can keep the mask off until the party. I sewed some pockets into the front." She showed him. "And you can slip your hands out of the paws through these slots here." Pulling the fur back she showed him how to slip his hands out. "You can keep the mask off so you can see, and slip it on for the costume award."

He fingered the amulet on the collar and remembered Sadie's words that morning.

Amulets will not work unless it's an old family symbol signifying safety and protection. If The Howler is wearing an amulet, he cannot be harmed. If you are wearing it, it will not save you from harm, but it will save you from death.

"What is this?" He'd never seen it before, at home or online.

"*That* is an old family amulet." His mother brushed off the costume. "Signifies safety and protection apparently. Got handed down through the generations on your father's side, but I thought it looked cool on a collar."

Sam stared at her, wondering why. Why did she make him a Howler costume? Why did she use that particular amulet? And why was that amulet in the family in the first place?

"Time to go," Geoff called from downstairs. "I want to take some photos before we leave."

Sam and his mother went downstairs and he posed for photos for his father. Donning the mask, he pretended to be a cat, but felt awkward, weird, as though he was in some weird dream where people did strange things and didn't know why. He removed the mask and tucked it into the pocket for later.

Riding in the back of the car to school just staring out of the window, he looked around for Elliot as they alighted in the car park. His parents were chaperones too, and he knew things wouldn't be easy for Elliot when he saw the costume.

Fortunately, he wasn't in the car park, but Sam kept an eye out as they made their way into the gym where the party was being held. He saw a wide assortment of TV and movie characters, odd costumes he couldn't put a finger on, and luckily not everyone was wearing their head or face mask, so his stayed in his pocket.

"You go and have fun and we'll be over at the refreshments table," his mother told him.

Sam nodded and went in search of Elliot, but found the rest of his friends instead. "Hey cool, love your costumes."

Ben Kingston had come as Rocky Balboa from the *Rocky* movies, Nathan Berry as Doctor Who. There were several Sherlock Holmes and Watsons, Eddie Murphy's *Beverly Hills Cop* character, Axel Foley, a ship's captain, and a plane pilot.

"And what are you?" Nathan arched a brow at Sam's costume.

Sam rolled his eyes. "My mother made me a cat costume. The mask is in my pocket because I couldn't see out of the damn thing." He pulled it out of his pocket half way. "God knows why she made me a cat, but it's all I've got."

"Give us a look at the mask," Ben said.

Sam pulled it out and showed them the blood-red eyes. "It's pretty cool I guess, but kinda creepy too." His fingers slid over the red plastic.

"Yeah, it's creepy," Nathan said. "When are you putting it on?"

"Only when I have to, otherwise I'll have no idea where I'm going or what I'm doing."

"Hey, is that Elliot?" Ben looked over their heads and they turned.

Elliot had come dressed as the Tin Man from *The Wizard of Oz* and made his way clunkily over to his friends.

"Cool costume, El." Sam high-fived his friend. "Glad to see you're out of hospital."

"So am I." Elliot looked at his friends' costumes then stopped at Sam's. "And what are you?"

Sam rolled his eyes. "A cat. Can't see through the mask, so it's in my pocket until later. Did you make yours?"

Elliot blinked at his friend. "A cat? What sort?"

Sam blinked back. "A black one," he joked, waving a hand at his body.

"With a really cool eye mask with blood-red eyes," Nathan cut in. "You should see it. Show him, Sam."

"Maybe later when I need to put it on," Sam deflected. "In the meantime, why don't we get something to eat and drink and see what everyone else is wearing."

Getting munchies and punch from the refreshment table, they stood around checking out all the other costumes. They saw Gretchen in a Dorothy outfit.

"Well, at least you can be her Tin Man," Sam joked. "Did you two talk to each other about your costumes?"

"No, we didn't." Elliot frowned. His outfit was silver sprayed cardboard; each piece hooked to the next so he could still move. The helmet was a bucket with a funnel stuck on top, and he had sprayed silver face paint on to make his skin silver to match.

Gretchen glanced over her shoulder. Her brown braided wig had ribbons in it, and her gingham dress was blue. She had a basket with her small dog Mr Twinkles in it, and she had sprayed her shoes red with glitter. She gave Elliot the once over, turned her nose up, and turned back to her friends who all giggled.

"God, she makes me so angry," Elliot growled through clenched teeth.

"But why?" Ben asked. "Jesus, Elliot, it's just a costume. We're here to party, not to care about who wins a cheesy trophy for best costume. Get over it. We're all sick and tired of hearing it."

Elliot flashed him a surprised look. "I'm just sick

of her winning year after year."

"Dude," Ben said. "After what happened to you this week, a costume and trophy aren't worth worrying about. No one cares; neither should you."

Elliot thought about it a moment and glanced at Sam's costume. "Yeah, I guess you're right."

"Good, let's dance then. I love this song." Ben led the way to the dance floor and they all stood around in groups awkwardly dancing in their outfits.

The hours flew past until they had the costume competition when Sam reluctantly had to put his mask on.

"Don't look, El, keep your back to me," Sam told his friend, who turned away to fume at Gretchen instead. Sam pulled his mask on and adjusted it so he could see out, then popped his hands back into the costume. The teachers and parents came around to judge the best costume, and Sam pulled the mask back off, hastily shoving it into his pocket before Elliot turned around.

Mr Bennett, the school principal, got up on stage and tapped the microphone. "Is this thing on? We have studied the costumes all night and have narrowed it down to three. The third runner up is…Nathan Berry as Doctor Who."

"Oh my God," Nathan blurted, taken by complete surprise. He ran up onstage to collect the ten-centimetre high trophy, waved to his friends, and slipped back into the crowd.

"Second runner up is a pair, Sherlock and Watson, Terry Lockerby and Paul Whatmore."

Terry and Paul high-fived each other and ran up to collect their trophies.

Elliot glanced over at Gretchen who was primping herself. *The arrogance,* he thought. *She thinks she's going to win. Again!*

"And the winner, of the 2002 Betton High School Halloween Costume Party is…" Principal Bennett waited for the drumroll.

Elliot saw Gretchen start walking toward the stage and seethed more.

"Elliot Gunfield as the Tin Man from *The Wizard of Oz,*" Bennett announced.

Gretchen stopped dead.

Elliot's eyes widened, and all eyes were on him. He saw Gretchen turn to look at him, horror all over her face. His friends were slapping him on the back, and Bennett was calling him up to the stage. It was all in slow motion. His lips curled into a smile, and he saw Sam lead him to the stage and push him up the stairs. He made it to Bennett who shook his hand and congratulated him before the school photographer took the picture. Elliot took his trophy and descended into the crowd. It was all a blur and sounded dull, as if he were underwater. His friends all gathered around him, taking him back to the floor to dance, and finally, his hearing came back and the noise blasted into his eardrums. He was back to normal and out of his shock.

"Oi, watch out, El, trouble's on the way," Sam said, spying a very angry-looking Gretchen over his friend's shoulder.

Elliot turned as Gretchen got to him. "Suck it up, princess, you lost, I won."

Gretchen seethed. "*You cheated. Your* parents are chaperones; they should not have voted for you."

"They didn't," Principal Bennett said from behind her.

Gretchen spun around. "What?"

"They didn't vote for him, Gretchen. Chaperones weren't allowed to vote for their children. You didn't receive as many votes as the others did. You didn't win this year, so deal with it. Sometimes we win, sometimes we lose. You need to deal with that for when you're an adult, so no more of these silly accusations. Elliot and the others won fair and square. If you don't like that, don't enter next year," he warned before walking away.

"Exactly!" Elliot exclaimed before turning away.

Gretchen gritted her teeth and clenched her jaw. Her eyes narrowed, her lips pursed. Clenching her fists, she stomped her foot and went back to her friends to complain to them.

"Geez, what a sore loser," Nathan muttered and they went back to dancing.

Sam glanced over at the refreshment table and saw his father leave. Hurrying over to the table, he spoke to his mother. "Where's Dad going?"

"He had to pop out for a few minutes. He'll be back." She smiled and handed him a cup of punch. "Thirsty?"

He pulled his hand out of his paw and took it, downing it in seconds. "Thanks. What's the time?"

"Nine-thirty," his mother said. "Half an hour left, so enjoy yourself."

He went back to the dance floor and partied with his friends until a loud bang on one of the gym doors interrupted them.

CHAPTER SIX

The boys looked up, having heard something, but not sure what it was from the centre of the gym. They saw the kids near one of the double doors moving away from them, looking at each other in alarm.

Bang!

The doors shuddered, but stayed locked.

"Okay everyone, away from the door," Principal Bennett called. "Probably some hooligans playing games."

Bang!

He quickly ushered the kids away as a growling howl sounded outside the door. It was so loud it was heard above the music which was quickly turned off. All stood silently in the gym, looking at the double doors leading to the outside of the building.

The howling stopped, but the banging didn't. This time it was another set of doors. Banging, trying to force its way in. Back to the first set of doors, back to the second set, another howl.

"Everyone up against the back wall. Meredith, call triple zero, tell them we've got a problem," Bennett said.

The kids and parents gathered against the wall of the gym while the teachers kept them all corralled. They cried, murmured, and clung to each other.

"Sam," Elliot whispered. "It's here." He clutched his best friend's arm, fingers digging nails through the fur and into his skin.

"We don't know that." Sam saw the wide-eyed fear on everyone's face except his mother's. "Mum, where's Dad?"

"He went to get supplies," she said calmly, eyeing the doors.

"Why aren't you scared?"

She gazed at him with catlike eyes. "Why would I be?"

That answer freaked Sam out. Here was his mother, as calm as can be, while there was some wild beast outside trying to get in. But she wasn't worried. Oh no, not worried at all. He turned back to Elliot who looked ill under all his face paint. "Ow, El, your nails." He pried his friend's fingers from his arm.

Bang. Howl.

"We have to get out of here," Gretchen cried, huddled with her friends.

Fear filled the room; terror filled their faces. To be trapped inside of a building while some beast was trying to get in was madness. Murmurs and cries grew louder, the crowd grew tighter, and they squashed themselves against the wall as if it would save them from whatever was outside.

"We have to get out of here," Sam whispered. "Is there another door out?"

"The door to the tech building," his mother whispered back. "Then there's a corridor to the main classrooms. We can trap it in here." She went in search of a teacher and told her the plan. They consulted with the principal who nodded, and the door to the tech building was unlocked.

"Move quickly and quietly," Bennett said, just as the door broke off its hinges. Panic hit his face. "One more and it will go. Move it."

"Yowwww," came screeching through the door in a half growl, half howl.

"Move, move." He frantically waved kids through the door as they were led by several teachers, and almost all had passed when the doors burst open and the most inhuman beast pounced into the room.

"Yowwww," it growled, saliva dripping from its foot-long fangs. Its lips were drawn back in a snarl. Its eyes were fiery blood-red, and it set its sights on the people left in the gym. It was taller than man, big, black and furry, and Bennett stood frozen to the spot.

"Go, go." Milly shoved the kids into the tech building, their screams of horror bouncing off the concrete walls. Racing back to the gym door she saw the huge black beast advance on the teachers and students left. She pulled them into the hallway, grabbing their arms, their clothes, pulling as hard as she could to get them out of danger. The beast sensed her, smelt her, and headed straight for those left.

"Mum," Sam screamed from the tech building,

trying to run back, but being held by his friends.

Milly pulled the last few into the hallway and slammed the door as the mighty black beast pounced.

"What the hell was that?" Meredith, the school secretary, gasped. "The cops are never going to believe this."

"Let's go." Milly moved them into the tech building and locked the door behind them, grabbing hold of her son as he ran to her. "I'm okay."

"Oh, Mum," Sam sobbed. "What *is* that thing?"

"Someone's idea of a joke I'm sure," she breathed, brushing his hair away.

"Well, that is some sick joke," Bennett said. "What *is* it? How would they have even made it?"

"Animatronics?" Milly shrugged. "Maybe they used some sort of bulldozer or something to knock down the door then manoeuvred that in."

"It didn't look like animatronics to me," Meredith said. "That looked very real."

"Yowwww," came through behind them.

"We gotta go," Appleby called. "Grab weapons and let's get out of here."

Bang!

They heard the door to the corridor give way and quickly rushed for the hallway to the main building, shutting it tightly behind them.

They stayed in the corridor, classrooms either side, hoping the police would make it soon. In the distance they heard sirens, and heaved sighs of relief as flashing lights bounced into the rooms and off the wall.

"It's The Howler," Elliot whispered to Sam. "It's The Howler come back for me. It's come to get me, Sam. It's come to get me." He slid to the floor, bending or breaking pieces of his costume. But he didn't care. He and his parents had gotten out of the gym, and for now, they were all alive.

"Yowwww," came from outside the building.

"What the hell was that?" Sergeant Dickson asked. He and his men had turned up to find the gym empty, and the doors busted off their hinges. They ran outside to see a huge hulking beast before them, and each pulled his gun from its holster. "Hold it right there," he yelled and then realised he wasn't talking to a human.

The beast turned to stare at them, lips snarling, teeth dripping. Its snout took in their scent, its eyes their shapes.

The police quaked in their shoes as the beast walked forward. It was taller than them, as wide as the patrol cars, and snarling its foot-long fangs at them.

"What the hell is that?" one officer asked, his voice shaking as badly as his arm that held his gun.

"Dunno. Some wild inbred beast I guess." Dickson levelled his gun at the beast so the bullet would land right between its eyes. The blood-red eyes stared into his soul, his brain.

"I am The Howler. You are my servant."

"Huh, what?" Dickson mumbled. "Who said that?"

"Who said what, Sarge?" a constable asked. He knew he had wet himself, but right now, that kinda didn't matter.

"Open fire," Dickson called and pulled the trigger of his gun.

But The Howler was too quick. With a swipe of its paw it decapitated all three officers.

"Oh." Bennett stumbled back from the window. He'd sneaked into a classroom to see what was happening and had seen the beheadings of the three officers. Rushing back to the hallway, he said, "Meredith, call the police and tell them to send the army, our officers have been killed. We need help now."

Meredith nodded and got on her mobile, telling dispatch they needed everyone because they were under attack.

The most frightening growl came from outside. It vibrated the glass in the windows and made them block their ears. It sounded as if a freight train was passing them there in the hallway.

"We've got to get out of here," Gretchen screamed and took off running. Several girls followed, while teachers yelled for her to come back.

"Oh, my God, look." Elliot pointed to the windows.

They looked, and saw the huge beast standing outside the building, staring through the window right at them with its blood-red eyes. It looked ready to spring.

"Let's get out of here," someone screamed, and everyone went running in two different directions as there were only two doors to go through.

"Stay together, or you'll get lost and possibly

killed," Bennett yelled, unable to control the crowd.

Pieces of costumes were left behind in the mad dash for the doors. Some kids went back to the tech building; some kids went upstairs to the second floor, others went to the adjoining Home Ec building, while others managed to get out the back doors and run to the nearest homes for shelter.

The beast heard the new sirens approach and quickly moved to a better vantage point.

Cops, ambulances, and fire engines all turned up. All saw the three dead officers; all saw the busted gym doors. But none saw the beast.

Sam had become separated from his mother, but he and Elliot managed to get back to the tech room and hide in a utility closet, shoving shelves in front of the door to block it. They shuffled back until they were against the wall, eyes never leaving the door.

"It's after me," Elliot whispered. "It wants me."

"Stop talking nonsense," Sam snapped. "If that's the way you feel, get out there and sacrifice yourself so the rest of us don't die." He looked around for weapons, but found only brooms and mops. "We can poke its eyes out with the handles."

"Why would you say that to me?" Elliot asked.

Sam glanced over his shoulder. "Because you're making it about you, and I don't think it has anything to do with you."

CHAPTER SEVEN

Elliot eyed Sam thoughtfully. "How do you know that?"

"Jesus, El. If it wanted to kill you it would have last week when you said you saw it. Why would it bother you now?" He handed him a mop stick. "No, I think it's after something else, *someone* else maybe." He pulled the brush head off a stick and prepared himself. "I don't think it's after you, El."

"Why did you wear that costume?"

"Huh?" Sam looked from the door to his friend, before flicking the light off and making his way back to Elliot in the dark. "Mum made it. I have no idea why. I didn't tell her about The Howler. She doesn't know. She said it's some Egyptian thing. They like cats or something."

A deep throaty growl wafted along the air outside the doors and stopped a moment before it grew louder, deeper, before becoming higher and turning into a yowl.

The boys couldn't see what was happening, but sometime during the howling they got separated, cowering against different walls, behind different shelving units.

The growl started low in the throat, slowly escalating in pitch until the door was pummelled in.

Elliot covered himself with a tarpaulin, hiding from its eyes. He didn't want to see those eyes again. Not ever. He couldn't fight it; he wouldn't dare.

The growl started low in the throat, slowly escalating in pitch until the beast grew into what it would become. It roared like the beast it would soon be.

Elliot knew it was inside the room, but if it didn't have him, that meant it had Sam. Digging deep and finding the courage, Elliot peeked out from under the tarp to see the unholy beast hovering where Sam should have been. In the light coming through the battered-down doorway, he could see Sam's costume lying on the floor, ripped and torn. But there was no sign of Sam.

The beast sensed, heard, smelt him, and turned in his direction.

And finding the courage he never knew he had, Elliot stood, held the mop handle out in front of him, and faced the growling beast. "What did you do to Sam? Did you eat him? Kill him? I'll kill you."

The beast levelled its eyes at the boy before it, dug in its paws, and let out an almighty roar that blew Elliot back against the wall into a shelving unit that toppled down on him, knocking him unconscious. Paint tins fell to add to the pain that Elliot would suffer when he would finally wake.

The beast sniffed the air and tried knocking aside the shelving in front of the door, but decided to simply jump over it. It loped into the tech shed and looked around, sniffing the many scents that wafted around it. It saw flashing lights outside, heard the men yelling, knew it wouldn't be safe to go out, but knew it had to feed. Its head turned to the left and it smelt it; the scent that would lead it. The scent it would follow.

Leaving the tech building behind, it made his way into the upstairs hallway of the main building. Padding without a sound, sniffing for what it sought, it found it in a police officer and a small group of children who screamed while it fed upon the scared man in the uniform.

The kids bolted from the floor and the beast finished up, licking its lips in delight at tasting blood for the first time. Hearing a sound, it moved on, down the hall, down the stairs at the other end and into the Home Ec building where it heard the terrified muffled cries in cupboards, under tables and behind benches. It sniffed the air and headed for the bench behind which the teacher hid. Snarling and growling, it backed the terrified woman up to the bench and zeroed in on her throat.

She tried to scream, but it was cut short as her larynx was ripped out. Rachael Merrin was dead within seconds from blood loss.

The beast fed, licking its mouth, lapping up the blood. The muffled cries of the children reached its ears, but it had no need for the children, just the adults. It finished the food and padded along the hallway. No one else had come into the building. Just the one officer; all the rest had stayed outside. It peered out the windows and saw the emergency services crowded around. The bodies of the officers had been removed, and children were being driven away. But it had a mission and it needed more food. Moving on, the beast found its way outside, sniffing the air, the ground, picking up the scent it needed.

"Hold it right there." An officer dashed out from behind a building and held up his gun. Upon seeing what was before him, he fainted, and The Howler feasted on the easy prey before making its way through the grounds to leave the school behind.

"It just left the grounds, but not before eating a cop," came through Police Chief Erickson's radio. "It just walked off like a normal cat."

"Well, it's not a normal cat, it's a god damn hell beast, so follow it," Erickson barked into his radio. "Everyone spread out. Get the rest of the kids out, go room to room, every building from the gym around. Move, move, move."

All emergency services personnel fanned out across the building and grounds. Teachers joined them, leading the way into each building, each room that was unlocked. They opened the utility closet Elliot and Sam had hidden in, finding Elliot unconscious and Sam's costume ripped to shreds. The paramedics saw to Elliot, and an officer stayed with them until they could get him out.

"We might have a missing child," the officer

radioed in. "I think I found a costume. It's a mess; there's some blood. Either it got the kid, or he's wandering somewhere." He kicked the fur with his foot and the mask was unveiled. "Jesus Christ," he muttered. "The kid was dressed just like it. What the—"

"Sergeant, get that kid out immediately and to the hospital," Erickson replied.

"Sir." Another officer led the paramedics with the stretcher in and stood guard while Elliot was loaded up and rolled out. Both officers followed and went off to the hospital with them.

"My son's missing." Milly Almaw pulled on the Chief's arm. "Sam Almaw, he was with Elliot, but he just got taken away, so where's my boy?" Her eyes were overflowing like Niagara Falls, her face red and blotchy. "My son, where's my son?"

"Your son was with the boy in the closet?" Erickson asked, towering over her with his six-five frame.

"Yes. He was wearing a cat costume. I made it from fake black fur, with big red eyes and everything." She allowed herself a moment of grief. "Where is he?"

"I don't know, ma'am, but we're collecting all the kids and are taking them to the hospital for observation. He'll end up there if he's not found here." Looking down at the petite woman clinging to his arm, he sensed she knew more than he did. He felt that she was different, and not as upset as she wanted him to believe. But then, it could have been the shock. "We'll find him, ma'am, don't worry." He patted her hand before removing it from his arm. "You stay here and watch for those coming out." He left her to see to his duties.

*****

The beast made its way through the streets, a low growl here, a hiss there. It fed upon a lonely jogger out for a late-night run, and a cyclist training for the local bike race. Both were decapitated before being consumed. It was easier to swipe a paw at them as it stopped them dead. So to speak.

It knew it was being followed, and knew it had to lose them, but it was having too much fun to care. What could they do to it? A bullet would not bring it down; a stun gun would have no weight. Besides, it was bigger than them and could kill in an instant. They'd seen it.

As it meandered along, its inner clock told it the time was drawing near. It had somewhere to be and it needed to get there. Now.

It just needed to lose them.

*****

Milly ran toward every child that was brought out of the school. Every group, every teen, but none was Sam. "Where is he?" she wailed. "Where's Sam?"

Chief Erickson kept an eye on her, wondering what her game was. Sure, her kid was missing, and sure she had a right to be upset, but this was different. "We've cleared every building, there are no more students," came through on his radio. He got onto the officer at the hospital. "Are all the kids accounted for?"

"All but one. Sam Almaw is the only one not here." The officer flicked through the list the teachers had complied for him.

Milly heard, as her hearing was impeccable, and she ran over to Erickson. "If my son is not here, and not at the hospital, then *where the hell is he?*"

"Ma'am, I don't know, but we plan on finding out," Erickson told her then turned to the men around him. "We have a missing child. Sam Almaw. His mother can give us a description." He turned back to her, but she was gone, gunning her car and peeling out of the parking lot. "Ah, Jesus. Find out if that thing had a kid with it. Search the grounds; maybe he's wandering somewhere. Get out on the streets and see if you can find him."

The emergency services of Belmont spent the rest of the night cleaning up the mess at the high school, awaiting word on the beast and the boy. But officers didn't find Sam, and they lost The Howler when it disappeared into the woods.

It didn't know what led it there. The scent, the instinct. But it knew that was where it needed to go. It prowled through the jungle like the beast it was. It was big, black, and beautiful. Lithe, smart, and quick footed.

The undergrowth was easy to get through, the

scent easy to follow, and it finally made its way to the last feed of the night before it needed to hibernate. It was already well fed, but just one more wasn't going to hurt. Its snout picked up the aroma of burning wood and cat urine, and saw the lights of the old lady's house in the distance. Silently, it walked up to her door, sniffed, dug its paws in, and growled.

The woman inside knew it was coming and knew what it meant. Her cats sensed it, had warned her, and now she removed her amulet, which she knew would not protect her, from around her neck. She had heard it last week in the woods. Heard its growl echoing, its howl piercing.

But this one was different. Not the same as the other. A son. A child on its thirteenth birthday. Hallows night. But Halloween was nearly over.

Her eyes peered at the wall clock. 11:50. It was nearly over. A boy child born on the ill-fated October 31st, forever destined to become The Howler on his 13th birthday. Forever destined to spend the rest of his life becoming it. Which meant his father was one too. It had to be the adult last week. Now it was the child. He would have been hungry, and if he was at the school's costume party, then he would have fed on them. *I wonder how many are gone?*

The beast pushed its snout against her door, trying to get in. It would have to break it down, but wasn't sure if it could even fit. *Oh well, I'll give it a go.*

Walking about ten feet away, it aimed itself at

the door and charged. The wood held, and all it gave him was a pounding headache. It yowled in pain, shaking its head to get rid of the stars that were circling, and narrowed its blood-red eyes. The growl grew in its throat and it backed up to try again.

The old lady slowly got out of her chair and made her way to the door. Peering through the small window, she saw the blood-red eyes glowing about ten feet away. They stood out in the full moon's beams as it shone down. Sighing, she opened the door and watched it pad forward, towering over her. It's bulk wider than her doorway. Its snout buried itself in her neck to take in her scent, and she knew she would be its last meal for the night. Staring it straight in the eyes she said, "Hello Samuel."

CHAPTER EIGHT

The beast blinked and took a step back, unsure of why the woman called it that. The growl gurgled in its throat and it bared its fangs.

"You are Samuel Almaw, are you not? Son of a Howler, born on Halloween night. Destined to become a Howler on your 13th birthday. It will end at midnight. You have eight minutes before it's over. Do as you will."

The Howler sat on its haunches, tilted its head and gently purred. Its tail softly flapped left and right, and if it weren't so big, people would think it was a normal household cat.

Except it wasn't a normal household cat.

It was a beast of epic proportions, carried down through Egyptian bloodlines from father to son for centuries and generations to emerge on its 13th birthday at the time it was born on Halloween night. It stared at the woman, perplexed as to how she knew these things, and why she was so calm in the face of death.

"Come, Howler, finish your feeding before your

hibernation," Sadie said. "It is my time, and besides, your father is waiting." She had seen the second set of red eyes in the woods, waiting.

The Howler turned its head, knew the scent, and saw it slowly approach. It was the scent it had followed, and now saw that it was bigger, more important. Saw it stop and wait for the job to be over. It growled.

The larger howler growled back and told him what to do.

Junior growled again and turned to Sadie. Its time was nearly over, and it needed one last feed before the night was done. Rising to its feet, it moved closer to the woman, sniffed her, growled at her, and before the clock struck twelve, howled and bit her head off. It chewed and crushed with its powerful jaw as her body fell to the ground before it. It devoured the rest of her while Sadie's hundred cats looked on, huddling together in the doorway, sitting on furniture, sitting in the entrance hallway. They watched while their mistress was eaten by the beast, a beast they knew better than to defy. They *could* run, they *could* stay, but this was their master either way.

The older, larger Howler growled and wandered away from the house to a clearing by the river.

The young Howler shook its head and followed, licking its mouth and swishing its tail. It was well fed now, but wanted to play, even though its energy was flagging. It halted at the river bank and lapped up the cool refreshing water before turning back to the other beast. It knew it wasn't to be reckoned with, being older and larger. So it did what it was told, clawed at the grassy sod beneath its feet, and walked around in circles a few times before settling down. It wrapped its tail around itself, closed its eyes, and twitched its ears. In the distance, a clock struck twelve, and it was time to sleep.

*****

In town, Chief Erickson closed the school down, bolted shut the doors, and wrapped crime tape around every crime scene. The bodies had been photographed and removed. The children and teachers were all accounted for except for Rachael Merrin, Sam Almaw, and his father Geoff who had gone out for supplies and not come back. As each emergency service packed up and left, Erickson scoured the school with the army and knew that the crime lab would come up with the clues needed. His officers had lost the beast in the woods, but they were preparing to go in at daylight. Other officers were looking for Geoff Almaw and had reported seeing Milly drive by in her car, frantically calling her son and husband's names out the window.

"At least she hasn't run off," Erickson muttered, watching as the army camped for the night. They would be keeping an eye on the school all night until it could be cleaned up and dealt with. Leaving them to it, he headed for the hospital to check on the kids and teachers, informing Principal Bennett he'd lost a teacher and a student.

"Who?" Bennett warily stood before him.

"Sam Almaw and his father Geoff are missing, and Rachael Merrin is dead." Erickson consulted the notes he'd taken at the school. "You also have an…Elliot Gunfield in critical condition."

"Oh, dear God." Bennett sighed. Weary to the bone, he collapsed into his chair. "What the hell is that…*was* that…*that beast? That animal?* What did it want? What was it doing?" His eyes burned, and he felt the grit every time he blinked, plus his head had a sand storm blowing through it.

"I have no idea, sir." Erickson stared down at him. "I didn't see it myself, but it killed five of my officers. Whatever it is, it can kill in an instant. Take a man out in a split second."

"Well, *I did* see it." Bennett looked up. "And it was an unholy beast made from the devil himself. Eyes that burned through to your soul, teeth that could rip your head off. It was as tall as us and had the power to do anything it wanted. I've never seen anything like it. Satan must have been controlling it."

"Yeah, well," Erickson scuffed a well-worn boot against the floor and hooked his hands in his belt. "I've never put much thought into the devil and hell and all that, so I'd rather call it an inbred anomaly that needs to be dealt with. Come light of day, we will scour the woods and find it and kill it. In the meantime, we need to find Geoff Almaw and his son."

*****

At daylight, the army and police from around the state combed through the woods one metre apart as they walked in a single line. They walked from the woods to the river bank and found nothing. At lunch, they moved down the road and started again. They made their way into the clearing where Sadie lived and found her house. They also found her remains and quickly set up a crime scene.

"Chief," someone called out.

Erickson walked over to the army corporal and looked to where he was pointing. When they had found the remains of Sadie, all stopped where they were, but now they continued the search and found something even stranger.

"What the hell is that?" Erickson slowly made his way over to the mass of coloured fur to discover Sadie's cats lying all over each other in a squirming pile. "What the hell are they doing? Shoo, shoo." He kicked a few hissing ones aside and the others jumped off. Underneath the furry mess was the body of Sam Almaw. "Oh, dear God." Erickson crouched down and felt for a pulse. "Gone," he called to the others. Examining the boy's body, he saw his t-shirt and shorts were ripped and bloodied. He had fur and blood matted to his hair and face; his feet were bare and dirty as if he had wandered on his own.

"Were the cats keeping him warm?" a constable asked. He was standing back a bit, not used to seeing so many dead bodies.

"Maybe." Erickson found the collar with its amulet still around Sam's neck. "What the hell?"

Fingering the pendant, he recalled the mother had dressed him as a cat. *The costume has been ripped off, but the collar remains. His shoes are gone, his clothes ripped, but the collar remained intact. Why? How?*

He stood up and let out a weary sigh. "Take photos and get the kid to the morgue. Anyone know where his parents are?"

"At home." Another officer flipped through his notebook. "Found the father there this morning. According to him he went out for supplies, but was hit with gut pain so he dashed home. Said he was going from both ends all night. He didn't look well, so the officers believed him."

"Mmm," Erickson grumbled. "Likely story. Let's go inform them about their son." They drove to the Almaw house where he spoke to a distraught Milly and a sick-looking Geoff. Upon hearing the news, Milly collapsed into Geoff's arms, and he collapsed to the floor. Erickson helped them up and onto a couch where he told them what had happened. When he left, they dressed to go to the morgue to collect their son's body. They didn't believe in autopsies and refused the coroner. They asked for him to be declared dead to be done with it.

Two days later, they took their son's body home for the prayer service before burial. It was a small affair and schoolmates attended. As the casket went into the ground, Milly and Geoff stood forlorn, crying, weeping when necessary, and when it was over, they went home to pack up their house. They couldn't stay there knowing their son had died there. Knowing *people* had died there.

But they also knew they had to be careful.

Erickson had a man watching them, still suspicious over Geoff's behaviour. Why hadn't he called his wife that night? Had their son wandered off, or was he taken? Regardless of the fact, no one had seen the boy with the beast when they tailed it.

Principal Bennett attended and organised the funeral for Rachael Merrin, the school's Home Ec teacher who had lost her life that night.

And Erickson organised for the funerals of his five officers to be with honours. They had died in the line of duty; they would get a burial of the highest standards. When he wasn't dealing with funerals, he kept a close eye on the Almaw couple, watched as they packed up their home and drove out of their driveway one week after their son's death. He found it strange. That parents could bury their son and then leave the place he was buried. He got the whole grief thing, not being able to stay where the loved one died, etc, but this was way too strange, even for him. He followed their car until they reached city limits and then let them go. The moving van followed. He was unable to solve the crime and probably never would.

Geoff watched the chief follow them until they reached the outskirts and heaved a sigh of relief when he stopped. "He's stopped following. We're in the clear."

"For now," Milly told him. "We should wait until

we're in another state before we relax. We could still be seen." She waited for another ten kilometres before reaching into the backseat to pull a blanket back. She gently brushed Sam's hair out of his eyes and checked his breathing. "Still in hibernation. But he should be coming out of it soon." He was curled, but comatose except for a twitch of his nose. "It's wearing off," Milly said.

They had pulled the old fake switcheroo upon the viewing in the house. His body had been on display in the coffin, but they replaced him with a long hessian bag filled with the exact amount of sand to mimic Sam's weight. Sam's initiation into the ancient Egyptian rite would last a week of hibernation. No one had guessed. No one had known. And if you looked up their name no one would find out, even if you ran it through a translation system because centuries of Almaw generations had shortened their name from Almawlul; Arabic for Howler.

Sam stretched a leg, yawned and blinked. It was the best sleep he'd ever had, but now, he was hungry.

*****

In the hospital, right at that moment, Elliot Gunfield flatlined. He'd been in a coma all week after slipping into it after admittance to the hospital. The paint tins that had fallen on his head caused bleeding, and he'd required emergency surgery where they drilled a hole in his head to let the blood run free. His coma had lasted since.

Until now. And it was no mere coincidence that it had lasted as long as Sam's change and hibernation. The doctors rushed into Elliot's room in ICU and started beating his chest to get his heart started. They flattened his bed, pulled in the defibrillator, and electrocuted him with a hundred CCs. It didn't work.

"Again," the doctor yelled. "200 CCs." Rubbing the paddles together he placed them on Elliot's chest. "Clear!" He charged, and Elliot's body flew upward from the shock. "No good. 300 CCs." The doctor electrocuted Elliot once more and finally got a heartbeat. "Okay." The doctor sighed and replaced the paddles. "He's back. Let's check him over and keep a close eye on him."

Giving him a thorough examination, the doctor pulled up each eyelid and flicked his light back and forth. Something struck him as strange. "What colour are the kid's eyes?" He thought back to the last exam and vaguely remembered them being dark brown.

"Dark brown," the nurse looking at the chart, said.

The doctor pulled up both of Elliot's eyelids and looked again. "Then why are they now a fiery amber colour?"

SHADOW WALKERS

CHAPTER ONE

Elliot Gunfield awoke from his coma on December 1st 2002. It was his 13th birthday, and he had been in a coma for a month since that horrific Halloween night when he faced the blood-red eyes of death. And paid for it with his life.

Doctors and nurses rushed in to check on him and gave him a thorough examination. Much to their surprise, he was fine, except for the change in his eye colour which fascinated the doctor.

Elliot had brown eyes from birth. Dark brown hair and dark brown eyes his best friend Sam Almaw had often said at certain times looked black. His eyes didn't look black anymore. They were fiery amber instead.

The doctor didn't understand why they had changed and called in experts, but they too were perplexed by the change, with none of them having ever heard or seen of such a phenomenon. Elliot's parents didn't understand it either, but they were just glad their boy was finally awake.

"Mum, Dad," he croaked, having not spoken in

a month.

"Oh, my baby," Sharon Gunfield murmured as she smoothed his hair away from his face. "You're awake. You're awake."

Elliot licked his lips and sighed. He was tired, even though he'd spent the last month in a coma. It wasn't sleep he'd had. He'd drifted between bad dreams and reality. The reality of hearing his parents sob his name and tell him what was going on in the world, and dreams that horrified, terrified, *tortured* him awake. If only he'd actually *been* awake, he could have run far away from those dreams and not had anything to do with them. But he was trapped. Trapped in a coma that kept him supine in bed, unable to move, unable to scream, unable to get away from the horrors he faced. He was awake now, but wouldn't talk about them.

"It's so good to have you back, my baby," Sharon cooed, staring into her son's changed eyes. "It's so good to have you back." And even though he was back, she worried for him. What had the head injury done? What damage was left behind? It couldn't *just* be the eyes, it had to be something else. But time would tell even though she didn't know how much time he had.

"So, what's happened?" Elliot asked, his eyes focussed on the clock ticking away on the wall in front of him.

Sharon glanced at her husband, Elliot's father, Mark Gunfield. They had already discussed how much they were going to tell him. The hospital psychiatrist told them to tell him the truth and not lie because he'd find out anyway. Taking a deep breath, she started slowly. "Well, you won the school's Halloween costume competition. Do you remember that?"

Elliot blinked and remembered his Tin Man costume. "I beat Gretchen. She was so pissed that she didn't win."

"Language," Mark said softly.

"Yeah, whatever," Elliot muttered. "Didn't think that was gonna matter considering what I've been through." His eyes stared straight ahead to the clock.

Sharon and Mark exchanged a worried frown before she went on. "We collected your trophy. It's on your bedside cupboard at home. I can bring it in if you like, and maybe some of your toys. I brought Mr Giggles in for you." She pointed to the bear on the trolley beside the bed. "I've been playing your favourite music. If there's anything you want, just let me know. I have an overnight bag with pyjamas and toiletries."

"Has Sam been in?"

She glanced sharply at him before moving her eyes to her husband.

"Has Sam been in?"

"Uh, no sweetie," she said slowly. "He hasn't."

"Is he dead?"

Sharon watched her son's face. "Why would you say that?"

"Because one minute we were in the closet then The Howler was there and Sam was gone. His costume was ripped to shreds…"

Another glance at her husband. "Ummm…" Remembering what the psychiatrist said, she added, "He was found later…he didn't survive."

"Found where?" Elliot frowned.

"Near the river. Near old lady Sadie's house. They think he wandered there dazed and confused."

"No!" Elliot exclaimed loudly. "He was in the closet with me and then he was gone, his costume ripped up and that thing was there instead. It ate Sam. It killed him in the closet." His fists were curled into balls, and the heart monitor went up twenty beats a minute.

"Calm down, El." Sharon stood to lean over the bed. "It's okay. Whatever happened, however it happened, Sam didn't make it. Neither did Ms Merrin the Home Ec teacher. Several officers died as well. But everyone else is okay. *You're* okay. *We're* okay."

"Where is he?"

"Who?"

"Sam…"

"He's gone, sweetie."

"I know that, you just said it." He finally looked at his mother's concerned face, his amber eyes flashing. "Where is he, *as in*, buried?"

"Oh." She leaned back and swallowed. Her son's eyes were unnerving her a little. "At the Belmont Cemetery."

"When?" His frown deepened.

"When was he buried?" Sharon asked in return and

got a nod. "Two or three days after the examination. It was quick. Then they left town."

"They left town?" Elliot's brain ticked over. He'd been haunted by The Howler in his coma, reliving the whole thing from beginning to end. "Why would they leave town? He's buried here. Why would they leave him?"

"Maybe they couldn't deal with it all." Mark stood beside his wife, one arm around her, one hand on Elliot's leg. "Sometimes grief makes people run away from the tragedy that caused it."

"Why would you bury your son and then leave him?" Elliot murmured, more to himself as his eyes went back to the clock on the wall. "Why would they leave him? Anyone else dead?"

"A couple of people not on school grounds," Mark told him. "But just Sam and Ms Merrin from school."

"Not Gretchen Merryweather?" Elliot's lips turned up into a snarl.

Sharon frowned again. What was going on with her son? "No. Gretchen's still alive."

"Still whining about not winning the costume comp, I bet. She accused me of winning because you voted for me, but Bennett pulled her into line. Didn't stop her whinging, though. Ran back to her friends and started again. Pity The Howler didn't get her."

"Elliot, what's The Howler?" Sharon asked him.

"The cat creature that was at the school. The beast that howled and growled and ate Sam. We'd seen it the weekend before." Elliot stared transfixed at the clock, as if it offered important information for him.

"Sweetie, we don't know *what* that was. The chief of police thinks it was some sort of inbred animal," Sharon said.

"It wasn't," Elliot persisted. "It was an ancient animal that had roamed the woods the week before. I saw it on my way home. It told me its name and to never mention it again. Every time I started talking to Sam about it I had those fits. Monday, Monday afternoon. I fitted when I mentioned it, so I didn't mention it again. It was horrible. Like death. Its eyes were blood-red, its fangs a foot long. It was taller and broader and powerful." The air rushed out of him and he closed his eyes. "It ate Sam; it was there in the closet with us. It growled so hard and so loud it blew me backwards. I hit the shelving and blacked out. I don't remember what happened after that. What happened?" His eyes opened and pleaded with them to tell him.

Taking a deep breath, Sharon told him the whole story as she knew it. How he had been hit on the head with the paint tins, and had been unconscious for a week. How they bled his head, and he went into cardiac arrest one week later. How the doctor said they needed to keep an eye on him to see what had changed, but so far, there didn't seem to be anything dramatic happening.

"Sharon," Mark warned.

She sighed and looked at her husband. "Well,

there is *one* thing." Picking up a small mirror from the bedside trolley she handed it to her son. "Take a look."

Curious, but also worried, Elliot took the mirror and looked at his face. "Jesus Christ look at my eyes." They widened as he stared back, astonished at how his eyes had changed colour. "How the hell did that happen?" He looked from left to right. Up then down.

"Watch the language," his dad warned. "The doctors aren't sure; they think it had to do with the brain damage. They've never seen anything like it before."

"Neither have I, whoa, look at them." Elliot pulled his eyelids up. "Cool! I've never seen anyone with this colour eye before."

"Neither have we." The doctor who had been looking after Elliot walked in. "Elliot, I'm Doctor Nevo, you've been my patient since you were brought in. I've looked after you since. How do you feel?" He stood at the end of the bed reading Elliot's chart.

"Old." Elliot stared at him. "Out of time."

Nevo glanced up. "Well, that's an interesting thing to say. Why do you feel old?"

"Because I've aged." Elliot blinked. "I've lived a thousand lifetimes, done a thousand things. I'm tired, and I'm old, and I've run out of time."

"Time for what?" Nevo asked, seeing a psychology paper before him.

"For life," Elliot replied mechanically. "For living."

"Interesting," Nevo muttered, seeing the concerned look on Sharon and Mark's faces. He stepped around to the other side of the bed and flicked a light across Elliot's eyes. "How old are you, Elliot?"

Elliot blinked. "A thousand and eighty-three."

Nevo's lip curled up. "Really? That's very interesting. And what have you done?"

"Oh, this and that." Elliot waved an uninterested hand. "Sailed the high seas, fought in wars, climbed the highest mountains, lived an ancient life."

"That is *very* interesting Elliot." Nevo straightened and crossed his arms. "Could you write it all down for me?"

"I don't have the time. When can I get out?" Elliot countered.

"Well," Nevo glanced at the parents, "we can do another full body scan and see if you're okay. If you are, then we can let you go home."

"You already know I'm all right. You found nothing in the last two scans. The injury has healed, the swelling dissipated. There's nothing wrong with me except for this eye colour. Which you clearly can't explain."

"No." Nevo smiled. "We can't. And you're very astute, Elliot. Heard the last few conversations about your test results, did you?"

"Something like that." Elliot's eyes wandered back to the clock.

"Okay then." Nevo walked around to Elliot's parents. "We'll schedule tests for tomorrow, and if he's okay, you can take him home."

"Oh, thank God," Sharon breathed. "It will be good to get him home."

"What about school?" Elliot asked. "There's a couple of weeks left. I could spend it with mates, catch up on work before the holidays. Otherwise, I won't see anyone until next year."

The adults turned to him. "I don't see why you can't spend a few hours with your schoolmates," Nevo said. "Provided you don't participate in sports or physical activities. Keep it light and non-violent."

"I guess we could let him go," Sharon murmured. "As long as he passes all the tests."

CHAPTER TWO

Three days later, Elliot stood in the Belmont Cemetery looking down at his best friend's gravestone. It was a small, simple one that stated, Sam Almaw 1989-2002.

That's all it said.

No…best friend of Elliot Gunfield.

No…son of Milly and Geoff Almaw.

No saying, no poem, no…nothing.

Just his name and birth and death dates.

He wasn't sure what he felt. There were a thousand lifetimes of feelings inside of him all vying to get out. Sure, he felt sadness and some pain. But it wasn't the way he thought it would be. He thought he'd be bawling his eyes out at losing his best friend. But here he was, dry eyed and not even wiping his face free from tears. Not one single tear for his best friend in the whole wide world. Not one.

Weariness overtook him, and he sat down in front of the gravestone cross-legged, picking at the blades of grass that had grown over the burial plot.

"Sam, I don't know if you can hear me. I don't know if you're even dead. I should miss you, and I'm sure somewhere inside I do, but for the life of me, I just don't feel much these days. Not of my own anyway. It seems spending time in a coma and dying has made me old. I *feel* old. Old and tired and worn out. Like I've lived a thousand lifetimes and all not my own. I have no idea what happened that night after we locked ourselves in the utility closet. But it got in, and it got you, and I'm sorry I didn't do anything to stop it. I'm sorry I didn't do anything at all."

Biting his lip, he glanced around at the other gravestones, trying to decipher what it was he *did* feel. But all the other feelings and voices in his head negated each other, and so, he ended up feeling nothing. "We could've had fun this year. Both of us are thirteen now; the school holidays are on, it's summer, swimming, biking, movies, pool parties with our friends. But no, not gonna happen now. Not with you dead and me an invalid. Mum's got me on a short leash."

He leant back on his hands, stretched his legs out, and crossed one over the other. "She doesn't want me going anywhere on my own. She's even waiting in the car park while I talk to you, and she doesn't want me going back to school. Scared I might get knocked on the head, I suppose. But still, she can't stop me for long. I want to get back to life while I still have it. Oh, did you see my eyes... they've changed colour." He lifted his sunglasses and stared down at the grass. "How's that! They changed to amber. Who would've thunk it? I get clobbered on the head with a couple of paint cans, and my eyes change colour. The doctors have no idea why, or what's going on, but the damage I sustained has fixed itself, so I'm good to go. If only I didn't feel so damn old and tired."

He sighed. "I better go, Mum's waiting." He clambered to his feet like an old man and dusted himself off. "See you next time, Sammy." As he walked away, he wasn't even sure there would *be* a next time.

*****

Elliot went back to school on Monday and, it being the last two weeks of the school year, it was all fun and games. His friends welcomed him with open arms and kind words about Sam.

"Dude, good to have you back." Ben Kingston slapped him on the back. "You okay? Everythin' all right with your head?" Ben was a schoolmate in the same class and year. At six feet tall, and thirteen years of age, he towered a head above his friends.

"Yeah, I'm doing good," Elliot replied, taking in the expressions of his friends who had gathered around him. "It's good to be back. Good to be doing things and not sitting around the house or hospital."

"The doctors gave you the all clear?" Nathan Berry asked, noticing Elliot's black sunglasses perched firmly on his face. "You goin' for the cool dude stakes or what? What's with the sunglasses?" He reached for them, but Elliot's hand flew up to his face to protect it and he took a step back.

"Need to protect the eyes, man. Something weird happened to them, and my olds and the doctors think I should protect them when I'm out in the sun."

"What happened to your eyes?" Simon Plattfield asked. He was in the same year and class as the others.

"You'll see once we're inside." Elliot smiled mysteriously.

They spoke for a few moments before the bell rang, and then headed inside to see what the activities were for the day.

"Elliot, welcome back," Ms Revesby said as she sorted through the books on her desk. "We were told you'd be coming today and to not let you get involved in physical activities. How do you feel?"

"Old," Elliot replied. "Really tired all the time. But it's good to be back doing something."

"And we've been instructed by your mother and the doctor to let you keep the sunglasses on if you want to. Apparently, something happened to your eyes. Are they okay?"

"Well." Elliot bowed his head for dramatic pause before pulling the glasses off. "If you call my eyes changing colour something happening, then yes, something *did* happen." He blinked, and the whole class saw his amber eyes.

"Whoa!" his friends all said at once.

"Get a loada those," Nathan crowed. The kids all

sat around large desks, and Elliot's friends all sat with him. "What happened to you?"

Elliot shrugged. "No one knows. They think it had to do with the brain injury, and so they want me to wear glasses in bright light." He glanced around the room, his eyes lighting upon each person in his class until they landed on Gretchen. He blinked, and it unnerved her, making her frown and glance away. Looking at the teacher, he added, "so don't think me rude if I put them on inside. My eyes might freak some people out."

"No." Ms Revesby stared back. "I find it fascinating. They're such a strange colour. You might even find me staring at you throughout the day."

Elliot smiled indulgently. "I understand."

The morning passed with colouring activities, origami classes, recess, and then quizzes before the lunch bell rang. Eating out on the quad, kids from other grades would try to inconspicuously pass by to get a look at Elliot's eyes, for word had gotten around at recess about their change in colour. But he noticed and kept his glasses on, and his friends stayed around him as bodyguards. They chatted about Sam's passing and what they were doing for Christmas.

"Do you know, have you been to the…" Ben let the sentence trail off.

"Yeah, I know. Mum told me after I woke up. I went to the cemetery on the weekend." Elliot shoved the last of his sandwich into his mouth. He didn't particularly want to talk about it, but knew it was going to come up. "I'm still dealing with it all. Trying to get my head around it."

"Yeah, I guess you would be," Nathan muttered. "Will you tell *us* about it?"

Elliot breathed in the warm air of December. "Don't know. Maybe, maybe not. Depends on how I feel."

The bell rang for the afternoon class, and they packed their lunch boxes back into their bags and walked off for the rec room. All three year eight classes would be together for the rest of the day.

Elliot lagged behind a little, aware of eyes on him. He turned his head to look at the tech shed as they passed and saw someone right behind him. His head turned to see who it was, but there was no one there. Stopping, he glanced at the windows to see a shadow. He looked behind him. No one there. Puzzled, his head moved back and forth between the two, but he couldn't decipher how there was no one behind him, yet in the window's reflection, there was.

"Hey, El, you comin'? You okay?" Ben called.

Elliot turned to the front and saw his mates waiting for him at the rec room door. "Yeah, comin'." He hurried after them, and they walked into the room and settled into their seats to listen to the teachers. The afternoon was going to be for having fun, reading, writing, telling stories, and hanging out.

Elliot kept his glasses on. He saw quizzical stares from the other two classes and hated being the centre of attention.

The class played hangman with the teachers drawing the figure on the chalkboard. They did more quizzes, told jokes, and talked about plans for the holidays, and still Elliot kept his glasses on. He knew he was probably drawing more attention to himself than if he'd sat there without them, but if he removed them, he'd be stared at, and he was over it.

When the bell rang, they gathered their things and waited for the teachers to let them go. Ms Revesby held Elliot back while the others filed out the door. "Will you be back tomorrow, Elliot?" she asked, straightening the pencil cans on the table.

"Dunno. Maybe, maybe not. The doctor said to take it slow. What are we doing tomorrow?"

"Tomorrow's sports day. But on Wednesday the class gets to go swimming, so that might be fun for you."

"Yeah, maybe." He hefted his bag onto his shoulder. "Maybe I'll come then. See you."

"Bye, Elliot." She watched him walk outside to his friends who had waited for him, and now crowded around, but noticed a strange figure who looked as if he didn't fit in with the kids. Blinking, she looked again, and just saw a blur as the kids rounded the corner. "Just a trick of the light I suppose." She shook her head and knew his mum was picking him up, so didn't worry about him getting home.

"How was your day, sweetie? Have fun?" Sharon asked when Elliot was buckling up.

"Yeah. It was okay." He sat back, leant his head against the headrest and closed his eyes. "Tired though."

"You can have a rest when we get home." Sharon manoeuvred out of the car park. "The doctor said to take it easy. Will you be coming back tomorrow?"

"Probably not. They have sports tomorrow, but swimming Wednesday. I'd like to do that." He felt every bit his thousand years, and his bones ached.

"You okay, El?" she asked softly.

"Just tired." He sighed, and when they got home, he rested in the lounge room watching TV until dinnertime and then went to bed early. He slept through the night until ten the next morning, when he woke to see his mother standing over him.

"You okay, El? You slept in."

He yawned so wide his jaw cracked. "Ow," he said, rubbing it. "Just tired from yesterday. Must have worn myself out."

"Well, the doctor did tell you not to overdo it. I'll get you some breakfast. I want you to get out in the sun for some vitamin D. Sit out in the backyard, read a book, or play with that poor dog you've neglected."

After breakfast, he did just that. Sat in the backyard getting some sun. The problem was, the dog didn't want to come near him.

"Buster, what's wrong with you?" Elliot slapped his leg, but the heeler cross wanted nothing to do with him. He just growled at whatever was behind Elliot, ears back, mouth snarling.

It reminded Elliot of The Howler and the way it growled at him. He shuddered, and saw Buster's eyes looking past him. Slowly turning his head to look, Elliot saw nothing.

But Buster kept on growling and inched closer, ears flattened against his head.

Elliot leaned around his chair to look some more, but all he saw was a fuzzy mess of a shadow of him in the sun. He lifted his glasses to look better with his fiery amber eyes and stared in shock.

He could have sworn he'd seen a face.

CHAPTER THREE

Elliot turned up at school on Wednesday, swimming shorts tucked into his bag along with a towel and not much else. He was buying his food from the canteen, and there was no need for school books or pens and pencils.

They spent the morning in the classroom watching movies, and after recess, Elliot watched while the rest of the class played games on the field. But he was never alone. There was always something or someone watching him, touching him on the shoulder.

The hairs stood up on the back of his neck, and a chill went down his spine. Unnerved, he got up from the grass and walked over to the trees surrounding the oval to sit in the shade. It was a warm summer day, and he was sweating from being out in the warmth, but on the inside, he was chilled. In the shade he felt better, not watched, not touched. Just himself. Old and tired, but himself. His eyes followed his classmates having fun until the bell rang. He joined them, and they headed for the canteen.

"Ah man, I don't feel good." Nathan rubbed his eyes. He was in line behind Elliot as they stood in the sun waiting to get in.

Ben, who was in front of Elliot, turned and grinned. "Must have been that ball you took to the head."

"Dunno, but I feel sick." Nathan fanned himself as they stepped inside. The sick feeling drifted away and he felt better. "Must've been the sun. I feel okay now."

"Get some food into ya, level your blood sugar out," Kyle Burrows said from behind him. He was another classmate, a diabetic, so he knew about blood levels and what the heat could do.

"Yeah, I guess. I do need a drink." Nathan grabbed a bottle of cola from the fridge and cracked it open to scull some back before ordering two meat pies and a cream bun.

"Yeah, because *that's* really gonna help," Kyle muttered from behind him.

"Hey, it's got my meat, my carbs," Nathan countered and stepped forward to pay for it all. "I've been drinking water all morning, time for cola." He waited for Kyle to pay for his food, then they followed Elliot and Ben over to a shaded table and sat to eat, huddling up when their other friends joined them.

Enjoying their food, they chatted briefly, wanting lunch to be over so they could hit the pool and the cool water of heaven after such a warm day.

Elliot spied Gretchen and her friends sitting at another table giving them an occasional glance and muttering amongst themselves. "Wonder what she's whinging about now," he said.

The boys all looked in her direction, but the girls quickly looked away.

"Did she say anything in the month I was gone?" Elliot asked, finishing off his chocolate éclair. "Like whinging about losing the costume competition?"

"Nah, man. She was pretty quiet after it. We all were," Ben said. He bit into an apple and chewed thoughtfully. "With everything that happened, the school was shut for two weeks. We had exams after that, so had to study while we were gone. We'd only been back a couple of weeks when you came back, and she's said nothing."

"Then why does she keep staring at me?" Elliot glanced away from the girls. "Like I don't feel like a freak show as is. People always staring."

"Must be your eyes bro, they're *so* sexy," Kyle joked. The others laughed. "But seriously, we've known you for years, and now you have different coloured eyes. It's creepy *and* cool and people just want to see."

"Yeah, I guess," Elliot muttered and pushed his glasses up to rub the bridge of his nose. "But I can get wicked headaches sometimes. The doctor said it's normal, but they're worse when I'm out in the sun or in bright light. When I'm in a room or the shade, I'm okay." He rubbed his eyes and placed his glasses over them. "Maybe it's just the sun, but I dunno. There's something…"

"What?" Nathan asked. "I felt sick before, but I'm okay now. It is warm today."

"Yeah, but…" Elliot shook his head. "This is different. Maybe it's from getting hit on the head…" He shrugged. "I dunno."

"How long did the doctor say it would last?" Kyle asked.

"Anywhere up to a year. They said headaches would be normal. That's why I need to see a physio for a while. To keep my neck and shoulders in check and keep my muscles supple." Elliot balled up his lunch wrappers and got up to put them in the bin.

The bell rang, and the other boys followed suit before racing off to the pool and lining up. While standing in line, Elliot glanced around at the rest of the kids. His gaze flew past the windows of the classrooms beside them, and he saw a fuzzy dark shape. There it was again. He looked behind him then back to the window. He saw Ben and nothing else. Lifting his glasses up a little, he looked behind him and saw the dark fuzzy shape standing at the edge of his shadow.

"Hey, dude, move." Ben pushed him ahead.

Elliot saw they were filing inside and hurried into the change rooms to slip into his shorts. Keeping his glasses on, he followed his friends out and jumped into the blue water. It hit him smack in the face and knocked his glasses off, but he didn't mind. He stood up and put them back on. It had been months since he'd been in the pool. Last summer in fact. And now all he wanted to do was swim with Sam and play games. Except Sam wasn't there, and he was.

Wading over to the corner in the shallows, he watched his friends frolic, jump, bomb and dunk each other. He wanted to join in, but didn't have the energy, the will. He just wanted to sit there in his little corner and watch. Besides, his mother wouldn't be happy if he was injured again, so it was best not to join in.

"Hey, El, catch." Nathan threw the ball at him, and he caught it and threw it back. "You not joining in?" Nathan threw the ball to Ben.

"Better not, don't want to get hit on the head," Elliot called. He felt uneasy in that moment and glanced over his shoulder. He didn't see anything; there was nothing *to* see, but he was uneasy nonetheless.

The boys moved a little closer so they could still chat to Elliot and throw him the ball. They dived for rings on the bottom and raced each other across and back. Elliot called time on the races and declared winners without participating. But for the most part, he sat in the corner and hovered just above the water.

Sam should be here. I should be here with Sam. Where is he? Why isn't he here? He should be here enjoying all of this. Why did his parents move away and leave him? Is he even there? Wouldn't that be funny, he thought, *if Sam wasn't even buried there, because I really can't fathom why his parents would leave him behind.* The water was above his lips and tickled his nose, and he blew bubbles as he thought. *Sam should be here. We should be here together.*

His gaze darted back and forth to his friends and their antics, watching Gretchen continually look in his direction. They weren't really his friends, just classmates, school friends, but not best friends. Sam was his best friend, but Sam wasn't there. What would he do without the best friend he'd had all his life? The best friend he'd played ball with, played cricket with, swum, rode bikes, and watched scary movies with. Who would he do that with now? He had no best friend now. He had no one. What was he going to do over summer now? Nothing, without his best friend, Sam.

His eyebrows scrunched down. What was he going to do without his best friend? The others were just his school friends, not his best friends.

"Hey, let's see how long we can hold our breath underwater," Kyle called out and took a great gulp of air. He disappeared below the surface and the other boys followed suit.

So did Elliot, who slipped beneath the surface without a sound. He opened his eyes and blinked a few times, letting them adapt to the chlorine. He saw his friends all staring wide-eyed and wide-cheeked at each other until one by one they went up gasping for air. But he didn't need to. Didn't need to gasp, didn't need air. He was fine where he was. Blinking, he felt his eyelids close.

Visions burst left and right past his pupils. Visions

of The Howler, Sam, death, destruction, blood, guts, gore, hell, the devil himself, the horrors, the terrors, the dreams that had terrified him while he was in a coma. His eyes started to burn and he blinked, but all he saw was blood. He wasn't in a pool of water anymore; he was in a pool of blood. Thick, red, sticky, and it trapped him. It was like thick mud or quicksand, and he couldn't move his arms, his legs, his head. It was thick and red, and it was drowning him.

He saw a face he didn't recognise, but the mouth was wide in an angry roar, its eyes non-existent, just black holes for sockets, no nose, no teeth, just a skull flying toward him. Bony hands reached out from the sides, bony fingers wrapped around his arms, dug into them. A bony hand came hurtling toward him from the bony body in front of him and shoved itself into his chest.

His mouth opened and his body sagged forward. The hand retreated and struck again, aiming for Elliot's heart. It found it, wrapped around it, clenched tight and pulled. Elliot saw the bony hand retreating with his heart firmly entrenched in it, and the bony figure disappeared into the distance.

He had no idea what it was about. It didn't hurt; he didn't feel it. He just knew his heart had been taken and he was dead. He had died that moment in the hospital, one week after that night. His heart had stopped, and he'd gone into cardiac arrest. That's when he'd first seen it. The bony figure, the bony hands. He'd seen them again in the coma. The blood cleared and he saw himself in an old house looking through ancient leatherbound books, crazed, the desperation evident as he pored through each page. Then Gretchen turned up in his dream.

Why the hell would she be here and where the hell am I?

He saw Gretchen talking, but no words came out. There was no sound. He looked up from the book he'd been reading and grabbed a random piece of paper to mark the page before shoving the other two books into his duffel bag. He pulled down his ski mask and quickly moved into the lounge room with the book in his hands.

Cut to Scene 2 where he raised his hands over Gretchen's body, read something from the book, and stabbed Gretchen under the ribcage. She jerked up, grabbed her stomach, and collapsed.

"Dude, should we pull him up?" Nathan asked, looking at his watch. He'd been timing the whole thing, and while they'd barely lasted a minute, Elliot was going on past four.

"Yeah, we'd better," Ben said. "His mum'll kill us if anything happens." The boys grabbed Elliot by the armpits and hauled him up.

He felt bony fingers dig into his arms once more and he was pulled upwards to break the surface. Gasping in air, he wiped his face and saw his friends gathered round. "Hey, how long was I?"

"Five minutes," Nathan said, watching Elliot remove his glasses and rub his face. "We were worried."

"Don't be. Me and Sam trained ourselves last

summer to see how long we could hold our breath underwater. Guess I could go longer than I thought." He caught a glimpse of his face in the pool's reflection and noticed something strange. Looking up, he saw his friends take a step back and other kids in the pool stop to stare.

"Whoa." The boys couldn't take their eyes off Elliot's face.

"Dude, they're glowing," Ben murmured, freaked out by what was going on in Elliot's eyes, but also amazed by it.

"Yeah." Elliot blinked and replaced his glasses. "They do that sometimes."

"No, like, *really* glowing," Kyle said. "Like you've got light bulbs in your sockets."

Elliot grinned. "Yeah, pretty cool huh! I'm gonna sit by the side for a while." Bouncing over to the edge, he climbed out and sat on the bleachers with his towel around him, watching his friends go back to playing. He glanced over his shoulder at his shadow to see the fuzzy mess. Lifting his glasses, he eyed the bony, eyeless figure behind him lurking in the shadows. "You're not getting me again," he murmured. "These are mine, and you're not getting them back."

CHAPTER FOUR

Elliot took a break on Thursday and went back to school on Friday. Being the end of the week things were easy, and there was barely a week to go before the school holidays. The class watched movies in the morning, played quizzes until lunchtime, and then the three grade eight classes got together in the rec room for the rest of the afternoon.

Elliot was busy joking with his friends when the teacher asked if anyone wanted to start a subject of conversation.

A kid's hand flew up and he yelled out, "I want to talk about Halloween."

The room grew silent, and the teachers glanced at each other.

"So do I," came a second voice.

"Same here," came a third.

"We never did get to talk about it," the first boy said. He was Jason Yu, an Asian kid who'd lived all his life in Belmont. "I think we should clear the air about it so we can finish off the end of the year. When we come back next year, it will be a fresh year to learn." His mother was a Feng Shui expert who dealt with big business clients from around Australia.

"Well…" Ms Revesby said, looking from the other teachers to the kids. "I guess you have a point." Her eyes lingered on Elliot as he sat with his back to most of the class. "Okay, Jason, do you want to start?"

"I want to know what that thing was and where it came from." Jason stood up. "How did it even get here to Belmont? Was it born, raised, hand-fed like the crocodile in the movie *Lake Placid?* Hand-reared from birth? What? Where did it come from, does anyone know? Why did it pick on us, on Halloween of all nights?" He crossed his arms and waited for someone to answer.

The teachers had no answers, but tried anyway.

"The Chief of Police thinks it was an inbred animal," Ms Revesby said. She was standing in front of the chalkboard at the head of the room. "We don't know for certain, because no one was able to find it afterwards. We don't know why here, why us. It just did." She put her hands out, palm side up. "I don't know, the chief doesn't know, no animal expert can help us. We just have to help ourselves."

"Why did it eat the adults and not us?" Gretchen asked from her table of her cliquey friends.

"We don't know that either," Ms Revesby told her. "We don't know who or what it was, or why or what it did. We have no idea why it chose adults."

Elliot, who had been trying his best to ignore

what was going on, had looked up sharply when the teacher said who. *It was Sam,* raced through his head. *Sam disappeared only to be found later. It was Sam.* "It was The Howler."

The fact that it had come out of his mouth at all surprised him, and he breathed silently, just as silently as the room now fell.

His friends all looked quizzically at him, frowning, with cocked brows or lips.

"What?" came from behind him.

"Did you say something, Elliot?" Ms Revesby asked.

With the authoritative calmness of an old man, Elliot slowly removed his glasses and blinked. He felt his eyes burning, knew they were glowing. Knew he was about to tell all. Slowly turning his head, he looked at Jason over his shoulder. "It was The Howler." The kids murmured and gasped in surprise at his eyes that were glowing like bulbs of fiery amber. "The beast that attacked us that night was The Howler. *Is* The Howler." His body turned to meet up with his head as he stood. "A wild beast of Egyptian origins that no one can stop." He watched Jason fall into his seat. "I saw it the week before, in the woods along the road. Sam and I heard it when we were riding home; it howled like a beast and started crashing through the underbrush towards us. Sam sped off, but I was rooted to the spot, unable to move even one foot to pedal out of there. Sam came back and shoved me into gear. We sped off to my house and locked ourselves away for the night. The next day when I was riding home I heard it, heard the howl that sent chills down my spine and I froze. I heard it crash through the underbrush and then I saw it. Saw the cat-like body, saw the dog-like snout, saw the foot-long fangs and the blood-red eyes. It got inside my head. It got inside my head and told me what it was. It was The Howler. It was of ancient scripts and faraway lands, and I was not to breathe a word of it. It frightened the crap out of me and I raced home."

He breathed slowly. "I'm surprised I made it to school the next day, and when I started telling Sam about it, I fitted. Even though I'd never had a fit in my life, and even though the doctors still can't figure out what caused them. And later that afternoon when Sam came in and we started talking about it again, I had another fit. Because The Howler told me never to speak its name or it would hurt me."

He took a step forward and held the room captivated. "I spent a week in hospital while doctors ran tests trying to find out why I had fitted, and when I came out, it was Saturday, the day of the costume party. And I go there, and everything was great, and I won best costume over Gretchen."

He stared pointedly at her and saw her blanch from his fiery gaze. "Who then turned around and whined like a brat about how I only won because my parents voted, and then that thing bangs on the door. It bangs and howls and bangs until it breaks in, and I know it's after me because I had seen it the week before. I knew it was after me. So, we run, and it follows, and it howls and growls, and Sam and I hide in the closet in the tech shed. But it finds us, and I told Sam it was after me, but he told me not to be stupid. He said it was after something or *someone* else."

He stepped forward and licked his lips. "But I knew. We ended up separated, and it banged against the door, and the next thing I know, it was inside the closet growling at me, and I faced it with courage I never knew I had. But it was too late. It already had Sam. He was already dead. His costume was ripped to shreds, and that beast was licking its chops like it had just enjoyed eating my best friend." His voice grew in pitch. "I faced off with it, but it growled with power I'd never known and I went flying backwards into the shelves and blacked out. But was that all I went through because of that thing? Oh no…"

He cocked a lip and had them in the palm of his hand. "I was unconscious for a week and then went into cardiac arrest because paint tins had fallen on my head and caused trauma. I died." He pointed to his chest. "*I* died. And *I* saw it. It was ready to take *me. I* saw death and destruction. Ghosts and ghouls, grotesque things that you will only see on a TV or movie screen. *I* suffered because of what that beast did. *I* went through hell. *I* lost my best friend, *I* lost my life, *I* lost a month in a coma and only came out of it on my thirteenth birthday just two weeks ago. *I* lost a month of my life, saw horrible, grotesque creatures and lost my best friend all because of that animal. The Howler. That decided it wanted to feed on us. Poor little school kids who couldn't defend themselves. We have to live with the horrors of that night. The families of the dead people have to live with never seeing their loved ones again, and *I* lost my best friend. So really, worrying about something none of us knew existed, and we haven't seen or heard of since, is a waste of time. It's a waste of time worrying about something we can't do anything about. We've all lost too much time to waste another second on a beast that clearly we have no idea about."

He threw his hands up in frustration. "You lot are alive; you lot don't have headaches and weird shit going on in your head. Be grateful nothing happened to you. *I* had brain damage, *I* lost my best friend, and *I* have a weirdo new eye colour that glows." He looked across the kids in the room. "*What did you lot get out of it?* Because *I* got hell."

The bell rang for home time, and Elliot dashed out the door, snatched his bag up from the hallway floor, and ran to the car park to find his mother waiting for him.

"How was your day?" She saw he was without his glasses and his eyes were glowing. "El?"

"I just wanna go home," he murmured, closing his eyes against the sun.

Sharon drove off, worried for her son. "Will you be going back next week?"

"Dunno. I ended up telling everyone what happened on Halloween." His face crumpled. "Jason started asking what that thing was and where it was from and just kept going on and on and on." He rubbed his eyes. They were pounding in their sockets and felt like they were bulging out. "And I just snapped and started talking. Telling them I've lost the most and they've lost nothing. I lost my best friend, a month of my life, my eye colour." He burst into tears, something he hadn't done since before that night. He'd had no feelings to cry for or over, but this was different. He couldn't put his finger on it, but there was a reason he was crying.

"Oh, sweetie." Sharon laid her hand on his arm. "We're nearly home. Why don't you go rest in bed until dinner? You don't have to go back next week. You've got all your things out of your desk and locker, and got an automatic pass on your exams. You don't need to go back. Here we are." She drove into the garage and collected her bags from the boot of the car before leading Elliot into the house. "You go and rest, El. If you want a cool shower, have one. It was quite warm today."

Elliot nodded and trooped upstairs in the cool shaded house to his bathroom, pulled off his clothes, stepped under the cool refreshing water and stopped crying. It was as if a switch had flicked. One moment he was, next moment he wasn't. Twisting off the tap he got out, dried himself off, found a pair of shorts and slid into bed. His eyes were no longer burning, and he'd noticed in the bathroom mirror they'd stopped glowing. He couldn't figure out why they did that. Why they glowed. It seemed to happen when he got emotional, which wasn't hard to do. But it wasn't as if he'd been feeling any emotions lately. Not since the coma, the night of Halloween. He hadn't felt anything, but when things got stirred up, his eyes glowed.

I wonder what they do when I get really emotional, like angry or crying. Do they shoot fireballs? Beams of fire? Rays of light? That might be fun to see. I wonder if I have x-ray vision. Maybe I can see through buildings and kids' notebooks and people's clothes.

Smiling, he drifted off to sleep, but sleep was not soothing or calm. Sleep was anything but.

Visions hit him from left and right. Long bony fingers and long bony hands and long bony arms reached out, grabbed him, pulled him left and right. The shadowy figure loomed in front of him, eyeless, toothless, faceless, reaching and clinging and silently howling. It whooshed left and feinted right before driving its bony hand into Elliot's chest. Its long bony fingers clasped his heart and yanked it right out of his chest. The hand closed around his heart and turned it to dust.

Elliot watched his heart flutter on the breeze before the burning feeling in the pit of his stomach flared up. It started as a butterfly, but turned into a dragon, and with power he didn't know he had, he unleashed an almighty roar onto the faceless figure floating in front of him, and his eyes burned fire, unleashing themselves on all before him.

The figure turned to dust and the bony arms holding him let go and retreated, and he was left floating in the air to look down upon an old house in a clearing by the river bank. He saw a shadowy figure ride up on a bike and lean it against the wall. That bike was familiar, and so was the figure. It was him, and he was breaking into the house.

Curious as to why he'd be breaking into a house he didn't know, Elliot watched while another figure followed him, came up to the house on a bike and left it around the side against a wall. The figure crept up to the door and peeked in before glancing over its shoulder. Gretchen? Why would she follow him to a house he'd never seen before?

Gretchen disappeared inside, and he waited. A third figure dashed up to the house and ran inside, followed by two more. Not long after, the third figure dragged him out, and he saw the figure's face in the moonlight.

CHAPTER FIVE

Elliot awoke before dinner and watched TV with his parents before going back to his bedroom. Everything he'd dreamed about made no sense. The bony figures, the black figures sneaking into a house he didn't know, and why would three of them be him, Gretchen, and Sam? Sam was dead, and why would Gretchen follow him? And whose house was it?

Feeling the beginning of a headache starting, he got a notepad and pen from his desk, sat cross-legged on the bed, and began at the beginning. He wrote everything down from the weekend before Halloween, right up until today. Every detail he could remember he wrote down, trying to make sense of everything that had happened to him. But the more he wrote, the more confused he became and the more questions he had.

Why did my eyes change colour?

Why do strange faces appear in windows behind me?

Why did Sam die?

Did Sam die?

Where's The Howler now?

Is Sam really buried?

Will my eyes go back to normal?

Knowing the list of questions would be endless, he sat pondering them as he stared out his open window at the stars twinkling in the sky.

Buster scratched at the door and whined, and Elliot got up to let him in. Buster padded over to his favourite spot beside Elliot's bed and slumped down with a weary sigh.

"Oh, now you want to come near me?" Elliot flopped down face first on his bed and let his hand hang over the side while he rubbed Buster's belly. "Who's a good boy then?" Buster cocked his legs and rolled onto his back for Elliot to scratch him.

Elliot obliged and gave him a tummy rub for a few minutes more before rolling onto his own back to stare at the ceiling with its glow-in-the-dark stars and moons. Twiddling his thumbs, he crossed his legs at the ankles and wondered why he had been chosen.

Why me?

Why did it have to be me that suffered?

Why couldn't it have been Gretchen who got hit on the head or eaten?

Why did it have to be me and my best friend, Sam?

Why us?

Why did I have to lose my best friend?

Why did I have to be haunted or hunted?

If only someone else was going through what I've been through then maybe I could understand what the hell is going on.

Elliot made some notes about googling several subjects and looking up the local library for books on his long list of things to do. He was determined to get to the bottom of what was going on, and come hell or high water he was going to do it. He dumped his pad and pen on the desk beside him, flicked out the light and drifted off to sleep.

*****

On Saturday morning, Elliot was determined to face it head on. He spent the morning googling The Howler, found the same stuff Sam had, and started on his search for creepy things in shadows and death experiences, finding a couple of websites about near-death experiences and what the people writing the stories had encountered. He found they were completely different to his. One piece of information he did find out was on the same website as The Howler info. Apparently, if you had a death experience and saw images, shadows, figures in reflective surfaces, faces, bodies, etc, they were called Shadow Walkers. These were ghoulish ghosts and spirits that attached themselves to the returning soul when it got sent back to the living world. They haunted dreams at night and memory during the day. They were always there in the shadow when the victim was in light or the sun, but never there in shade or dark. *It was,* said the information, *as if a devil is breathing over your shoulder and looming over you. It could feel suffocating and terrifying, especially when you have visions of death.*

So far, there had been only one reported way of getting rid of a Shadow Walker, but the information had been lost, and no one from now knew what it was.

Elliot printed the information off, along with The Howler page, and collected it all into a folder. He had no idea what he was going to do with it, or what the one way to get rid of it was. He went in search of how to get rid of a Shadow Walker, but found nothing.

"It had what it is, but not how to get rid of it," he mused, highlighting several passages and lines in the printout. "How the hell am I going to solve this shit then?" Flicking his pen back and forth, he stared out his window. The sun radiated down warmly, the sky was as clear as day, and Buster was snoring at his feet. "What am I gonna do, hey, Buster?" He rubbed the dog's stomach with his feet. "What am I gonna do?"

Buster opened one eye at him, cocked an ear, sighed, and went back to sleep.

"Yeah, you're no help," Elliot complained and went back to searching. He found nothing, and by the afternoon was exhausted so took a nap. When he woke, he padded downstairs with Buster behind him, grabbed a drink from the fridge, and heard his name called from the lounge room.

"Elliot? Your teacher dropped your sunglasses off. I left them on the kitchen table," Sharon called out.

"Thanks, Mum." He slipped them on and went outside to sit on the back steps with Buster, who eagerly wagged his tail. "Don't let me stop ya."

Buster bolted for the back yard, racing down to the garden at the back fence to cock his leg and pee over the flowers. He raced back, sat on the concrete path in front of Elliot, cocked his leg, and licked himself before looking up at his master expectantly, tongue wagging, tail bouncing left to right and back again.

"Ew, Buster!" Elliot screwed his nose up. "I am *not* touching you now." Finishing off his drink, he got up and turned the tap on for Buster to drink and cleanse his palette.

But Buster's ears went back and he stopped drinking long enough to growl at something behind Elliot.

Yawning, Elliot stopped to look over his shoulder at his shadow. There it was. The messy blackness that hovered there. Curious, he stepped fully out into the light so the sun was behind him, casting his shadow out to the front. Lifting his glasses until they hovered just above his eyes, he stared at the Shadow Walker.

It was a vague outline of a person, or thing, bony, as in his visions. Bony head, eyeless sockets, no teeth. It floated there, rising from the ground.

He moved, left, right, stepped forward, stepped

back, turned left, right, went around in a circle. It was always there, always in his shadow, always attached to him. He reached out to see if he could touch it. It floated backwards, but stayed planted in his shadow. He flicked his hand back and forth then retracted it. He quickly thrust his hand forward, but it was too quick. No matter what he did, it floated away like a boxing opponent. Its feet stayed still while it feinted left, right or back.

Elliot waved his arm, hoping to go through it, but it moved. Putting some more thought into it, he kept his right foot in place, but lunged forward on his left, so his shadow was corrupted.

So was the Shadow Walker, having no idea which foot to stay attached to. It hovered from Elliot's left foot, but didn't have much room to manoeuvre, shrinking on the spot. As Elliot's shadow was smaller, so was it, and it floated right in front of Elliot so he was easily able to move his arm through it.

It felt cold, just like normal cold air. There was nothing special about it. He didn't feel a solid mass, no bones, no nothing, just cold air. He waved his hand back then stood up. "Mmm." He looked down at a growling Buster. "Well, what are we going to do about that then, Buster?"

The dog looked from the shadow to Elliot, licked his lips and looked back, baring his teeth as the shadow stared back.

"So, what are we going to do?" Elliot asked the dog. "How do we get rid of this thing? It wouldn't be here if I hadn't've died last month. I wonder how many other people have had one of these." He frowned. "I wonder if they've figured out how to kill it, or get rid of it, or whatever it is we're supposed to do. Maybe I should post something online?"

Staring at his shadow, he danced across the yard to see how it kept up. It kept up well, twirling like a natural born ballet dancer. Elliot's frown deepened, and he hunched down and zigzagged back to the house. The shadow was there the whole time.

"Mmm, clearly I'm not getting rid of you in a hurry." With a sigh, he went back inside with Buster, and after dinner typed up his story into a word doc so he could get it right before pasting it into websites.

He found several sites where you could post questions about anything, and pasted his story into five different ones. He wanted to go as wide as he could to get the most attention on his post and fingers crossed, get decent replies. He hung around on the internet for a few hours before hitting the off switch and going to bed.

*****

On Sunday morning, he had replies from all over the world. Many shared his story and pointed him in the direction of several website forums for people who had experienced death and all it entailed. He read the replies, but no one had dealt with a Shadow Walker, so he clicked onto the other web urls and found a whole host of ghosties who had come back with souls. None were described as Shadow Walkers.

People had named them different things, so no wonder it was hard to find anything. They had left their stories about dying and seeing grisly things after death and then coming back with the unearthly presences. The feeling of someone watching when no one was there, seeing figures in reflective surfaces, feeling headachy and sick, having dogs growl and cats hiss every time they came near. There was a wide assortment of eerie happenings, and Elliot had experienced all of them, and regardless of what name people gave it, no one had the cure or a way of getting rid of it. He scrolled all the way back to the beginning of the forums and blogs, hoping whoever originally started them might have an idea, but no one did.

The next thing he posted was asking if anyone knew of a witch doctor, guru or soothsayer who could help and who was around the Belmont area. He needed to see someone now. No matter what they were called, he wanted to get rid of this thing and wanted to know how to go about it. He didn't want to live the rest of his life with a ghoul attached to his shadow; especially one he saw rip his heart out in dreams and visions.

Not finding any answers, he went in search of why eyes change colour from brain damage and found nothing. There was absolutely nothing to say how or why, or even if eyes can change colour except through puberty. No one had ever come across anything like it.

Not getting what he wanted, he got permission to ride into town to go to the library. He raided medical books, looked for ghosts, ghouls and spirits, and checked a load of books out. He even asked for help from the librarian, but she couldn't find what he needed. Flagging in energy, he hefted his heavy bag onto his back and pedalled home, stopping to stare at the wooded area along the main road to his house.

Was The Howler still there? Did it come back at night? Was it gone for good? Or, was it just there for Halloween?

Discouraged, Elliot continued his way home and lugged his bag upstairs. Sorting the books into piles, he left them for another time, because right now, he was tired and flopped onto his bed to rest before dinner.

Buster padded in and rested his head on his master's bed, wondering what was making him twitch and gasp, murmur and rasp in his dreams. He whined softly and carefully jumped on the bed to lay his head next to his master. Whatever it was, it couldn't have been good.

Visions flew back and forth in Elliot's mind. Shadow Walkers, ghosts, ghouls, spirits, other people's stories, images and pictures all bombarded his brain as he tried digesting the information.

Why did he have a Shadow Walker?

What was it for?

Was it good or evil?

Did it want him back, or was it there to protect him?

What did it want?

When would it leave?

What was its purpose?

Did it mean him harm?

Did it really want to rip his heart out and clench it until it turned to dust?

What was its purpose?

He could see it without glasses on, and clearly Buster saw it and didn't like it.

Was it his eyes? Is that what it wanted?

Did he have some sort of x-ray vision, super sensory eyesight? Was that why he could see them? Because of the change in his eyes, he could now see dead people?

CHAPTER SIX

The last week of school was a short one; Monday through Wednesday and then they were off for another year. The activities were much the same as the week before, games, quizzes, swimming, spending time chatting and watching movies.

For Elliot, things were a little different. He was the freak of the school due to his outburst the Friday before. He'd told everyone what the beast was called, how he'd seen it, and that he'd been affected more than anyone else.

He refused to talk to anyone outside of his year, and only then spoke to those he wanted to speak to. His friends stayed huddled around him and kept everyone at arm's length. They acted like security guards or minders, putting their arms out and telling people to back off and walk away. In general, everyone stayed away from Elliot anyway. Many saw him as the freak show, many saw him as fascinating. He saw himself as haunted and in trouble.

He found himself in the canteen line behind Gretchen.

She turned around to see who was behind her

and flinched. "Elliot."

"Gretchy baby." He grinned and lifted his glasses to give her the eye.

She frowned and repeated the line. "*Gretchy baby?* Where do you *get off* calling me Gretchy, let alone, baby?"

"Calm your farm, Gretchy baby." Elliot pretended to yawn and patted his hand over his mouth. "It's the last week of school, no games, no bullshit, just face it, you have a thing for me, and that's why you're always watching me."

"What! A thing!" she exclaimed, her face screwing up in displeasure. Her friends laughed behind her. "You've *got a hide,* Elliot Gunfield. Thinking *I've* got a thing for *you.*" Rolling her eyes, she turned her back to him.

Elliot stood on tiptoes so he could talk over her left shoulder. "Sam used to think you did. He'd tease me all the time that you had a thing for me which is why you couldn't take your eyes off me all day."

"Sam!" Gretchen stepped forward to get away from him. "What would Sam know?"

Elliot shrugged and moved closer. "Clearly a lot more than you and me, Gretchy baby."

"Ooohhh," she growled. "*Don't call me that!*" Shoving ahead of her friends to get away from him, she left him grinning like an idiot and being slapped on the back by his friends.

During lunch, he kept giving her the eye, lowering his glasses and wiggling his eyebrows at her, much to her friends' amusement and her chagrin.

Gretchen got up and stormed away, and her group up and followed.

The boys laughed.

"What is *up* with you today?" Nathan asked light-heartedly. "You never flirted with Gretchen before."

"Dunno." Elliot sighed. "Something's come over me since the whole coma thing. It's like I'm a different person. I'm doing stuff I didn't do before, reading books that didn't interest me before. Sleep a lot…" He shrugged. "I'm just different. Maybe it's losing Sammy. He used to tease me that Gretchen and I had the hots for each other. That's why we were always staring at each other and fighting."

Snickers went around the group.

"Is he right?" Ben asked. "*Do you* like her?"

Elliot thought for about 0.00002 seconds. "God no! The only *thing* I had was that I didn't like her always winning best Halloween costume every year. It annoyed the hell out of me. And then she got pissed that I won and accused me of winning because my parents voted for me. After that, shit happened, and here we are. But she's always staring, so what does *that* mean?" He shook his head in bewilderment. "Does she like me? Do I still infuriate her, or is she just after me for my eyes?" He got more laughter.

"Dunno, El, but what are you gonna do about it?" Simon asked.

Elliot's shoulders sagged, and he felt every bit of his one thousand and eighty-three years. "I don't know. The year's almost over. Do I do anything or nothing? And I don't even know if I like her." He sat up straight. "I mean *seriously*. What am I even *talking* about this for? I *never* liked her, and she *hated* me. Sam was wrong."

But Sam was never wrong, went through his head. *Sam was right about everything. Everything. So, was he right about Gretchen?*

There was only one way to find out.

After lunch, Elliot purposely sat near Gretchen and her friends. The boys followed suit, sitting at the table next to the girls. They laughed and joked, called out to the girls, made them blush and turn away in embarrassment.

All Elliot had to do was stare at Gretchen and she'd flinch and turn away, but then look back, unable to help herself. When Elliot lowered his glasses and stared at her, she became hypnotised, unable to look away until he smiled and looked away. Oh, yes, he had her.

*****

On Monday night, Elliot read through the books from the library. They were intriguing and got the hair on the back of his neck to stand up. He set down the book he was reading and made sure his window was locked and the curtains were drawn tight before continuing.

In one book, he read about the cultures of different countries and how they deal with the dead.

In some cultures, the dead were revered and those left behind celebrated with marches through the streets and big parties. In other countries, the dead were feared and buried quickly to ward off evil spirits, so they didn't latch on and make the dead rise. This was something which other countries and cultures believed as well; that the dead could *and* would rise if they weren't buried properly. No wonder there were so many zombie movies.

Another book was all about how the heart could slow down so much that doctors could not feel a pulse or heartbeat, and thus declared the person dead. Many had come alive again on the coroner's table; many in the coffins before or after burial, and so some cultures believed in burying their dead with a string leading from the coffin so they could pull on it and a bell would ring above ground, letting everyone know they were still alive. In other civilisations, they buried their dead with enough supplies to last ten lifetimes, like the Egyptians who gave their dead all they could want in the afterlife.

A third book spoke of magic and witchcraft, how evil could put a spell on people and witches could kill them. Witch doctors were still very prevalent in many African countries, and followers revered them while others shunned them. Of course, it all came down to what you believed personally and to whether you were predisposed to interest in hoodoo and parlour tricks. Some thought it was all about hypnotising their followers into doing what they wanted. Others thought the witchcraft voodoo was very real, regardless of who thought what and which country believed it.

None of this got Elliot any closer to an answer for his problem.

He read the rest of the books and scanned many pages into the computer to print them out. He had quite a pile of papers now, but none helped him with what to do. Knowing what his problem was and knowing what to do about it were two very different things, and he needed to know about it now so he could get rid of his Shadow Walker and stop feeling like an old man of one thousand and eighty-three.

Time was running out fast.

*****

On Tuesday morning, the classes got to go swimming, and Elliot made a beeline for Gretchen. "Hey, Gretchy baby. How are ya today?" He waded through the water, glasses on top of his head, waiting for Gretchen to reply.

She glanced his way, irritated at being called Gretchy baby *again*, but got hypnotised by his eyes. *What is it about them?* she thought, unable to tear her eyes away. *Why do I...have such a hard time...?*

"Gretchy baby, why are you and I always staring at each other?" He pushed himself into an upright position to stand in front of her, looking eye to eye. "What *is it* about us that we're constantly staring at each other? Tell me, Gretchy baby, do you actually *hate* me?" A devilish smile crossed his lips. "Do you *really*, Gretchy baby, or do you just secretly have the hots for me and want to *get it on*?"

"Ew, Elliot," Katie Rogan cried. As one of Gretchen's friends, she had been privy to all of Gretchen's innermost thoughts. "You're being gross. Come on, Gretchen." She tugged her friend's arm and broke the spell, pulling Gretchen away from Elliot. Melissa Wong, Yvonne Wellmond and Susan Belford followed. They were the year eight Belmont High clique and stuck together at all times. The girls crowded around Gretchen and got her away from Elliot.

"What *was* that?" Nathan asked as he and the boys waded over. "You said you were going to have a chat, but she couldn't stop staring. What did you do to her? Hypnotise her?"

"It's all in the eyes, boys, all in the eyes." Elliot turned around to show them they were glowing before flipping his glasses down. "They must be magical if they can captivate the girls going around."

"Ha!" Kyle laughed. "Magical! We know they're *somethin'*, but that ain't it."

"No, but I'd love to know *what* they are," Simon added. "Dude, seriously, you're like Superman. They glow. Did you get hit by a meteor rock or something? Maybe some kryptonite?"

Elliot grinned. "I'd love to know, believe me. I can't figure it out, and the doctors can't. No one knows why my eyes changed colour. *I* don't know why they glow, and I sure as hell can't tell you why they interest and fascinate people so much. Maybe it's my magnetic personality."

"Well, whatever it is," Nathan replied, "I'd love to get my hands on some."

*****

That afternoon, Elliot wouldn't take his gaze off Gretchen. He'd removed his glasses and was all but staring a hole into the back of her head.

She felt the heat burning her and swiped her hand through her long light brown hair. She knew it was Elliot, and while she didn't want to, she knew she also couldn't help herself. Glancing over her shoulder, she found him staring without his glasses and quickly looked away.

Melissa Wong noticed and shuffled her seat so she sat in Elliot's line of sight. Frowning at him, she saw his eyes flash angrily and felt the power behind them hit her. She gasped and clutched her chest as his eyes bored into hers and her breathing became laboured.

"Miss, Miss," Susan yelled. "Melissa's having some sort of seizure. Tell Elliot to stop looking at her with his weirdo eyes." Susan quickly stood with her back to Elliot so he couldn't see Melissa. Everyone in class turned their way.

"Melissa, are you okay?" Ms Revesby rushed over to administer first aid.

Melissa's breathing slowly calmed and got back to normal. "I'm okay now. Elliot's eyes were doing things to me."

The boys groaned and rolled their eyes. "Yeah sure, blame the poor kid who died and came back to life," Nathan muttered.

Ms Revesby turned to look at Elliot. "Elliot?"

He shrugged. "Seriously? I get hit on the head with paint cans, get brain damage, and my eyes change colour. And what do I get accused of? Putting some weird hoodoo on the girls. Get real!" he exclaimed. "My eyes changed colour; they didn't suddenly gain magical powers. I'm not Superman. I can't burn through things with my heat vision. I can't see through things with my x-ray vision. Jesus." He scowled. "Like I haven't been through enough. Now I'm copping crap from girls who can't keep their eyes off mine." He crossed his arms and his scowl deepened. "I'm not some freak show for everyone to stare at and then blame stuff on, you know. I'm not the easy cop-out excuse. Get over yourselves." Slumping in his seat, he saw his friends trying to conceal their grins.

Ms Revesby knew he was right. "Melissa, Susan, it wasn't fair to blame Elliot. Melissa, you clearly had some sort of asthma attack. It wasn't fair to put that on Elliot."

The girls stared at each other, shock all over their faces at having been told off by the teacher. The boys just sniggered at their displeasure.

CHAPTER SEVEN

On Tuesday night, Elliot scoured the internet websites he'd left posts on. There were a couple of responses to his plea for help about witch doctors or anyone that could help near the Belmont area, and a couple of people suggested websites. While looking up the urls, he found a site for a man who lived a couple of suburbs over. The site claimed he was a healer who laid hands on people, could rid those of evil demons, and all manner of things otherworldly. Elliot read every page with interest, and found an email address. He shot off a letter, and while checking out other sites received a reply.

Dearest Elliot,

I am so sorry about your ordeal. I have heard of Shadow Walkers, but by another name and I am willing to try and help you. While I'm not sure how, I can do some research and advise you to the best of my ability. If you can't make it to my place of residence I am more than willing to come to you or meet you somewhere that's more convenient. I look forward to hearing from you.

Regards,
Trevor Longfield

Elliot's brows rose. Willing to come here, huh? Cool! He emailed back more information and suggested times and places.

Trevor replied promptly and added that he had thought of someone who might be able to help. He also asked about the Halloween incident.

Elliot gave vague details about that, didn't mention losing his best friend, but did say several people were lost that night. He suggested meeting up on Saturday.

Trevor told him Saturday was fine and he'd do some research until then.

The whole conversation made Elliot feel better. He was finally getting somewhere with finding a way out of his mess and couldn't wait. But he still had four days to go and felt he needed to be doing something. With a day of school left before summer break, he wanted to get rid of this thing that was attached to him now.

Frowning, he grabbed a sketchbook and pencil and tried to draw what he'd seen in his visions, to see if it was the same as his Shadow Walker. "So, they're haunting me in real life and my dreams," he muttered, using the edge of the pencil to shade in the picture.

Holding up the pad, he cast a critical eye over his drawing. Definitely an eighth-grade sketch, not Picasso or anything. It did look a bit like that painting, *The Scream*, but the Walker wasn't clasping its face, and it didn't have eyes.

He added bony hands coming in from the left and right of the page and got out his chalks from art class. Using the red and brown shades, he smudged up the background to look bloody and dirty. When he was done, he laid the pad on the desk and stared at it, expecting the image to move, or to spring to life and haunt him. But it didn't.

He revisited his visions and tried to decipher if they meant something. Did they signify the past? The night he died, went into cardiac arrest; was that what it was about? Was it why the main Walker thrust his hand into his chest and pulled out his heart?

Was that to signify the death I experienced and I'm just reliving it over and over? Or, is it something more sinister? Does it signify my future death? Death by the hand of a Shadow Walker. Is that what it's about? Is that why I feel so old and like time is running out?

His ears picked up the ticking of his wall clock and tuned in while his eyes moved to look at it. He sat there, fascinated by the second hand as it found its way around and just kept on going and going. When he came to, an hour had passed.

"Jesus," he muttered, blinking his tired eyes. *What is going on with me? Why does time capture my attention, or is it simply the mechanical nature of it being a clock?*

He remembered his time in the hospital and how he'd stared at the clock all day. It had lulled him into sleep, like a hypnotic swinging fob watch being waved in front of him. Did it have to do with the Walkers? Was it all a part of some big scheme? The eye colour, the clock, the Walkers, feeling old and tired. Why did he think he was one thousand and eighty-three all the time? Did he come back as someone else? Was he another spirit and not Elliot? Had Elliot really died, and he was someone else? Was there another person's soul inside him; was that it? Two souls had been switched or jumped back into the wrong bodies? Is that why he felt old? But one thousand and eighty-three, where did that number come from? How could he be one thousand and eighty-three years of age? Maybe he should write down some more.

I've got Thursday and Friday to do it. School's over tomorrow, and Trevor doesn't get here until Saturday. Who knows, maybe I can turn it into a book when it's all over.

He rubbed his eyes and stared at the drawing. His fingers lightly traced the outline of the Walker; its eyes, its mouth, its bony head. *What are you and what do you want? More importantly, how do I get rid of you?*

*****

Wednesday was the last day of school, and Elliot knew it was his only chance to get to Gretchen before next year. He stalked her from afar, staring at her with his magnetic eyes. But she was smart. She stayed away from him, sitting across the room, and eating on the other side of the schoolyard. She avoided him all day until she didn't, and he cornered her against the wall well away from her friends and his.

"Gretchy baby." He put his hands either side of her against the wall, blocking her from leaving. "It's the last day of school, and you need to tell me now if you have the hots for me, because we won't be seeing each other until next year, and I don't even know if I'll make it that long. I died you know." He leaned closer, so their faces were nose to nose. "I died and saw things I should not have to see. My eyes changed colour from brain damage; I lost my best friend. I'm a different man, Gretchy, and so it's time to be truthful with one another." He stared into her green eyes, knowing full well his eyes had her attention. "Do you really hate me, or is it all an act to cover up how you really feel?" The glow emanated from his eyes, and he could feel the heat down to his core. He definitely had some sort of superpower; it was just a pity he didn't know what. "Tell me, Gretchy!"

She blinked, captivated by his fiery amber eyes. They also scared her. She had no idea how she felt about Elliot. She hated him for hating her, no doubt, but she certainly didn't like him, or, ew, love him and have the hots for him. Gross!

Unable to put her words together, her mouth moved open and closed.

Elliot took his chance. Grabbing Gretchen's head,

he slammed his lips onto hers, kissing her as he'd never kissed a girl before. Which he hadn't coz he *was* only thirteen. He recalled all the times Sam had teased him about having never kissed a girl and felt a stirring in his pants. He even tried shoving his tongue in, but Gretchen put a stop to it post haste.

She got her arms up between his and broke the hold he had on her. Planting both hands on his chest, she shoved him backward. "How dare you do that, Elliot Gunfield, you horrible, horrible boy!" With a quick slap to his face, she raced off to find her friends.

Wiping his mouth with the back of his hand, he breathed hard. He'd made sure to watch her shadow as she ran, but had seen nothing. Slowly turning his head to his own, he saw the Walker was still there.

"Damn it!" He flung his head back in frustration. He'd been hoping to transport it to Gretchen. That's why he'd kissed her. But no, it was still attached to him. "Why didn't that bloody work! Argh!"

*****

All day Thursday and Friday, Elliot got to writing more information down. He filled an A4, 250-page notebook with his thoughts, his fears, and his ideas about what was going on. They were a bit of a messy jumble, but at least it was all out of his head. With a few emails back and forth to Trevor, he made a plan to meet him the next day at a house by the river at ten a.m.

*****

After looking up an old road directory, Elliot found his way down the long, rickety driveway through the woods to an old house buried in greenery that he recognised instantly. "What the hell!" he breathed, knowing it from his death visions as the house he, Gretchen, and Sam had all turned up at. Hearing a car come up the drive, he slipped into the shadows and waited.

The car came to a stop and a man alighted. With grey hair pulled back into a ponytail, and a long flowing purple robe, he held his hands up toward the house, as if feeling its vibes drifting off it.

Elliot came out of the shadows. "You Trevor Longfield?"

The man opened his eyes and set them on Elliot. "And you, dear sir, must be Elliot Gunfield. The poor boy in need of help." He spotted the messy shadow behind him. "Ah, I can make it out." Hurrying over to Elliot he walked around him, hands up, trying to pick up a signal. He stepped into Elliot's shadow and felt instantly sick, then stepped out to feel better. "Curious." He waved his hand through it and felt the cold. "Fascinating." He stood in front of Elliot. "I don't know if I can help you, but I'm going to try. Do you know if Sadie's home?" He rushed to the door and knocked loudly. "Sadie, you in? It's Trevor."

"Sadie?" Elliot screwed his face up trying to remember where he'd heard the name.

"Yes." Trevor turned to him. "Sadie Blunt. I've conversed with her a few times. Apparently, she has some books on all worldly things. We were talking just a month or so ago about a beast creature. The Howler, she said it was." He eyed Elliot closely for any recognition, but the boy remained stone faced. "Of course, I was fascinated by it all, so when you emailed me about it I had to come. I had to help you. You were involved with it." He stepped closer to Elliot, hoping to get some sort of vibe from him. "You saw The Howler," he all but whispered.

Elliot flinched. "Yeah, whatever. Now I need to get rid of this thing that's attached itself to me. I have no idea what it's here for, how it came back with me, or why it's picked me. I want it gone."

Trevor nodded. "Since Sadie's not home I can't use her books, but I'll do my best with what I've got." He hurried back to his car and retrieved a bag from the back seat. It was a small suitcase, and he carried it over to the house. "Okay, let's work here in the fresh air. Take a seat." They sat in the chairs on the front pathway, and he opened his case. It had small pockets and compartments full of bottles and powders. He pulled out a book, flicked to a page, crossed himself, and started chanting in some foreign language Elliot didn't understand.

Elliot watched curiously, trying to temper how he was feeling while it was going on. No different to five minutes ago. And even though Trevor was flinging his arms around, Elliot didn't believe he was doing anything effective.

Trevor pulled a small bottle of clear fluid from his case and splashed it over Elliot. "Come stand in the sun so we see your shadow."

They moved to the sun and Elliot was splashed with water that burned his skin.

"Ow!" Elliot slapped a hand over his arm. "That burns."

"It's holy water, and it's burning the Shadow Walker." Trevor feverishly splashed the shadow, seeing a black mess swaying from side to side, trying to avoid being hit by the water. "It's working," Trevor announced and emptied the bottle. He started preaching to God Almighty, holding up the silver cross around his neck, taking it off and waving it over the shadow whose mouth was wide and horrified. "Be gone demon creature, be gone from Elliot I say, be gone."

He raced back to his case and produced more fluid and powder which he threw over Elliot. "Protect this boy from this creature, protect him from this curse, protect him from this demon that followed him back to this earthly soil. I will lay my hands upon thee to rid thee of this demon." He laid his hands on Elliot's head and heart, chanting something in another language, different to the last.

Elliot was feeling sick. Whatever Trevor was doing to him must have been working because he was feeling something odd. It was as if his insides were wrestling.

Trevor made a big production of sprinkling powder and water then ran back for more, plus a mirror. "Be gone evil demon, be gone. Take a look at yourself in this mirror and be gone with you." He held it up to the face of the Walker, who seemed to be deteriorating.

The Walker saw itself in the mirror and silently wailed. Bony hands on face, mouth open, eyes empty, it flailed from side to side.

Trevor appeared to be winning the war on the Shadow Walker, but the Shadow Walker knew better. Nothing would get rid of it except for one thing, and no one had ever figured it out in years. Well; two things if you include killing yourself. But if you wanted to get rid of a Walker, there was only one other thing to do.

It shrank down and dissipated.

Trevor looked at clear air. "Elliot, my boy, we've done it. We've done it."

Elliot looked around to see nothing behind him and heaved a sigh of relief. "Oh, thank you, Mr Longfield, thank you so much." He shook his hand rapidly then did a little dance as Trevor packed up his bag.

"I'll have to give Sadie a call to find out what she knows. I haven't been able to get in contact with her." He stood staring at the house before turning to Elliot. "My work here is done, Elliot, my boy. It's on the house since I've never actually gotten rid of this Shadow Walker before. If you have any more problems, let me know. Right now, I need to be off." After shaking hands once more, Trevor offloaded his case into the back seat and got into the front.

Waving out the window, he drove off down the driveway and onto the road.

Turning, Elliot stared curiously at the house and walked around it, looking in windows, seeing if they opened. The house was locked up tight, and he racked his brain for where he'd heard the name *Sadie* before. Going back to the front door, he did what he'd seen people do on cop shows. He looked under the welcome mat, checked the pot plants and rocks beside the door, and felt along the top door sill until he found what he was looking for. Lowering his hand to his face, he stared gleefully at an old black key.

Down the road, Trevor was congratulating himself on a job well done. Having never beaten a Shadow Walker before, he felt it would be one for the books. Preening a little, he glanced in the rearview and tucked a few stray wisps of hair away, and that's when he saw the messy shadow in his back seat right behind him.

A bony hand came flying through the seat and out of his chest. It held his heart in its bony fingers, and they curled around the beating muscle and crushed it until it was dust in its hand.

Trevor collapsed onto the steering wheel and drove across the road into a light pole and the fence of someone's home.

He was dead in an instant.

CHAPTER EIGHT

Elliot rode past the wooded area on his way home and saw the car being hauled onto the back of a tow truck. It was on the corner of his street, and he passed slowly so he could look. He recognised the car as Trevor's and skidded to a halt.

"Jesus Christ!" he breathed, watching the truck drag it onto its back. "Oh no." Fearfully, he glanced behind him and saw the Walker was back. "How did you—?"

He spied his neighbours gawking over the fence. They had the house across the road from the crash. "Hey, Mr Trusdale, do you know what happened?"

"Oh, hello Elliot. I heard the words *heart attack* mentioned by the paramedics before they carted him away." Trusdale was the street's biggest gossip.

"Oh." Elliot's face fell. "That's bad." He wondered if it had to do with earlier.

"Well, it is for him," Trusdale said.

Elliot said goodbye and rode home. He climbed the stairs to his room where he sat on his bed thinking about everything. Halloween, his brain damage, The Howler, his eyes, the time, the clock, his age, the Walker. Now Trevor was dead *after* he'd supposedly rid him of the Walker. Was it all connected? Trevor's death to his? And why did the name *Sadie* make him remember?

Hitting the internet, he googled Belmont and Halloween 2002. Newspaper reports came up and he read all of them, finding the death of Sadie Blunt. Parts of her body were found at her house by the river. The body of Sam Almaw was also found on the premises. Sadie lived alone with a hundred cats that were found to be covering the boy in some weird way of keeping him warm. But it didn't work. Sadie left behind no relatives and just her property, which would revert to the government and be auctioned off in January 2003.

"That's next month," he murmured. "If I'm gonna get in there and get those books, I'd better do it now." Holding up the key, which he'd slipped into his pocket, he made a plan.

*****

That night, Elliot dressed in black, sneaked downstairs, and rode his bike all the way to Sadie's; just as he'd first pictured in his vision. Using the key to unlock the door, he slipped inside, turned the lights on, and searched for the books.

Trevor had mentioned them, and he'd seen them in his vision.

"In a side room," he muttered and moved to the

left of the house. He found two small bedrooms full of junk and picked the room that looked like the one in his vision. There on the shelf against the wall were three black leatherbound books; large, heavy, and very old.

Setting his duffel bag on the ironing board between him and the cupboard, he picked up a book and started going through it. "Speed Demons, Gnome Busters, Killer Bees, The Howler..." He stopped to read that one before moving on. "Ghost Dogs, Puppet People, Graveyard Ghouls, Screaming Armour, Walking Mummies, Full Moon Fever, Ghosts in Mirrors, The Shadow Walkers, here." Running his finger down the page, he mumbled as he read. "Return with soul, attach self, makes feel old, only two ways to get rid of it..." He read a few more lines and his eyes widened. "Jesus!"

Gretchen stopped her bike outside Sadie's house. Her friend Susan lived across the road from Sadie, and she'd seen Elliot out of the bedroom window take a right down the long drive. The girls had been having a sleepover, but she couldn't sleep and had been staring out at the sky. She'd quickly dressed and sneaked out without disturbing anyone. Leaving her bike against the side of the house, she tiptoed to the door and quietly opened it. The lights were on, but she didn't see Elliot.

Stepping in, she closed the door behind her, wondering what he was up to. She could see the lounge and kitchen from her spot by the door. He wasn't in either room. Inching forward, she saw a light to her left coming from a hallway. Trying not to make a sound, she stealthily moved toward it.

Elliot couldn't believe his eyes. There were only two ways to get rid of Shadow Walkers and while one was understandable, the other was pure insanity. His ears pricked up at a sound coming from the front of the house and he knew it was Gretchen. Shoving a random piece of paper into the page, he closed the book and hastily shoved the other two into his bag. He zipped it up, slung it over both shoulders like a backpack, pulled his black ski mask down and picked up the first book. It was now or never.

Slowly, he moved forward, listening for Gretchen.

She reached the hall and saw his shadow looming in the doorway, and turned to run back to the front door.

But Elliot was faster. He dashed into the main room. "Oh, Gretchy baby."

She turned her head, a frightened expression on her face, and copped a huge black book to the head. She did a full spin and fell down, unconscious.

He stood staring over her, holding the book for dear life. Besides dying, there was only one other way to get rid of Shadow Walkers and he had to do it now. Breathing hard, he went into the kitchen and looked for a knife. Finding one in a drawer, he rushed back to Gretchen, put the book and the knife down, pulled off the duffel bag, and opened the book to the correct page.

Rolling Gretchen over, he inched closer, grasped

the knife in both hands, raised it above his head and read from the book. "I transfer mine Shadow Walker onto mine victim. I transfer mine Shadow Walker onto Gretchen Merryweather." He slammed the knife down into Gretchen's stomach.

She gasped and lurched up, her eyes widening in horror as her hands went around Elliot's on the knife.

Elliot glanced dazedly from the knife in Gretchen's stomach to his shadow, watching the messy figure dance between the two bodies, one foot in Elliot's shadow, one foot in Gretchen's.

A dark shadowy figure raced to the cottage and through the door. *"El, no, what have you done?"*

Elliot looked up in a state of shock. "Sammy? Is that really you?"

Sam saw the Shadow Walker as he passed through it and pulled back his lips to snarl at it.

The Shadow Walker knew of Howlers and didn't like them, so it slid into Gretchen's shadow, awaiting for the transfer to finish.

Gretchen's eyes went to Sam's. She was freaked out of her mind by all that was happening; the pain, the hallucination of a dead classmate, and silently pleaded for help as he fell to Elliot's side.

"Oh, El, what have you done?" Sam released Elliot's hands from the knife, stared into his best friend's glowing amber eyes and said, "Let's get you out of here. Come on." He helped a stunned Elliot to his feet and together they stumbled out the door. He saw his parents race inside from around the corner, but didn't mention it.

"Sammy," Elliot sobbed, pulling his best friend to a stop outside. "I knew you weren't dead. I knew you weren't dead." Grabbing his friend in a bear hug, he broke down, finally shedding the tears he hadn't since coming back from the dead.

"Oh, El, I'm so sorry. I couldn't tell you. We're only back now because we saw the notice about Sadie's house going up for auction." He pulled back and wiped Elliot's face. "What have you done, El?"

"I had to get rid of it, Sammy. I had to get rid of the Shadow Walker. I had to, Sammy." He wept. "Look at me. My eyes have changed, I feel old and tired, and I'm haunted by dreams. It's horrible, Sammy." He wiped a hand over his face. "It's horrible."

"Oh, El, I'm so sorry you had to go through all of that because of me. I never meant to hurt you; I just wanted you out of the way. And how was I to know that was going to happen on Halloween?" Sam babbled.

"You were The Howler, weren't you Sammy?" Elliot's face crumpled.

So did Sam's. "Yeah, El. I am."

Inside, Milly and Geoff Almaw, Sam's parents, got to work on Gretchen. Milly poured a special tea blend down her throat while Geoff read from one of the books and sprinkled a special powder on the wound before grabbing the knife by the handle and yanking it out.

Gretchen jerked and screamed, but Milly quickly poured amber fluid into the wound. Geoff poured more powder on top and lit a match, setting the powder on fire.

"Ah," Gretchen screamed, before passing out.

The Shadow Walker stared forlornly down at Gretchen. It knew its work here was over and there was no reason to stay. It dissipated into thin air.

Hearing the screams, Sam pulled Elliot behind him. "We have to go, El, now." They grabbed Elliot's bike and raced off through the woods.

"Gretchen…is she…" Elliot gasped, stumbling over branches.

"She should be okay." Sam breathed and skidded to a halt just before the trees ended. Ahead of them was a beachside car park blocked from the road by sand dunes. Sadie may have lived on the river, but that river fed into the ocean less than a kilometre from her house.

"Sammy?"

Sam looked at his best friend. "El."

"You're a Howler."

"You had a Shadow Walker."

Elliot's tears started again. "I've missed you so much."

"And I've missed you, El." Sam enveloped him in another bear hug. "But I have a new email, so if you want to communicate that way we can. Just don't let anyone know it's me. Okay." He pulled a crumpled piece of paper from his pocket and shoved it into Elliot's. "Email me. Because I don't know if we'll see each other again, El. At least not until after my 20th birthday."

"What happens then?" Elliot wiped his tears away.

"I only become The Howler every ten years instead of every year."

"I won't see you for seven years?" Elliot mumbled in despair.

"But we can email and talk," Sam said as his parents came out the woods.

"Let's get you in the car and out of here. We'll get you home, Elliot." Geoff quickly unlocked the car and lifted the boot to put the duffel bag of books and Elliot's bike into it. He closed the lid as quietly as he could.

Sam bundled Elliot into the back. "Get down, stay low; no one can see us." He lay on top of Elliot as Elliot lay facing him.

Milly and Geoff got in, removed their beanies and put on reading glasses so no one would recognise them with their new haircuts and colours. Pulling out of the parking lot, Geoff flicked on the headlights, and Milly poured a small cup of tea with extra added herbs and handed it into the backseat to Elliot. "Here you go, drink this, it will stop the shock."

Elliot lifted his head and took the cup, drinking the warm, sweet brew. "Sammy," he said softly. "We will keep in touch, won't we?"

"You have my email, El." Sam smoothed back Elliot's hair and kissed his cheek. "Best friends forever, El. In life and death."

Geoff turned into Elliot's street and drove a couple of kilometres down the road to an open field before doing a u-turn. He drove back and stopped just before the last house in the street with his lights off. Leaving the car running, he slipped out and got Elliot's bike from the boot and quietly closed it before opening the back door. "Here you go, Elliot. Time to go."

Elliot sat up and looked around. "Where are we?"

"Just down the road from your place. We'll follow you back to make sure you get there and then leave. Say goodbye to Sam," Geoff said.

Sam followed him out the door, and they stood hugging. "I've missed you, El, but we'll email, okay." He kissed Elliot's cheek before letting go.

"Okay, Sammy. I've missed you too." Elliot kissed his friend back and threw his leg over his bike. "Bye, Sammy."

"Bye, El."

Elliot pushed off and rode up the incline to his house.

Geoff and Sam got back in the car and followed until Elliot rode into his yard.

Sam placed his hand on the window as they passed and Elliot waved goodbye.

"How long will it take?" Sam asked as they turned onto the main road and he lay down so no one saw him. "His eyes were dark again. It's already working. Were they like that from dying, or from the Shadow Walker?"

"About half an hour," Milly told him. "Enough time for him to get upstairs to bed. And his eyes changed from both of those things, but mainly the

Shadow Walker. They make you feel old because *they're* old, and make you feel tired from sucking on your energy. The potion reverses everything, and it should all be back to normal now the Walker's gone."

Elliot watched the car turn the corner, walked his bike to the back of the house, and quietly let himself in. He made it upstairs without waking anyone and fell into his bed fully clothed.

"And he'll be okay and remember nothing?" Sam frowned at the events of the night.

"He'll be back to his old self by morning."

"And Gretchen?" Sam stared at the roof of the car as he settled on the back seat.

"She should sleep for about eight hours. The potions will heal her wound and keep her alive long enough for it to happen."

In Sadie's cottage, Gretchen lay silent under a blanket on the couch where Milly and Geoff had placed her. The powder and potion were doing the job of healing her, but something else was happening. The Shadow Walker was gone, but in its place loomed something bigger, darker, deadlier.

Her brows turned down, her lips twitched. Her body jerked up, arching her back so her head dug into the pillow, her feet into the couch arm. The blanket rose into the air, levitating above her as her wound sizzled, burned, healed and disappeared. Her body spasmed in the opposite direction, lurching her up into a sitting position, her head facing the ceiling. Her eyes flew open to reveal a bright burning light that changed to bottomless pools of black oil before she fell back into unconsciousness.

The blanket settled back over her, and she slept deeply until morning.

FADED

CHAPTER ONE

Gretchen Merryweather woke.

Blinking slowly and yawning, she stretched her back, focussed, and realised she was not in Susan's house, not in Susan's room. In fact, she was nowhere near one of her best friends at all.

"What the hell!" She jerked up and swung her legs to the floor. Brushing aside the blanket, she looked around. "Where the hell am I?" Standing, she made a beeline for the door and flung it open to see she was in a clearing in the woods. "Whose place is this?"

Curious, but also scared, she tried to remember how she could have possibly gotten to a strange house in the middle of nowhere. Seeing her bike against the wall, she calmed somewhat. *I obviously rode here, but when? And where's here and whose house is it?* Glancing around, she quickly grabbed her bike and pushed off, looking over her shoulder as she followed the driveway back to the road. Skidding to a halt, she realised she was across the road from Susan's and frowned. *Why would I be waking up on some strange person's couch when it's right across the road from Susan's? Did I go for an early morning bike ride? Was I kidnapped and left there? Did I sleepwalk? I've never sleepwalked before,* she thought. *I've always woken up in my own bed and never on someone's couch.*

Puzzled, she rode to her friend's house and parked outside the back door. Luckily, Susan's parents were up, and Gretchen nervously slipped inside. "Hey, Mr and Mrs Belford." She hoped they didn't have too much to say about her whereabouts.

"Oh…hello Gretchen." Mrs Belford looked up in surprise from making waffles. "When did you go out?" She went back to pouring batter into the waffle maker.

"A while ago," Gretchen replied casually. "Couldn't sleep, so I went for a bike ride."

"Didn't go too far I hope," Mr Belford said. "You're under our supervision while you're here, and if anything happened to you, your parents would have our guts for garters."

"Um…" Gretchen hesitated. "No, not far. Just across the road along the woods."

"You didn't go to old Sadie's house, did you?" Mrs Belford frowned and dumped waffles onto a plate. "The mayor's warned everyone away from there after the death of Sadie and the weird way Sam was found."

"Yeah…" Gretchen bit her lip. "A whole bunch of cats, right? Something out of a weird horror movie."

"Yes, something like that," Mr Belford mumbled

as he read the paper. "Just remember to stay away from there in future."

"Yes, Mr Belford," Gretchen murmured. "Is Susan up yet?"

"Don't know, but you may as well go and see."

"Okay. Breakfast smells good, Mrs Belford. I'll tell them it's ready." Gretchen went upstairs to Susan's room to find her friends waking. Melissa Wong and Yvonne Wellmond were there as well, whereas their other friend, Katie Rogan, was away for the holidays with her parents. "Breakfast is ready." She sat down on Susan's bed, waiting for the girls to rise.

"How come you're dressed?" Susan yawned and stretched her arms above her head.

"Got up for a bike ride," Gretchen replied. "Got some early morning summer air."

"A bike ride." Melissa groaned. "*Why?* It's school holidays."

Gretchen shrugged a shoulder. "I woke up and couldn't get back to sleep, so I went for a ride." She wasn't about to tell anyone that she'd woken up in old Sadie's house. Having no idea *how* she got there, what would be the point? She wouldn't be able to explain it when she didn't know herself.

"Ugh." Yvonne crawled out of her sleeping bag. "Did you say breakfast was ready?"

"Mrs Belford's making waffles." Gretchen got to her feet. "And they're getting cold."

The girls traipsed downstairs to devour waffles with fruit and cream before showering and dressing for the day.

"So, what are we doing today?" Melissa asked as she fixed her headband in place. Staring into the mirror on Susan's dressing table, she adjusted it until it sat right. "It's school holidays. We're down the road from the beach, and up the road from the shopping centre. What are we doing?"

Gretchen pulled on her boot and thought about it. After whatever adventure she'd had the night before, she felt okay. Her head was a little achy, and she'd noticed a lump on her head when she was brushing her hair, but other than that, there were no marks on her body. No scratches, bruises, or scars. Nothing except a lump on her head, and she had no idea *how* she got that. Did she fall over and hit her head, or get hit by something or someone? With no recollection, whatever *had* happened eluded her and she didn't like it. "What about the centre? We can hit the shops and see what's in for summer. The stores get new stock on the first of the month, but with Christmas just around the corner, they'd be marking stuff down now."

"It's only a week until Christmas, I can't believe the year has gone so quick," Yvonne said. "The last few months especially."

"We did get an extra two weeks off," Susan reminded them. "After Halloween, the school was a wreck."

"Yeah, but we had to study because we came back to exams." Yvonne moaned. "Two weeks off and then back for exams. That just sucked."

"Not as much as Halloween night," Melissa

added to the conversation. "We lost a teacher, police officers were killed, and people on the street. Even that old lady who lives across the road in the woods. What was her name again?"

"Sadie," Susan and Gretchen replied at the same time. They glanced at each other in surprise.

"Isn't that where Sam Almaw was found?" Yvonne asked. She checked her purse and put it in her handbag. The girls went quiet for a moment.

"Yeah," Gretchen murmured, feeling dread flow through her. "Yeah, it was."

"Yeah, that sucked." Susan grabbed a light jacket from her closet. "It's right across the road for God's sake. Talk about creepy. That beast thing went through the woods and ate old Sadie and left. And Sam wandered in and died only to be covered by Sadie's cats in some weird thing to keep him warm or alive or something. But it didn't work."

"Yeah…that *was* weird," Gretchen mumbled. "I take it the shopping centre is it?" The other girls held up their bags. "Shopping it is."

*****

Elliot Gunfield woke, groggy and face down on his bed.

It was Saturday, school holidays, and he was dead tired. Rolling over, he realised he was fully clothed and *on top* of his bed. He lifted his head, looked down at his body, and saw black clothes and high-top sneakers. "What the hell?" His head fell onto the bed and he breathed deeply. *Why am I dressed? Did I go out last night? What the hell has been happening?*

The Shadow Walker.

Do I still have it? Is that why I'm dressed? I did something to get rid of it last night? With a hundred thoughts running through his head, he got up and sprinted downstairs and out into the summer sunshine. Spinning around, he looked for the Shadow Walker, but found none.

None.

No messy shadow lurking, no toothless, eyeless, screaming creature there to haunt his shadows anymore.

"Oh, my God it's gone," he shrieked.

Buster, the heeler cross, was sitting nearby panting, watching his master spin in circles. His tail thumped the ground, and he wanted to join in, so he leapt up and bounced around Elliot, dancing through his shadow and having no cares in the world.

"Hey Buster, you don't see it anymore!" Elliot exclaimed, grabbing his dog's paws.

Buster barked his excitement at having his master back to normal.

"Oh." Elliot collapsed onto the grass and lay spreadeagled, the sun shining on his face. Buster licked it and tripped all over him. "Buster." Elliot giggled, pushing the dog away. "No licking. I know where that tongue's been."

But Buster was having none of that. He was happy

to see his master back to normal.

"I can't believe it, Buster. It's finally gone. After everything I've gone through it's *finally* gone. I'm not being haunted anymore. Woohoo." He double fist pumped, and Buster jumped on him. "Buster!" Pushing him off, he laughingly ran inside and found his parents in the kitchen. "Can I go to the shops with the boys today?" Pouring a glass of orange juice, he didn't notice his parents staring.

"Elliot."

"Mmm?" He turned from the fridge to see his parents. "What?" Their quizzical expressions made him curious. "What?"

"El, have you looked in the mirror today?" his mother asked, stepping over to her son to take him into her arms.

"No, why?" He looked up into her eyes; the glass paused midway to his mouth.

Mrs Gunfield picked up the small mirror from the kitchen cupboard and held it up to her son's face. "Take a look."

Elliot stared into the small round mirror and saw his face. "What?"

"Your eyes, El," Mrs Gunfield said. "They're back to normal."

Elliot stared at them. They were back to normal all right. Normal old brown eyes so dark that sometimes they looked black. His normal old brown eyes were back and weren't the glowing fiery amber they had been for the last few weeks. Blinking, he frowned. He'd gotten used to having unusual eyes these last weeks. Freaking everyone out with them, especially how they glowed when he got emotional. Freaking Gretchen out. Gretchen! Didn't he have to do something where she was concerned? And what else did he have to remember? Something to do with Sammy…

"El?" Mr Gunfield said. "You okay?"

"Huh? Yeah, I guess…" Elliot looked from the mirror to his parents. "I guess I'll just have to get used to having normal eyes again. I'm not the freak show anymore."

"Well, I suggest we get back to the doctor so they can do some x-rays and scans in case something's gone wrong," Mrs Gunfield said.

"Ugh!" Elliot's head fell back. "Do we *have* to? *It's Saturday.* I wanna go out with the boys."

"You're right about it being Saturday." Mrs Gunfield put the mirror away. "I'll have to ring up for an appointment, and I don't think the doctor works on the weekends. I'll make it for Monday, and we can get you checked out to see if you're okay. Let's hope nothing's happened in your brain for them to change back."

"So, I can go to the shops with the boys?" Elliot's brows rose in anticipation.

Mrs Gunfield smiled. "Yes, you can. Just shower and change out of that outfit. What *is* that all over it?" She pulled at the black hoodie Elliot was wearing. "Is that mud, dirt, blood?"

"What?" Elliot looked down in alarm and grabbed at the hoodie. "Aw…I thought it was clean."

"Throw it in the wash and get something else. How long will you be gone for?" Mrs Gunfield asked.

"Dunno, probably till closing time, but maybe earlier." Elliot raced upstairs, showered, dressed in a t-shirt and shorts, then raced back down for a quick breakfast before hitting the streets on his bike.

*****

Gretchen, Susan, Melissa and Yvonne got dropped off by Susan's mother. "I'll pick you up at five," Mrs Belford called out the window. "Be here on the dot on this exact spot. Not a second after. Do you understand?"

"Yes, Mum." Susan rolled her eyes, turned, and linked her arm through Gretchen's. The girls started their day on a high note, but it soon turned sour.

CHAPTER TWO

"Ugh." Yvonne rolled her eyes. "Don't look now, but it's the boys."

"Which boys?" Susan asked, turning her head to look at Yvonne.

"From school." Yvonne cast a glance over her shoulder as they stopped to look at a table full of sparkling goodies out the front of a clothing store.

"*Our* school?" Melissa asked, examining a glittered purse.

"*Of course, our* school." Yvonne double eye-rolled. "*Who* else, from *where* else. Geez!"

The girls finally turned to look, seeing a group of boys all animatedly chatting in the middle of the centre.

"Ugh! Elliot!" Gretchen groaned, seeing the back of his head as it turned from side to side as he talked to Nathan, Ben, Kyle and Simon.

Nathan noticed the girls and pointed to them. The boys turned swiftly to look then turned back.

"Well, we've been spotted now," Susan said. "Should we go over and say hello?"

"Do we have to?" Melissa put her old purse away after purchasing the glittered purse she'd been looking at.

"Well, it would be rude of us not to." Susan smirked and led the way over. "What *are* you rejects doing here? It's not like you'd need to buy anything," she told them as they gathered together. "Loitering and being general pains in the bum."

"Christmas shopping actually," Nathan said pointedly. "Just like you."

"Yeah right." Susan rolled her eyes and crossed her arms. "Because boys know how to shop." She noticed Elliot wasn't wearing glasses. "Not incognito today, freak?"

"Not anymore." Elliot blinked at her.

Susan straightened. "Your eyes are different." The other girls finally stopped ignoring them and turned to look.

"Yes. Yes, they are. They're back to normal. It's a miracle," he mocked.

"What did you do? Hit yourself on the head?" Yvonne joked.

"The last time I was hit on the head it resulted in an aneurysm and me dying," Elliot crossly replied. "I don't want to go through that again, *so no*, I *didn't* hit myself on the head." He turned his attention to Gretchen as a picky little naggy feeling pulled at his insides. "Gretchen."

"Elliot." She stared at his eyes, even now unable to tear her eyes away.

He couldn't figure out what it was. What it was

pulling at his gut, his memory. He just couldn't put his finger on what Gretchen had to do with it. His brows slid down and he continued staring at her.

She shifted uneasily, unsure of why he was staring, why he'd kissed her, and why she hadn't told her friends about it. Why was he tugging on her memory about something she couldn't remember? And *why* couldn't she remember? Did it have something to do with why she was in Sadie's house? What had happened last night? How had she ended up there, and *when* did she end up there? All of that was a mystery that she couldn't figure out. Like why she kept staring at Elliot's eyes. The kiss had freaked her out, and it's not as if she liked it or anything. She thought it was kinda gross, but kinda nice. Nice! Oh, my God, how could she think that was nice? A boy's lips on hers, kissing her. It was Elliot, for God's sake. She didn't even like him, so why would she think a kiss from him was nice? Just because it was her first didn't really mean anything. There would be plenty more, but geez, he had her under some sort of spell.

And everyone noticed the staring contest between Elliot and Gretchen. The girls stepped between them.

"Let's go." Susan hooked her arm through Gretchen's and pulled her along. "We don't need to hang out with losers like that. And what *is it* with Elliot, the freak. Staring at you all the time. He can't take his eyes off you."

Gretchen blinked, trying to put her thoughts into place. "Yeah," she mumbled. "I have no idea why he can't either. It creeps me out."

Yvonne linked arms with Gretchen on the other side. "It creeps *all* of us out. More so now his eyes are back to normal. That whole drama was just… well…drama we didn't need. Everything he did to you was horrible. Ugh, boys!" She delicately screwed her nose up.

"I think his whole eye thing is incredibly fascinating," Melissa said from the other side of Susan. "Just a simple hit on the head from a paint can, and his eyes change colour. Now they've changed back. I find it fascinating." She noted the girls' displeasure. "Purely from a scientific point of view, of course." Melissa was the class nerd and always got top grades in science.

"Oh, of course." Susan rolled her eyes. "Although… I do agree it is fascinating. Did you see the way they glowed when they were the other colour? It was freaky, creepy, and quite interesting. So yeah, I guess I'm with you on that one, Melissa."

"How *could* you find that interesting? Boys, ugh!" Yvonne scoffed. "How could you be interested in boys?"

"We're not interested *in* boys," Susan scolded as they walked along in the centre. "We're interested in *why* Elliot's eyes changed the first time, and more importantly, *why* they've suddenly changed back to normal."

"Can we stop talking about them please?" Gretchen pleaded, coming to a halt. "I don't want to talk about Elliot Gunfield anymore. Not today. Just look around, it's Christmas this week. We're on holiday and out of school, we survived an attack by a beast on Halloween. We're alive and here and doing Christmas shopping. Can we *please* stop talking about the boys?" She stomped her foot for emphasis.

The girls laughed, and Susan added, "Yes, let's put the boys out of our heads and Christmas shop."

As they walked from store to store, buying up the Christmas bargains, Gretchen's mind kept wandering back to Elliot. She felt it. Felt that he had something to do with her blackout from last night. Because she must have had a blackout, right? A blackout or she'd been sleepwalking. What else could it be for her to get dressed, ride her bike over the road to Sadie's, and end up sleeping on the couch until morning? Did she fall asleep? Did someone knock her out? Did Elliot have something to do with it? Was he there? Did she see him and follow him there? Did he leave her on the couch? Why was she getting such strong vibes from him that he had something to do with it?

Sighing, she watched her friends try on clothes and buy trinkets from different shops, but she was no longer interested in the festivities around her. She wasn't even interested in lunch when they sat around chatting about their purchases so far.

"What's wrong with you?" Melissa nudged Gretchen's foot under the table.

Gretchen came back from dreamland and shrugged lightly. "Dunno."

"Do *not* tell me you've let Elliot get you down?"

Susan bit into a French fry.

"No…" Gretchen breathed deeply and looked away. "I don't know."

"You *have got* to be kidding me?" Susan burst out. "Got a crush, have we?"

Gretchen blushed and rubbed her sweaty hands on her favourite hot pink summer pants. "No."

"Well then, what's the problem?" Susan pushed.

"I don't know," Gretchen cried. "It's a weird feeling that something happened and Elliot has something to do with it. It's nagging at my mind and my stomach, but I just can't figure it out."

"What do *you* think it is?" Melissa asked, swirling a French fry in the burger sauce.

Gretchen heaved a sigh. "I don't know. I can't put my finger on anything. I just know something is going on and it's kinda scary."

"And what's Elliot got to do with it?" Yvonne asked from beside her.

"I don't know." Gretchen shook her head. "It's just a really bad feeling I've got."

The boys spied the girls across the food court. They'd spent most of the day talking about Elliot's eyes and what they were getting their families for Christmas. But now they were eating fried chicken and burgers.

"So, El, what's going on with you and Gretchen?" Nathan asked after swallowing a mouthful of burger.

"What?" Elliot frowned and shoved hot fries into his mouth. "There's nothing going on with me and Gretchen."

"Well, there's gotta be somethin' if you keep starin' at her. You did it at school the last two weeks and kept sayin' there was nothin' there, but I dunno. I think you're keepin' somethin' from us. Was Sam right? Do you and Gretchen have the hots for each other?"

"What! *Of course not.*" Elliot scowled. "We *don't* have the hots for each other. She gets on my damn nerves. Whinging about the costume party at Halloween, and then blaming me for burning a hole in her head in school that day. Bah!"

Simon laughed. "Yeah, blaming you for making Melissa sick. You soon turned that around and put it back on them. The teacher sided with you. The girls *did not* like that one bit. But *it was* funny."

"Yeah, like getting hit on the head with paint cans." Elliot's scowl deepened before his eyes wandered to Gretchen.

"And here he is moonin' over her again," Ben complained, throwing his hands up in the air.

"He's *clearly* got the hots," Kyle joked. "He can't keep his eyes off her."

"She did something," Elliot murmured. "But I can't remember what."

"Who did what?" Nathan asked. "Gretchen? What did Gretchen do?"

"I don't remember. But it's picking at my brain to remember." Elliot's scowl turned to a frown so deep his brows almost met.

"Well, whatever it is dude, I'd love to know," Nathan said. "If you and Gretchy baby get up to somethin' that we don't know about, then I *really* want you to remember so you can tell us."

Elliot sighed. "I don't think it's good. I have a bad feeling that whatever Gretchen and I got up to it wasn't good."

"Oh." The boys' brows rose. "Now it's what you and Gretchen *got up to*. Which was?"

Elliot shook his head. "I don't know. I wish to God I could remember, but I can't. What I *do* know, is it isn't good. And I don't even know *how I know* that."

*****

Not long before home time, Gretchen stood staring at herself in the dressing room mirror of a popular teen store. The dress looked awesome and was in her favourite colour of pink, but for some reason it was making her look pale. And at this time of the year, she was never pale. Stepping closer to the mirror she turned her head left and right. She pulled down the skin under her eyes to look into them, checked her gums and tongue, and felt the lump on her head. It had gone down a little, but was still there. *God, I look so white. What's wrong with me? Am I sick?*

She had dark circles under her eyes and bags too. At thirteen, she'd never had these in her entire short life. So why did she have them now? Was her sleep disturbed that badly? She did end up on Sadie's couch, but as far as how she got there, who knew. *But I should know because, hello, I got there on my bike. Which meant I had to wake up, get dressed, sneak outside, ride over there, go inside and fall asleep on the couch. How could I do all of that without knowing? That's the problem. I don't know. I don't remember. I don't remember anything after going to bed last night. And how is Elliot involved? Or is it just because he's been causing problems since Halloween and then he won that damn costume trophy. How dare he!*

She scowled, but caught her reflection in the mirror. She didn't look good. White, sickly, not well. Not sick, but not feeling a hundred percent. There was something in her gut about it all. *Something bad happened last night and I need to find out what it is in case I did something bad, or something bad happened to me. Was I drugged? Kidnapped from Susan's house? Did devil worshippers kidnap me and use me for a sacrifice? Could that be it?*

Considering that was Sadie's house and she was known as the old kook of the town, she'd heard all the warnings. Witch, devil worshipper. Had she been sacrificed for something to do with Sadie or The Howler that Elliot told the class about? And how did Elliot know about that? Is that what it had to do with? And why did Sam Almaw keep coming to her mind? Had Elliot done something in Sam's name? Was that why he was popping up in her head? Had Elliot done something like try and sacrifice her to some devil worshipper to get Sam back? Were they trying to resurrect Sam? Was that why she didn't remember? They had drugged her so she couldn't remember because it was too horrible and too horrific to remember?

CHAPTER THREE

The girls sat in Susan's room after dinner, going over their purchases, wrapping presents, and chatting about Christmas.

Susan noticed Gretchen's quiet mood and asked what was wrong. "You can't still be thinking about Elliot? *Do you* have a crush on him?"

Gretchen looked up from examining the pink glitter bag she'd bought and felt her anger rise. "You know what! I have absolutely no freakin' idea *what* I feel. I don't feel like myself. I know something has happened, and I know Elliot has something to do with it. But it's definitely *not* a crush. Why he stares at me, I don't know. It's like he knows something I don't about me, and it's creepy and I want it to stop." Sighing, she put the bag down, got up from her sleeping bag, and went and sat on the window seat in Susan's room. It overlooked the side yard so she could see the driveway to Sadie's house.

"So…" Susan glanced at Melissa and Yvonne who'd stopped what they were doing. "Do *you* think he's obsessed?" She wandered over to sit beside her friend. "He *did* stare at you a lot before the

Halloween party, and he always looked angry. But after that, when he came back, it was different. His eyes were different, and it was creepy, but fascinating. But it had *definitely* changed. Like he had another reason to stare at you."

She tucked a strand of long blonde hair behind her ear and licked her lips. "Maybe seeing that beast, losing Sam, and getting hit on the head made him a nutjob. Maybe he's dangerous, although I got the feeling that he's different again. When his eyes changed, he went from being angry at you over the costume party to being obsessed with you. But today," she shrugged, "dunno. I didn't get either vibe. It was more like…" Glancing at Melissa and Yvonne, she sought backup for what she was saying. "Like he was worried."

Gretchen frowned. "What! Worried? About me?"

Susan gave a half grin. "Yeah, kinda. It was weird. The way you two looked at each other, like you were trying to figure something out and you both looked worried about something…or someone…each other maybe?"

"That's ridiculous!" Gretchen retorted, staring out the window. "Why would I be worried about Elliot Gunfield?"

"Not so much *about* him, but something *to do* with him," Susan went on.

The frown slid over Gretchen's face. Considering how she felt it made sense, but what didn't make sense was she couldn't put her finger on exactly what it was.

"So what are you going to do about it?" Melissa asked, intrigued by the whole thing.

"I don't know." Gretchen turned to look at her friends. "I don't know if I *should* do anything about it. If there's anything *to do* about it."

"Ask him point blank." Yvonne smeared her new berry lip balm over her lips. "Just go and ask him what's going on."

"I can't do that!" Gretchen exclaimed. "I got a bad vibe from him."

"I doubt he'll do anything," Melissa said, watching her friend.

"Yeah, but still." Gretchen frowned. "I don't want him doing anything *to* me. What if he does?"

"Do you want us to go with you?" Susan asked, throwing herself onto her bed.

Sighing, Gretchen thought about it. "No. I guess I should talk to him myself. Not that I can do it at school because school's out."

"You should do it face to face," Melissa said. "Then you can gauge his reaction. If you do it over the phone, he could lie to you."

"Yeah, I suppose," Gretchen conceded. "Guess I'll have to bite the bullet and go and see him in person."

"When will you do it?" Susan asked, lazily swinging her arm off the side of the bed.

"Tomorrow…I guess…" Gretchen flopped down on her sleeping bag and gathered her shopping. "It's Christmas this week. I should get it over and done with before then."

"What if you don't like what you hear?" Melissa

asked, going back to her wrapping.

"Then I'll not like it and leave." Gretchen shrugged.

The girls spent the rest of the night listening to music and talking about their favourite celebrities before turning off the light for some sleep.

Gretchen lay awake in her sleeping bag, twiddling her thumbs, staring at the ceiling. She heard the others breathing and wondered how they could sleep so soundly.

Because they don't have your problem, wafted through her head.

Yeah, but what is my problem? I don't feel the way I did yesterday. I feel different. Like something's happened, but I don't know what. I wish I could figure it out. Ugh!

Rolling onto her side, Gretchen tried to put words to her thoughts. *I feel like my body is not my body anymore. Like I'm not me anymore. Have I picked up a bug and it's making me sick? I feel… blah. Like something is missing. But why would Elliot know? Maybe he doesn't, and he's trying to figure it out as well. Has something happened to both of us and we're both trying to figure it out…?*

Gretchen fell into a deep sleep, tired after the last two days. But the sleep wasn't peaceful for long.

She was standing on a grassy plain, the breeze floating through her hair, lifting it gently. The grass was thick and green and lush, the sky blue with fluffy white clouds.

"Where am I?" she murmured, her head moving from side to side. Spinning around, she saw nothing but grass and sky.

Running forward, she stopped short of the edge of the grass where it met the sky, flailing her arms to back pedal. What the hell! Puzzled, she knelt and ran her hand along the edge of the grass. It ended in mid-air.

Carefully leaning forward, she peered over the side of her magical carpet ride. What she saw made her recoil in horror. "No, no, it can't be. I must be dreaming it." Seeing no one else, and no*thing* else, she inched closer to the side and looked down.

The world below her was the red of hell. Fires, blood, fighting, killing. The heat wafted up and it burned her face and brought tears to her eyes. *What's going on? Where am I? What is this place? Why am I looking down on it?*

Smoke drifted across the scene, and she broadened her view. In the distance, volcanoes were blowing, buildings were crumbling down; horned beasts were killing the humans they fought with. Blood was shed by the bucket loads and filled the streets with rivers of red. Cracks appeared in the ground, shook, opened to swallow all that was upon it, and man and beast fell into the molten lava boiling crevice that closed upon itself. But the men and beasts were not gone for long as more appeared to replace them, and the fighting resumed from where it had stopped. The humans were not winning. The world beneath her was falling apart, and she was floating on a magic carpet of grass in the sky.

Crawling along the edge, she found it wasn't a very big chunk of land on which she was levitating, and regardless of which side she looked over, she saw the same scene; the devastating horror of destruction.

Her eyes flew open, her body jerked slightly, and she found herself back in Susan's room in her sleeping bag. *What the hell,* she thought. *What was that about?*

She felt her bladder about to burst, so quietly slipped out of her bag and into the bathroom connected to Susan's room. It was also connected to Susan's brother's room, so she hoped he didn't need to go.

Closing the door, she flicked on the light, did what she needed to do, and washed her hands. While standing at the basin, she examined her face in the cabinet mirror. Pale, withdrawn, eyes sunken, cheeks hollow. *God, I look awful.* She dried her hands and leaned in for a closer look. She didn't look herself. *Is this what I look like in the middle of the night? God, how horrible.*

Staring into the mirror, she became mesmerised by her eyes. Under the white light the green of her irises began swimming, like whirlpools of emerald, but quickly became overwhelmed by the black that invaded them, covering them like a blanket of evil, enveloping all that they were. Her fists banged on the mirror as she saw herself on the other side.

Gretchen looked up from the fires of the hellish destruction below to see a swirling black mess open to show herself on the other side of it. "What the hell?" She ran to it and placed her hands on the smooth surface of the wormhole, or vision, or mirror, or whatever the hell it was. But she was also on the other side with eyes as black as night.

"What's going on?" she yelled. "Hello. Is that me?" The wind whipped her around, flinging her hair across her face. She brushed it aside. "Hello. Who are you? Why are you here? How can I see you? Is that me? Why am I not in my body? How is this happening?" The questions came thick and fast, and all went unanswered as she stared at herself through the two-way mirror floating in the sky.

"What the hell!" Gretchen murmured, seeing herself on some grassy knoll floating above the sky. "Who are you? Are you me? Wait, I just dreamt about you. Am I still dreaming? I had the dream about being on a grassy knoll and seeing hell over the side, and now I'm looking in the mirror at the exact same thing. It can't be possible. It just can't be. I can't be seeing this. I must still be asleep. I *have* to be dreaming this."

A gnawing sound came through her ears and into her brain, growing louder and louder. "What *is* that?" She grasped her ears and placed her hands flat against her head, trying to block out the noise. "What *is* that? What's going on?" The only way she could put it was that it sounded as if something was chewing on her brain, eating it from the inside out. "Ugh, what *is* that?" She doubled at the waist, bending over, almost falling to her knees.

"No, no, what's going on?" Gretchen yelled from her grassy knoll, banging on the window. "Where are you? Where did you go? Come back. Why am I seeing myself? What is this world? Come back. Who are you? Are you me? What's going on?"

Bathroom Gretchen slowly rose to her feet as the sound had calmed and she could stand again. "Ugh." Blinking, she looked in the mirror to see herself fading away. "Wait, come back. *Who are you? What* are you? *Where* are you? Are you me?" She planted her hands on the mirror and saw herself fading into the distance. "Wait, come back." Banging her fists, she burst into tears, feeling a part of her was leaving, being wrenched away from her. She felt empty, soulless, as if she was losing her mind.

Collapsing onto the bathroom floor, she cried. For what, she wasn't sure. But it felt like the weight of the world. For Halloween and not winning the trophy. For her teacher and Sam, for Elliot, for the world, but for herself. Whatever was going on inside of her, it felt as if life was over. *She* was over, and she didn't know what to do about it.

Who was that in the mirror? Was it her? How could it be? Was she still dreaming or was this real? How was it happening? How was she seeing herself in a mirror?

Confused, she cried harder, letting months of grief flow forth. But grief for what she didn't understand. And she didn't understand how or why she had just seen herself in the bathroom mirror.

Slowing down, she wiped her face and heaved a

shaky sigh. *This is ridiculous,* she told herself. *Look at you. Sitting on the bathroom floor crying because you think you've seen yourself in the mirror. How ridic! Get up and get back to bed before someone finds you.*

Climbing to her feet, Gretchen glanced in the mirror, but saw nothing. *See, nothing there. You were just dreaming. You're not in there. You're here.*

"Gretchen…Gretchen…"

She turned from the mirror to look at the door. Uh oh.

"Gretchen wake up…time for breakfast."

Gretchen's eyes slowly opened and she yawned.

"Come on. Mum's got breakfast on." Susan was wrapping herself in her dressing gown. "Get up."

Gretchen frowned and lifted her head. "What?" She was back in her sleeping bag on her side and waking up to Sunday morning.

Wasn't she just in the bathroom?

"Get up and come down. It's waffles again." Susan ran into the hall with Yvonne and Melissa behind her.

Gretchen quickly got to her feet. "Wait, just a minute…" Racing into the bathroom, she looked at herself in the mirror and found the pale version of herself from the night before. Blinking, she saw her eyes were normal, but different.

What had just happened the night before?

CHAPTER FOUR

"Elliot, washing," Mrs Gunfield called from her bedroom. "Get your clothes and sheets. I'm putting on a load."

Elliot opened his eyes to Sunday morning. Buster was snoring by his bed, and the sun was creeping in around the curtains. "Ugh…Mum…it's Sunday," he called.

"It's eight o'clock. I want your washing."

"Argh!" Elliot rolled out of bed and landed on Buster. "Oops, sorry Bust." He ruffled the dog's head before stripping his bed and dumping the sheets out in the hallway.

"And your clothes and bath towels," Mrs Gunfield said as she carried a basket of washing out of her room and down the stairs.

Groaning, Elliot rolled his eyes and went back into his room. Flinging open the curtains and window, he felt the cool morning breeze float in. Spying his clothes all over the floor, his desk, the chair, and falling out of the laundry basket, he gathered everything and dumped it all in before noticing a crumpled piece of paper had fallen to the floor.

"What's that?" He picked it up, smoothed it out, and saw an email address. Catnip2002@gmail.com. He gasped. Sammy! The vision came flooding back. He was in the car with Sam and they'd dropped him off down the road from his place. "Sammy's alive!"

"Elliot, washing."

Shoving the paper under his laptop, he stripped off and dumped his bedwear in the basket, took a quick shower, and carried the basket downstairs.

How could he have forgotten Sammy was still alive? That he'd given him a new email address and he couldn't see him again until he turned twenty. Sammy was The Howler after all, and he had a lot to explain.

After a quick breakfast and helping his mum hang the washing out, he dashed upstairs and turned on his computer. An hour later he was hitting send on a lengthy email to his best friend. Telling him all about what had happened since Halloween and asking about other things.

An hour later he got just as lengthy a reply in return. Because of Sam's Egyptian heritage, not that you'd know it with him being so white, becoming The Howler was destined and not under his control. Plus, he didn't even know about it because his parents had kept it from him. He was glad Elliot was all right now and no longer had a Shadow Walker, but told him to be on the lookout for other weird behaviour.

Elliot typed up his reply. *I can't believe what's*

going on with Gretchen. I still don't believe you were right, Sammy. We don't have the hots for each other, but something is definitely going on. Do you know what?

No, Sam typed back. *You said you hated Gretchen before. I teased you by saying you had the hots for each other coz I figured you did. But with your eyes changing colour and going through what you went through, it's no wonder things changed for you. I'm glad you're back to normal.*

Elliot smiled before typing. *Yeah, so am I,* he wrote. *But I was getting used to freaking people out with them. Especially when they flamed up.*

Did you ever have any powers? Sam typed back.

Not that I know of, Elliot wrote. *They glowed brightly, but that was about it. No heat vision, x-ray vision, nothing.*

Lol. Pity.

Yeah, it was, now I'm back to normal, Elliot wrote. *But there's something going on with me and Gretchen, and not in a good way. It's a bad way. Like we're both involved in something we shouldn't be. Like we both did something we shouldn't. But I can't remember.*

Maybe you only wished it happened, Sam wrote, trying not to give anything away.

No Sammy, something definitely happened and I plan on finding out. You were there. Do you know?

Sorry El, I don't, Sam lied. How could he tell his best friend that he'd stabbed Gretchen in the stomach so his Shadow Walker transferred to her?

Well, someone knows something, and I plan on finding out. I'll let you know when I do. How do you like where you are?

Like it lots. It's sunny, bright, and there's lots of stuff to do. But I miss my old life, my old school, my friends. You.

You trashed half the school and ate a teacher, three cops, and two men, plus killed countless more.

Yeah…um…that wasn't actually me. Yeah, the teacher was, two officers were, and the jogger and cyclists, and Sadie, but the others, not me.

If not you, then who?

Ah…not something I can get into, especially over the internet. Maybe one day I'll tell you, El. When we're twenty-one and laughing over a beer.

Yeah, maybe, Elliot replied, hearing his mother call him downstairs for lunch. *Gotta go. I'll email soon.*

We're home on Sundays and you can email at night. I faff around doing stuff online.

Okay. I'll talk to you then. Bye, Sammy.

Bye, El.

Elliot switched off and went down for lunch. Afterwards, he helped bring the washing in, made his bed, and took Buster for a walk to the local dog park and playground.

Gretchen was walking along the road to the park. She'd been home since morning and was now heading for Elliot's to talk to him, but she found him at the park with his dog playing chasy. She stopped to watch as Elliot threw the stick and Buster chased it, chomped into it, and trotted back to his master.

Upon seeing Gretchen, Buster growled and raced towards her.

She screamed and ran for the jungle gym, climbing up just as Buster jumped up and nipped at her sneakers.

"Buster, down," Elliot yelled, finally catching up and pulling Buster back by his collar. "What's wrong with you? Bad dog. Bad Buster."

Buster growled at Gretchen who sat perched atop the bars staring down at the growling beast.

"What's wrong with him?" she cried. She was scared of dogs, which is why her family didn't own one.

"I don't know. Maybe he senses something about you." Elliot clipped on Buster's lead and attached it to the jungle gym. "Sit Buster!" he commanded, and Buster sat. Looking at Gretchen, Elliot suggested she get down the other side.

Not taking her eyes from the dog, she carefully crawled down and gave Buster a wide berth.

Elliot walked over to her. "You okay? He didn't bite you, did he?"

"No…no…" Her eyes were locked on Buster who was giving her a throaty growl.

"I don't know why he's acting that way. He got like that when I was different." Elliot looked from his dog to Gretchen. "You're different."

Gretchen finally tore her gaze away from Buster to look into Elliot's eyes. "Yes, and it's creeping me out. *Freaking* me out. And I don't know what it is. Do you?"

Elliot sighed. "No. But I have a feeling something's happened. It's connected us somehow. Maybe we should talk about it."

Gretchen's lips turned up into a small smile. "That's what I was coming to talk to you about."

Surprised, Elliot could only nod and point to a nearby seat that kept them out of Buster's range. They walked over and sat. "So…"

"So I have no idea where to begin." Gretchen nervously clasped her hands in her lap.

"At the beginning," Elliot said, noticing the hand movements. It was a warm sunny day, but there was a chill creeping down his back.

"Well…I'm not sure where the beginning is…" Gretchen licked her lips and eyed Buster who was panting and wagging his tail. "I *think* it happened Friday night."

"Friday? Like two days ago?" Elliot frowned.

"Yep. I don't know how, but I got dressed, rode my bike to old Sadie's house, and somehow woke up Saturday morning on her couch under a blanket." Shaking her head, she looked at Elliot for some form of confirmation, but got a puzzled expression in return. "I have no idea how I got there. Why I went there, what happened, *how* it happened? *Nothing.* I'm confused and a bit scared."

"Yeah, I guess you would be." Elliot tried remembering his own experience, but couldn't get a clear grasp on it.

Gretchen went on to explain the dream in detail. "And then I'm having weird dreams and wondering why you're always staring at me. Why *do* you stare at me, Elliot? Everyone keeps stirring me that we've got the hots for each other."

Elliot blinked and looked up in surprise. "Same here. I have no idea where they got it from, but I *think* they're joking." He shrugged and glanced away. "I don't know why I keep staring. I think I'm trying to figure something out that involves you. But I'm not sure how or why or what it is. I just have a really strong feeling it involves you."

"Same here," Gretchen said. "I think you're involved in what's happening to me, but I don't know how or why. My mind's drawing a blank."

"Mine too," Elliot agreed. "It's there in my head, but I just can't put my finger on it."

"Same here. I feel it in my gut that we're involved in something, but I have no idea what or how or why. Why would *we* be involved in *anything* together? I don't get it. If neither of us has a crush on the other, what's making us stare at each other or feel this way? This weird physical attachment to each other… Why would we *have* that? Why would we *do* that? I don't get it, Elliot. I really don't."

"Neither do I, Gretchen." Elliot heaved a long sigh, feeling all energy leave his body.

"Yeah…I feel like that," Gretchen murmured. "I feel tired and worn out and not myself. I have bags and dark circles under my eyes and look way too pale. And considering the weird dream I had *last* night, I feel like my soul is disappearing, or missing, or something. I don't feel like myself, Elliot, and I know it has something to do with you." She looked expectantly at him hoping he had an answer or could come up with one.

He couldn't, because he didn't know what was happening himself. He knew his Shadow Walker was gone, but couldn't remember how it happened, where or when, except sometime Friday night. *Wait, didn't Gretchen mention Friday night? So, if something happened to us both Friday night…what was it?*

"Have you thought of something?" Gretchen eagerly asked, seeing the thoughts fly over his face. "Do you know?"

"Ah…no…" Elliot said. "But you just mentioned Friday night, right?"

"Yes. I was staying at Susan's and somehow left her place and rode my bike to Sadie's during the night. Why?"

"I think something happened to me Friday night as well." He racked his brain for ideas, but didn't want to reveal the details about Sam.

"What! Tell me!" Gretchen grasped his arm and he jumped.

Staring down at her hand, Elliot had flashes of Gretchen's face, Gretchen's body, Gretchen lying on the floor with blood all over her. "Argh!" he gasped and jumped up from the seat. "Argh!"

"What, Elliot? What do you remember?" Gretchen saw the terrified look on his face and knew something bad must have happened Friday night. "What! Tell me." She got up and followed him as he turned and bolted across the park without Buster. "Elliot," she yelled, keeping up with him.

He stumbled on an uprooted tree branch and face planted into a pile of leaves.

Gretchen pulled him up and grabbed both his arms. "What did you see? What did you remember? Was it about me? Was it me? What was I? *Where* was I? Was I at Sadie's house? What was I?" She shook him as he gazed dazedly up at her. "Tell me. What was I?"

"You…" Elliot blinked and stared up at her pale face. "You were dead."

CHAPTER FIVE

"What?"

Elliot crumpled into the pile of leaves, hearing Buster bark at him in the distance. "You were dead."

Gretchen let go of his arms. "What?" barely came out in a whisper.

"I don't know; I don't know. When you touched me, I had flashes. I don't know where you were, or if they were real. I don't know," Elliot sobbed, unable to get a grip on his emotions or the images in his head. His hands moved to his bowed head and his fingers dug into his skull. "Why would I see that? Why would I think that? That was horrible."

"What did you see?" Gretchen whispered. "What did you see?"

"I don't know." Elliot's head moved mechanically from side to side. "You on the floor, blood all over. I don't know where it was, or when it was, or if it even happened. You're alive." He looked up sharply. "You're standing here in front of me, so clearly you didn't die and you aren't dead. Why would I see such things that clearly didn't happen unless..." He drifted off.

"What?" she prompted. "Tell me, Elliot. What?"

"Unless." He glanced around them before looking back at her. "Unless it's *going* to happen."

"What?" Her brows slid down. "A premonition? You had a premonition about my death? Don't be stupid."

Elliot got to his feet. "*You are not dead.* I saw you dead on the floor. I have no idea where, when, how, who or why, so *you* explain it to me!" He stuck his finger in her chest and stomped away.

She thought about what he'd said, but none of it made sense to her either. Racing after Elliot, she stopped him. "What else can you tell me? What was I wearing? What was I doing?"

"I don't know," Elliot cried, continuing on his way back to Buster. "I don't know. Black, I think."

"Pants? Shirt? T-shirt? Jumper? Skirt? What?" Gretchen demanded.

"Argh! Gretchen," Elliot growled. "Jeans and a jumper thing. *I don't know.*"

She thought back. "I had that on when I woke up in Sadie's place, but I was lying on the couch, not the floor."

"*And clearly not dead.*" Elliot waved a hand at her.

"No. But I still want to know." She grabbed his arm again. "What do you see now?"

He gave her a wide-eyed look. "*Nothing!* Now let go." He shook her off and kept going. "It doesn't work like that. I don't even know how it worked before. I don't know why. It just happened when it did, but not anymore. I don't know any more than you, now just leave it."

"I can't, Elliot." Gretchen sped after him. "If something's happening to me or you or both of us we should know. And if it didn't happen Friday night, then it's going to happen sometime, and I need to know."

"Well *I* don't," Elliot snapped and untied his dog from his prison. Buster growled at Gretchen, and she backed off.

"Look, I just want to figure out what's going on. Why I'm having weird dreams and how this is all related to you," Gretchen said, keeping an eye on Buster.

Elliot sighed, and his shoulders sagged. "I don't know what's going on myself so how can I tell *you*?" Shaking his head, he looked at her. "I'm sorry. But I can't help you. Come on, Buster." He pulled the dog along and headed home, leaving Gretchen more puzzled than ever.

When Elliot got home, he emailed Sam again and told him about his conversation in the park with Gretchen. He gave every detail he could think of and waited for Sam's reply. It came through about fifteen minutes later.

Have no idea what's going on El. Have you developed supernatural powers?

Hardly, Elliot replied. *But I definitely saw something today. Whether it happened Friday night, or it's going to happen, I don't know. But Gretchen's freaking out, I'm freaking out, and Buster's freaking out. He did that when I had the Shadow Walker, so maybe Gretchen's got something too.*

Maybe she does and doesn't know it. Or maybe Buster just doesn't like girls, Sam typed.

Lol. He likes girls plenty; it's just Gretchen he growled at.

Then he's clearly sensing something. But if neither of you knows what it is, there's not much you can do. It's not like Buster can tell you.

Baha! If only he could it would make it a lot easier to figure out. What happened that night, Sammy? Last Friday night at Sadie's, I mean. I was clearly there, you were there, your parents were there. You drove me home, and Gretchen was staying across the road at Susan's, so it would all fit. If only I could remember. Tell me what happened, Sammy. Were we at Sadie's house? Is that why I was there? And why you were there? I can't remember.

It took a while for a reply to come through.

Mum, Dad, and I were there for something from Sadie's house. I saw you in the woods and got you out of there. I don't know why you were there. But we took you home.

Not enough detail, Sammy. I know there's something you're keeping from me.

I have no idea what happened after I got you through the woods. I have no idea what happened after we took you home because we left. I have no idea what Gretchen has or had to do with it.

Elliot scowled at the email and sat biting his lip while mulling over it. Sammy wasn't telling him the whole truth and he felt it. If he wasn't going to get it out of him, then what? Who could he turn to? Trevor Longfield was dead, as was Sadie. There was no one else. Another email beeped.

Gotta go, El. Talk soon. Keep me updated, Sammy.

"Yeah, right I'll keep you updated," Elliot muttered. "You can't even tell me what's going on."

*****

Gretchen lay on her bed in her room staring up at the ceiling. The late afternoon sun poured in through the pink sparkly gauze curtains and made the room twinkle with lights. It was a pink room. Her favourite colour. And she was lucky enough to have a double bed with four posts and a gauzy canopy, frilly pink bedding, pink carpets, pink painted walls and curtains, with white bookshelves and a desk against one wall. A walk-in closet and shared bathroom completed the little pink haven she had created.

But it didn't feel too safe now. It was trying to protect her, but whatever was going on in her head, it was doing a good job of pulling it all apart. The gnawing sound was quietly eating away in her brain, and she wished it would stop. Whatever it was.

Sighing, she crossed her legs in the opposite direction, trying to find a comfortable position. Her hands rested on her stomach, her head on her pillow, and she watched the canopy softly flutter on the breeze from the window. She loved her room and didn't want to leave it. Didn't want to leave her pretty pink things.

Glancing around, she saw rainbows, hearts, stars, bags, hats, jewellery all hanging from every space possible. From the shelves and walls, the door knobs, and even hanging off the back of her desk chair. She had star lights wrapped around the canopy and posts of the bed, and flamingo and palm tree lights hanging on the walls. Every available surface was covered in something bright and sparkly. Or pink.

Rolling onto her side, she stared out the window and racked her brain. What did Elliot know? Did he see more than he said? More than he could or would tell her? And, why couldn't he? What was he holding back? Was it horribly life-ending? Did it have to do with seeing herself in the mirror on that grassy knoll? And why was she seeing that in her dreams? Why did she see herself somewhere else? She frowned, perplexed by the whole mystery of the thing.

Deciding to write it all down, she got up and grabbed a notebook and pen from her desk and sat cross-legged on the window seat so she had light. Starting from the beginning, she wrote everything down, going all the way back to Halloween and listing it all in bullet points. By the time she was finished it still didn't make sense, and she still couldn't figure out what was going on. Or how Elliot was involved.

Biting her lip, she stared out the window. She needed answers, but where was she going to get them from? Besides Elliot with his freaky eyes, and Sadie who was dead, there was no one else. Did that mean she was alone in all of this? That she had to put up with it and deal with it on her own? Could no one help her, tell her what she had to do or how she could get rid of it? And what did she have? Or was it all a figment of her imagination and she was going bonkers instead?

Sighing, she gnawed on the end of her pink sparkly pen and heard the sounds again. Why was there something eating the inside of her brain, or at least, sounding as if it was? And why did she feel so…blah? As though she wasn't herself?

"Something had to've happened Friday night," she growled and stalked around her room. "Something had to happen for me to feel so weird, and for Elliot to keep popping into my head. Argh! What! What is going on?"

Pain crawled into her head, wrapped itself around her and made her double over. "Argh what the hell!" Stumbling into the bathroom, she clung to the basin, unable to open her squinting eyes from the bulging pain she felt behind them. They felt as if they were going to explode out of her sockets. "Ugh!" Her body stiffened, her head flung back, her face toward the ceiling, her arms by her sides. Her whole self was unmoving, as straight as a stick, and she felt her insides writhe away.

"Ugh." She sagged and grabbed the basin. "What the hell?" Propping herself up, she looked in the mirror and saw her eyes change. Black bottomless swirling pits had replaced her green eyes, and they freaked her out. "What's happening? What's happening?" she cried out, planting both hands on the mirror while staring at her eyes. Her hands went to her face, pulled up her eyelids, pulled down her cheeks, poked her eyeballs. But the black pools were unchanging. "What the hell?" she breathed, unsure of what to say or do. Was she imagining it like last time? Was she dreaming again? This couldn't be real, it just couldn't be. She could not be standing here in her bathroom looking at herself and seeing her eyes change.

The gnawing sounds grew louder. It had been in the distance, but was moving closer and closer to her brain. Her insides quivered and felt thin, as though she hadn't eaten in weeks and there was nothing inside of her. Clutching her stomach, she looked down.

I'm still in one piece, but I feel empty, like there's nothing inside me. Like I have no intestines or bladders or kidneys. Is my heart even still beating?

Her hand flew to her chest. *Is my heart still beating?* She felt the thuds, but couldn't hear them because the sound of munching was too loud in her head. Looking in the mirror, she saw herself on that grassy plain looking down over the edge.

Is that me? Am I there and not here? Her brows slid down. *Is that me, the real me, and this is an imposter? Or am I the real me and she's just a bad dream?*

Fear weaved its way through her insides, clutching

each organ and filling it full of dread. The fear found its way to her heart and squeezed tight, making her gasp for air. *What is this? What is happening?* Clutching her throat, she managed to look back in the mirror to see other-world Gretchen staring back at her.

Other-world Gretchen had seen the wormhole open and ran to it. Unable to get through, she stood watching her other self disintegrate from the inside out. *Is that me? What's going on? Am I me? Why are there two of us?* She panicked, banging on the glass window. "What life is this? What life is that? Hello," she yelled, banging harder. "Hello, can you hear me?"

Watching closely, she saw bathroom Gretchen set her head against the glass, and other-world Gretchen did too. She stared into the black swirly eyes of bathroom Gretchen and saw the pits of hell open before her. Saw the same hell that was below her now and knew without a doubt that if she didn't do something, she would end up there forever.

CHAPTER SIX

After a restless night, Gretchen stood in front of the mirror after her shower. It was Monday morning, Christmas was four days away, and she didn't want to be going through this right now. Let alone ever.

"What is going on?" she murmured, studying her face. Her eyes were back to their normal green, but they were pale and lifeless like the rest of her. Her skin was almost translucent; she saw veins and arteries pumping blood, but it was thin, barely covering her face and body. Gaunt, bony, she didn't look well.

I'm fading away.

Frowning, she examined the rest of her body and found the same sickly look. Scared, she ran through the house looking for her mother. "Mum," she screamed. "What's wrong with me? I look so sick."

Mrs Merryweather took one look at her daughter's sickly face and said, "Get dressed, we're getting you to the hospital."

Gretchen ran back upstairs, dressed in the first things she grabbed, and was downstairs before her mother had finished locking up the house.

"Sweetie, how long have you been like this? You didn't look like this yesterday?" Mrs Merryweather asked as she reversed out of the driveway. "Did it happen overnight? It must have for you to look like this!" Worried, she drove as fast as she could to the local hospital's emergency room. "My daughter's sick, she needs to see a doctor," she demanded as they stood in line. "Look at her. Anaemic, pale, gaunt, sickly. She *was not* like this yesterday. Look at her." She stared expectantly at the nurse who took one look at Gretchen in her anorexic state and hustled her into a cubicle behind a curtain.

"How long has she had wasting disease?" the nurse asked, providing a gown for Gretchen to change into.

"What?" Mrs Merryweather frowned. "She doesn't have wasting disease. She was perfectly fine yesterday, last week, last month. This has happened *overnight.*"

The nurse stopped and looked at Mrs Merryweather. "Just last night?"

Mrs Merryweather rolled her eyes and heaved a heavy breath. "*Yes.* That's why we're here *now.*"

The nurse bustled out of the cubicle leaving them for a few minutes.

Mrs Merryweather helped her thin daughter into the gown and carefully folded her clothes and shoes into a neat pile.

The nurse came back with a man in a lab coat. "Doctor, this is the girl."

"Hello." He smiled as his eyes examined Gretchen.

"I'm Doctor Nevo. Apparently, you aren't well."

"No," Gretchen said, eyeing the good-looking doctor. "I look like death."

"And *why* is that?" Nevo poked his glove-clad fingers into Gretchen's neck, feeling for any lumps and bumps.

"Don't know," Gretchen murmured, feeling uncomfortable that a man was touching her. She was glad her mother was by her side.

"And how old are you, Gretchen?" he asked, feeling her armpits for lumps and bumps.

"Thirteen."

"And where do you go to school?"

"Belmont High."

"Oh, you must know my other patient from there, Elliot Gunfield." He flicked a light back and forth across her eyes. "I'm seeing him today. Apparently, his eyes have changed colour again."

"Yeah." Gretchen blinked a few times when the light was removed. "He's in my class." And now she was intrigued. Elliot was coming in today? Of *all days*. Coincidence?

"And now it looks as if you've come down with something, but I can't say what." He went from examining Gretchen's face to staring at her mother's. "This just happened last night?"

"Yes," Mrs Merryweather told him. "She looked fine and healthy yesterday, but *now* look at her." She waved a hand in her daughter's direction. "She's fading away."

"Right, we'll do a full check-up. Nurse, I want

full blood panels, tox screen, MRI, CAT scan, and that's what we'll start with and go from there. Does your daughter have any chronic diseases?" He turned from the nurse to Gretchen's mother.

"Not that I know of," she said, worried that there was something terribly wrong with her daughter.

"We'll find out, one way or another. And we'll start with the bloods," he said and prepared Gretchen for blood samples. The nurse brought in the trolley and set up needles and tubes, but the doctor was having a tough time finding a vein to use. "You're very thin, Gretchen." He squeezed her arm and let it go to see how much blood flowed through. "It seems your veins and blood have thinned out and that's not good." Slapping on an arm cuff, he gave her arm a good rub to get the blood flowing before tightening it. He managed to stick the needle in and draw some blood, but not much. "Okay, that's really not good." He stared at the tube. "We'll have to take it from other parts of you."

"Like where?" Mrs Merryweather asked, alarmed at his words.

"Her legs or fingers. She's not producing a lot of blood." He did the same to her right arm and managed a bit more than what he'd got from her left. "This will have to do for now. We'll try again in a half hour. Meanwhile, we'll get some sugar into you to try and produce more." He glanced from Gretchen to her mother. "We'll sort this out."

"Thank you, doctor," Mrs Merryweather murmured, squeezing her daughter's hand.

"In the meantime, we will get you the MRI and CAT scan." Nevo labelled the blood tubes and popped them into a plastic Ziploc bag. "Get these down to the labs straight away. Take them yourself, don't stop," he told the nurse.

She nodded and left.

Nevo wrote notes on his chart. "We'll get someone to take you up soon. It shouldn't be long. In the meantime, I'll get someone to bring in some food for you."

Five minutes later, Gretchen was munching on chocolate bars and drinking chocolate milk, and ten minutes after that, she was taken for her scans. An hour later Nevo was checking over the results.

"The MRI shows no abnormalities, no discrepancies, same with the CAT scan. No fractures, breaks, etc. Nothing, so we know it's not physical," he told Gretchen and her mother. "At least for now. Next stop is the blood and tox screen to see if there are any infections or toxic substances in her blood."

"Like what?" Mrs Merryweather asked, confused as to why there would be toxins in Gretchen's body, and how they would affect her so.

"Well, she could have inhaled something, or touched something. Maybe it's the laundry detergent you wash your clothes in. Prolonged exposure to something won't show symptoms from the beginning. They usually come after a decent amount of exposure. But if you say she was fine yesterday, and this happened overnight, then something is seriously wrong. I think we'll do a hair screen as well, but I'll need a sample.

"Of what? My hair?" Gretchen asked, fretting about getting a haircut.

Nevo opened a plastic bag ready for the sample. "Yes, but I'll have to pull it out by the roots; we need the whole shaft for testing. Don't worry." He stood before her. "I'll just take a couple of strands. Lean forward for me."

Gretchen leant forward and felt the doctor run his gloved hand through her hair. She felt a pinch. "Ow. That was sharp."

Nevo pulled his hand away. He didn't just have a couple of strands, he had a handful. "Oh…" Staring at the hair, and the bald spot on Gretchen's head, he gently moved his hand through her hair again and more came away easily.

"What the hell," Mrs Merryweather breathed, going from wide-eyed to a frown. "What's making that happen?"

"What?" Gretchen asked and sat back. She saw the pile of hair in the doctor's hand. "Is that mine?" Her hand flew to her head and found the bald spot. "Oh, my God," she cried. "No, no, I can't be losing my hair. No." Her cries turned to screams and she was pulled into her mother's arms to sob.

"Something is obviously going on," Mrs Merryweather said scathingly. "Find out *what* is wrong with my daughter."

Nevo placed the hair in the bag and sealed it up. "That's what we're trying to do. But tests take time."

"Gretchen doesn't have time, clearly," Mrs

Merryweather replied, stroking her daughter's head. More hair came away and attached itself to her hand. She looked at it in horror and stopped doing it.

"We're doing everything as fast as we can. We may have to give Gretchen a transfusion, but not until we get the blood and the tox panel back, otherwise we won't know what to treat her for." The case was as puzzling as Elliot's, and he wondered if it was all connected. "Gretchen." He turned his attention back to her. "Elliot's your schoolmate and his case is just as intriguing. Have the two of you shared anything, like a drink, or food where germs may have passed between the two of you? Have you touched the same thing, sneezed near each other, etc?"

She stopped sobbing long enough to say, "No".

"Have you talked recently, outside of school? Breathed the same air?" Nevo went on, trying to figure it all out.

"I saw him at the shopping centre on Saturday. But he was with the boys and I was with my friends. None of them are sick as far as I know." She gave a coughing hiccup.

"Do you know that for sure?" Nevo pressed. "I need their names and numbers, because if they've come down with something too…"

"I guess I could write them down. I know my friends' numbers, but not the boys'." She took the pad and pen he offered.

"That will at least be a start. I can get the boys' contact details from Elliot when I see him later." He took the list she'd written. "You rest while we wait for the bloods and I'll start calling." Exiting the cubicle, he didn't hold out much hope for Gretchen. Whatever it was, it was eating her from the inside out, and she was, simply put, fading away.

He made calls to Gretchen's friends and found out they were all fine. No symptoms, no illnesses. The parents were worried about them catching it from Gretchen, but he assured them at this stage it wasn't contagious. Still, he told them, if symptoms did start up, to bring the girls in for treatment immediately.

He hung up the phone more puzzled than ever. A quick glance at the clock told him he'd overstayed his allotted time in emergency and had other patients. But there was one patient he wanted to see more than the others. He called a colleague about taking his bookings for the afternoon, telling him he would take Elliot Gunfield personally as his case may be connected to another case. He also checked in with his secretary to let her know to send Elliot and his mother to emergency to see him.

The lab work for the bloods finally came back in, and he thoroughly went over it. For all the tests, and they double checked as asked when the second sample had been taken down, they found absolutely nothing in Gretchen's blood that was causing her illness. No parasites, worms, germs, bugs, diseases, *nothing* that would indicate what was making her sick. She didn't even have wasting disease, but still, something was making her waste away and to do so this suddenly, overnight…none of it was making any sense, just like Elliot's case.

Between the MRIs, CAT scans, blood and tox screens, there was absolutely nothing to indicate why those two kids were going through what they were experiencing.

Why had Elliot's eyes changed colour? Why did he think he was one thousand and eighty-three years old? Why was Gretchen suddenly fading away when she'd been fine yesterday and her friends weren't sick? Did the fact these two went to the same school and knew the same people make it connected, or was it just a huge coincidence?

"I don't believe in coincidences," Nevo muttered and leant back in his chair. "There is *no way* these two kids' conditions aren't related in some way."

CHAPTER SEVEN

When Elliot and his mother turned up for the appointment, they were directed to emergency where they met Nevo.

"Sorry for the inconvenience. I have a case I'm working on and thought it would be easier to see you here. Now, Elliot, let me look at your eyes." He examined Elliot's pupils and irises, stuck him in a retinal camera, and made him read letters from the chart. He gave him an MRI and CAT scan, and declared him perfectly normal. "I have no idea why they changed in the first place, so have no idea why they've changed back, except to say they've fixed themselves." They sat in an office off the emergency room. "You seem absolutely fine."

"So, there's no brain damage or eye deterioration?" Mrs Gunfield asked, gripping the handles of her handbag.

Elliot looked from his mother's face to the doctor's, and knew there was something going on that was yet to be spoken.

"No damage, Mrs Gunfield." Nevo leaned on the

desk. "But there *is* something Elliot can help me with." He studied Elliot's face.

Here it comes.

"And what's that?" Elliot asked.

"We have a schoolmate of yours in today. A Gretchen Merryweather. She's very ill, and I've rung the friends she was out with on Saturday. They're okay, but she said she ran into you and your friends as well. I need their phone numbers to see if *they're* okay. Can you write them down for me?"

Handing over a pad and pen, he watched Elliot's frown deepen.

"What?" Elliot questioned. "What's wrong with Gretchen?"

Nevo blinked. "She's very sick and needs help, but so far we have no idea what's wrong with her. All of you were the last to see her. I need to know if your friends are sick."

Elliot's forehead started throbbing from frowning so hard, but he quickly scribbled down his friends' numbers. "Can I see her?"

Nevo took the pad and pen. "I don't see why not. We'll put you in a mask and gloves to be on the safe side, and you can chat. Follow me." He led them down the hall, gave them masks and gloves, walked across the corridor and down another hall, turning right, he stopped at the cubicle and pulled the curtain back. "Gretchen. A visitor."

Elliot finished putting on the gloves and stepped forward. He gasped, and his eyes went wide. Gretchen looked like death.

Gretchen's eyes went to Elliot's. "I heard you had an appointment."

"We'll leave the two of you alone." Nevo indicated for Mrs Merryweather to follow them out and she moved into the hall.

"Oh, Grace, I'm so sorry," Mrs Gunfield said. She knew about the waiting for a child to get better, and comforted her friend. "What's wrong with Gretchen?"

"They don't know, Sharon," Grace sobbed. "They have no idea what's wrong with her." They stepped aside to talk, and Nevo went in search of the toxicology report.

"Oh, Elliot," Gretchen murmured, staring soullessly at him. "What have you done to me? Why have you done it to me? What's wrong with me?"

Elliot's head moved back and forth slowly. He was in a fog of disbelief. Gretchen was withering away before him and he couldn't say anything. Couldn't *think* anything. "Gretchen, I…"

"Yeah, whatever, Elliot." She rolled her eyes listlessly. "You didn't do it. Nothing happened on Friday night. Yet I keep having this weird vision that I'm on a grassy knoll looking down on a world that's burning and breaking apart. Like I dream that my eyes turn to swirling pits of black hell, and that something's eating me from the inside out. Yeah, I'm just making that stuff up for my own benefit and amusement." She watched his eyes. They looked traumatised, and even behind the mask she could tell he was horrified.

"But I…" Elliot managed. "I saw you… We saw

each other…in the park…yesterday. You were fine. You climbed the jungle gym to get away from Buster. You were fine. What happened?" He stared miserably at her, unable to comprehend the full extent of the problem. All because he couldn't remember. What *had* gone down Friday night, and what was *his* role in it?

"I *was* fine yesterday," Gretchen told him. Her energy had left her and lethargy had set in. She could barely raise her arms or keep her eyes open. "But overnight something went terribly wrong."

Elliot was sick to his stomach. Whatever had done this was now killing Gretchen, and as much as he had once hated her, all he felt now was remorse for something he couldn't remember doing. But it was something he knew he had to fix. No matter what it was.

"Help me, Elliot," she pleaded, through sick eyes. "Whatever it was, whatever you did, fix it and help me."

Nevo and the nurse came in with trays of blood bags and the mothers followed. "I've gone over your tox report, Gretchen, and can't find anything wrong with you." He eyed Elliot and Gretchen, hoping for something, but Elliot looked worried, and Gretchen just looked sick. "The only thing we can do is give you a transfusion and hope it boosts your system enough to recover from whatever's ailing you."

"Are you saying with all the tests you've done that nothing is wrong with my daughter?" Grace Merryweather asked. "There's no way."

"We're still working on the hair sample, but all bloods, tox, MRI, CAT scan have shown there is nothing wrong with your daughter." He moved into high gear at her distressed face. "But we won't stop doing tests, and we'll hope this souped-up blood will help get rid of whatever is causing this. If not, we may have to flush her blood, clean it, and put it back in."

"What?" Grace fanned herself. She was faint, and Nevo helped Mrs Gunfield get her into a chair.

"We have no idea what's wrong with Gretchen, Mrs Merryweather." Nevo knelt before her and checked her pulse. "But we will do all we can for her. She doesn't have a disease or parasite or anything. There are no toxins in her system. In test results, she's perfectly healthy."

"But she's not," Grace cried out. "Look at her." Pointing to her daughter, she knew Gretchen was on her death bed. "My baby's dying."

"We're not going to let that happen, Mrs Merryweather." Nevo got to his feet and prepared the blood bags. "We just need to get a needle in and this blood can start pumping into your daughter. Let's hope it will work."

He tried three times to find a vein to get the needle in, and finally succeeded in setting up the IV. He primed the blood for entry, and they all watched the blood flow down the tube and into Gretchen's arm. With bated breath, they watched for an hour as the oxygenated blood flowed through Gretchen's body, filling her with the lifesaving fluid.

Examining her, Nevo ordered another bag, and watched as Gretchen's colour came back and her skin returned to normal colour.

She opened her eyes.

"How do you feel, sweetie?" Grace went to her daughter's side.

"Better," Gretchen murmured. "I don't feel like I'm wasting away anymore."

"That's a good sign." Nevo removed the third bag from the metal rod attached to the bed. "We'll keep an eye on you through the night. You look better. You'll have a bed in ICU and be moved soon. You rest for now." Pulling the nurse aside, he added quietly, "Stay here and keep an eye on her. Get me if anything happens." He got a nod before leaving.

"I guess that means we should go too," Sharon Gunfield said. "I'm so glad you're feeling better, Gretchen." She patted the girl's arm. "But we've already stayed longer than we should have. Come Elliot." She bustled him out the door with a small wave of her hand.

Elliot sat mulling it all over on the way home then went to his room to mull it over some more. There was only one person who could help.

After flicking on his laptop, he emailed Sam, typing in the words, SAMMY, I NEED YOU THIS IS URGENT, in all caps in the subject line. Underneath, he explained about Gretchen and what she had mentioned to him about seeing herself somewhere else and how her eyes changed as well.

He waited an hour before getting a reply.

El, I've discussed this with my parents and looked in Sadie's books. It appears that she might have a Soul Feeder. That's an unseen creature that feeds on souls from the inside making them lethargic, thin, and translucent. She needs to be exorcised by a proper expert, but it will be tough. How is she now?

Doing okay after a transfusion of three bags of blood.

Yeah, but that will be eaten by the Soul Feeder. New blood for them to drink. It won't last long.

So, what about the visions she has of being in another world?

That's her soul. The Soul Feeder transports the soul to another world, mainly the one it comes from, and takes possession of the new body. The soul is trapped in that world until the Feeder kills the host, or the host gets its soul back.

And how does she do that?

Fifteen minutes went past. *She doesn't,* Sam typed. *The person who killed or injured her in the first place has to.*

What! Who! Who killed or injured her?

Another fifteen minutes silence. *You did, El.*

CHAPTER EIGHT

I what?

You tried to kill Gretchen last Friday night.

A lengthy silence.

You can't be serious?

I'm very serious.

So that means you lied to me?

Kept the important part from you.

Which was?

That to get rid of the Shadow Walker, you had to die or kill someone so it transferred to them. You tried to kill Gretchen.

What! How?

You stabbed her in the stomach with a knife, and from the looks of it, had read the incantation from Sadie's book. But I got you out of there, and my parents fixed Gretchen.

So, it's your parents' fault then! They didn't fix her properly.

No. It comes down to the person taking life. That was you. You have to be the one to fix it.

How?

There's an incantation you'll have to say, and a potion Gretchen will have to drink. But it all needs to be done precisely as before with a few extra things thrown in.

Like what?

Like another living being for it to enter upon evacuation of Gretchen's body. You must kill Gretchen for it to leave, and another living being needs to be nearby for it to fly into, otherwise it floats around until it finds one.

Are you saying I have to kill Gretchen again for this to happen?

Yeah, pretty much. And we'll need a rat or cat or something. You'll have to protect yourself from the Feeder so it doesn't fly into you, but that's easy enough.

Easy for you to say.

Yeah, it is. But we'll be there with you helping every step of the way. My parents are already packing.

You're coming back?

We need to stop the Feeder so it won't kill Gretchen. My parents know about these things.

So does that mean we need to get her back to Sadie's?

Yep. It has to be in the place where it happened the first time. And that means getting her back to Sadie's.

But she's in the hospital. I doubt she'll leave anytime soon.

When she does, or even if we can get her out of the hospital, we have to do it. We'll be there tomorrow.

She'll have tonight to recover, so hopefully they'll send her home then. But her resurgence won't last long. A day or two at most and she'll be right back in there getting another transfusion. It's best we do it fast, so she's okay as soon as possible. We have to do this, El. It's the only way to save her. To make her better.

You're telling me, I have to kill her…again… after I already killed her last Friday night and brought all this on both of us?

Yep.

How?

You snuck into Sadie's for the books and hit Gretchen. You thought it was the only way to get rid of it onto her.

It clearly didn't work.

Well, the Shadow Walker disappeared, but now it looks like a Soul Feeder has taken its place. Not uncommon, but not common either.

So why can't I remember?

Do you remember the tea Mum gave you in the car?

No.

Forgetful potion. You forget horrible things you've done. You stabbed her, you forgot.

And Gretchen?

Similar thing. Mum and Dad healed her wound from the inside out. Gave her the forgetful potion as well.

So, that's how we both knew something had happened but couldn't remember?

Yep.

That's why it's been nagging at us. For God's sake, Sam, why didn't you tell us?

Because the potion also helped you get back to normal. Once the Walker was gone, you were back to normal.

But Gretchen wasn't?

No.

What time do you get here?

We'll be there early.

And what time do we get Gretchen?

As soon as we can. If she goes home, from home. If she's staying in the hospital, then we get her from the hospital.

That's gonna be tough.

You don't know my parents.

*****

At 9:05 Tuesday morning, Elliot rang the hospital to ask about Gretchen. The good news was she was doing much better after three more transfusions. The bad news; they didn't know if she was going home.

At 9:30 Sam rang Elliot. "Well?"

"Not sure if she's coming home. I'll have to ring again later."

"I'll call at one."

At one Sam rang back. "Well?"

"She's still having tests. No word yet."

"Okay. I'll ring back at five."

At five Sam rang back. "Well?"

"She's gone home. The doctors are happy with her recovery and she's home."

"Call her. Tell her you need to meet. If she can sneak out, we'll pick her up after dark. Don't mention us. I'll call at seven."

At seven, Sam rang back. "Well?"

"She wants it to be over. I've got to try and explain it all to her. She wants to know. What do I tell her?"

"Tell her you need to go back to Sadie's for it to be over. Mum will pick you up and take you over there. Get ready. We're on our way at nine."

At 9 p.m., Milly Almaw picked up Elliot down the street from his house and drove him to Gretchen's. She parked down the road while Elliot sneaked back to the house.

Gretchen, who had been on the lookout, lifted her sash window and whispered loudly, "Elliot?"

"Yeah. Can you come down?" he whispered back just as loudly.

"Yeah." Gretchen climbed out, carefully moved across the roof of the downstairs veranda, and with help from Elliot, slid down the column at the side of the two-storey house. Once down, she turned to him and said, "This had better be worth it, Elliot Gunfield. Now let's go."

He led her to the car and they climbed into the back. "This is um…"

"Someone who's helping," Milly said, glancing in the rear-view at a very sickly Gretchen. "Put your seatbelt on. This should be over soon."

Not even recognising Mrs Almaw, Gretchen sat back in trepidation and anticipation. Whatever was going on, she wanted it to be over. She was sick and tired and on the verge of collapse and didn't want to die. Especially at Christmas, and especially at thirteen. What an unlucky number to die at.

Turning into Sadie's driveway, Milly parked close to the house and turned out the lights. "Let's go," she whispered, and they quietly got out of the car and walked into the house. No one was evident, but hot tea was brewing in the pot on the kitchen counter, and two cups were already set up. Pouring some in each cup, she told them to drink it. "It will help you."

"Do what?" Gretchen asked, suspiciously eyeing the cup and the woman.

Milly smiled. "Even in bad health you're stubborn. It will relax you, protect you, and help you. Drink up."

Gretchen tasted it. "What's in it? It's awful."

"Herbs, spices, a little bit of everything," Milly said, opening Sadie's book to the Soul Feeder page. It had been left on the counter next to the tea. While the kids drank, she read through the incantations.

"Done." Gretchen set her cup on the tray and tried to remember why they were there. "Where are we and why are we here?"

Milly looked up from the book and smiled. "Working already."

"What is?" Elliot asked.

"The tea you just drank." Milly's smile widened.

"What tea? You haven't poured any," Gretchen said before yawning. "God I'm tired."

"Good. You're nearly ready." Milly hung a rubber thong with a glass-like amulet around Gretchen's neck. It was carved into an ancient Egyptian symbol. "You need to wear this; it will protect you. Here is yours, Elliot." She handed it to him and picked up a small bowl from the tray. Dabbing her fingers in it, she drew lines across and down Gretchen's face.

"What are you doing?" Gretchen asked.

"Protecting you," Milly said and did the same to Elliot. Finishing with him, she drew lines on her own face and hung a pendant around her neck. "We're ready," she called.

Sam and his father, Geoff Almaw, came out of one of the bedrooms.

"Sam." Gretchen frowned. "Aren't you dead?"

"No," Sam replied. "But you will be soon."

"What!" Gretchen's frown deepened, and she saw paint on his face.

"If we don't help you tonight, Gretchen, you'll soon be dead. Now, do as we say and it will save your life." Taking her hand, he pulled her forward and told her to lie on the floor.

"Why do I need to lie on the floor?" Gretchen complained, but got down anyway.

"We need to re-enact the moment," Sam said, moving her arms and legs so they were just right. "How do you feel?"

"Tired." Another yawn hit her.

"Good. It will soon be over." Milly handed the

book to her husband, and they kneeled in the exact position around Gretchen as they had been in last time. "Elliot." She handed him the same knife he'd used and which she'd kept. "You need to do it again. She needs to go to the brink like last time."

"But I—" Elliot shook his head. "I can't."

"You have to, El," Sam encouraged him. "It's the only way to save Gretchen and bring her soul back."

"But I…" Elliot stared forlornly into his best friend's eyes. "I can't."

"You have to," Sam insisted. "And you have to do it now."

During the conversation, Gretchen had been looking around. "Why's there a cat in a basket?"

They all looked at the orange and white cat locked up in a basket, ears back, hissing and baring his teeth.

"It was the closest thing we could find to transfer the Soul Feeder into," Sam explained. As The Howler, he'd made the cat do exactly what he wanted it to. Even though the cat didn't like it and completely disagreed with him, it had no choice. Sam bared his teeth and the cat stopped hissing.

"We have to do this, Elliot. Do it exactly the same way you did it Friday night," Milly told him. "You have to re-enact it perfectly. Are we all ready?" She looked around the group.

"Ready for what?" Gretchen asked and watched Milly roll her top up to bare her stomach. "What did you do that for?"

"For this," Milly said, with a nod at Elliot.

Elliot panicked, his eyes widened, and he gripped that knife with both hands.

"Take it easy, El," Sam soothed him. "Just raise and stab. She'll be okay. Mum and Dad will take care of the rest. I promise, El." He squeezed his arm. "It will be just fine."

"What will be?" Another yawn escaped Gretchen, and she fell asleep.

"Now," Milly told Elliot. "Now."

Out of pure desperation and in fear for his life, he sobbed, raised the knife in both hands, and with tears falling down his face, plunged it into Gretchen's stomach just as he had last Friday.

Gretchen sat up, eyes wide, mouth wider, drawing in a raspy breath, both hands clasping Elliot's around the knife.

Other-world Gretchen had watched the whole thing from her grassy mat floating God knows where over Gods knows what hell and grasped her stomach as the pain flooded through her body. Glancing down, she saw blood pouring through her hands and fell to her knees. Looking up, she saw the other Gretchen fall back on the floor with two adults and two kids around her. She collapsed on the grass, passed out cold.

In Sadie's house, Gretchen fell unconscious, and Elliot scrambled backwards. Sam went with him, and they watched his parents work their magic.

"Leave this body, renew its soul, so it is one and you are gone. Leave this body, renew its soul, take cover in the being we behold." Geoff pointed to

Sadie's cat, hissing and scratching and trying to claw its way out of the basket.

Ears back, teeth bared, the cat was fighting for its life.

Milly removed the knife and poured a liquid into Gretchen's wound, dusted a powder concoction over it and set a match to it to burn and heal.

Geoff repeated the incantation and all four of them saw a messy black swirling whirlwind leave Gretchen's mouth.

She arched, and her eyes opened. They went from that swirling pit of black to fiery amber back to green, and that black mist flew from her mouth and around the room looking for the cat to land in. It needed a living being, and all four humans were protected by the ancient paint and pendants. Spying the cat, it headed for it.

But the cat was not willing to be sacrificed, and finally managed to fight its way out of the basket and run for the cat door. It escaped by centimetres, and the swirling black fog followed.

The cat ran for its life straight through the woodlands, across the road where it hit a fence, and veered off to the left.

The fog followed, but instead of getting the cat, it hit the fence, flipped up and landed in the teenager who had been standing on the fence looking out at the night from the back yard.

Back at Sadie's, Gretchen's soul slid back into Gretchen's body and she jerked awake. "What the!" she gasped and fell silently into Milly's arms.

"She's healed," Milly said and handed her over to Geoff who carried her out to the car and covered her with a blanket.

Milly cleared up while Sam pulled Elliot out of the house and into the car. "It'll be over now, El. I promise."

Milly closed up Sadie's house, and they piled into the car.

"What do you think happened to the Feeder?" Sam asked as they drove to Gretchen's to leave her sleeping peacefully on the front porch lounge chair.

"Who knows," Milly replied. "But that will be their problem." They made their getaway without being seen or heard.

When dropping off Elliot, Sam gave him a bear hug. "Go and sleep, El. You'll forget all about this by morning. I promise."

"Do you Sammy?" Elliot was in a state of shock at what had just happened.

"You won't remember a thing." Sam hugged him and said goodbye.

Elliot trudged upstairs, lay down on his bed and cried.

In the backyard, the teenager jerked up and arched their back so their head and feet dug into the ground. Their body spasmed in the opposite direction lurching them into a sitting position, their head facing the sky. Their eyes flew open to reveal a bright burning light that changed to bottomless pools of black oil before they fell back into unconsciousness.

No one knew Susan was out there in her backyard

as it was well after her bedtime. But passed out on the grass in the cool summer air, she slept deeply until morning.

THE BONES OF WRATH:
GHOSTS

GHOSTS OF OP SHOPS PAST

"Come on, Michelle, we're running late."

I rolled my eyes and groaned, watching my mother trot off towards the small secondhand op shop she volunteered at. It sat between a hairdressing salon and a pizzeria in the small shopping complex in our neighbourhood.

I reluctantly got out of the car and looked around while shutting the door. A deli, a pet shop, and a takeaway joint finished off the centre in the quiet neighbourhood. Mum volunteered during the week, but since it was school holidays, she had me volunteering as well. I dragged my feet and slowly made my way into the store.

Like with most op shops, it had that weird smell of mixed aromas. Dust, mould, old age, old people, mothballs, no oxygen, can't breathe, can't breathe, help! I gagged.

"Oh, it's not so bad." Mum came toward me with an apron. "Put this on and let's get to work."

"Work?" I took the apron and held it out in front of me with two fingers. "Happy Trails Opportunity

Shop," I read aloud, looking at the picture on the front of pine trees and a creek with horses standing nearby. "You get paid to work. Are we getting paid? You said we were volunteering." I grimaced at the stain on the apron and delicately sniffed it before slipping it over my head. I think my face was still screwed up because when I finished tying it, I looked up and saw Mum with her arms crossed, staring at me in disapproval.

"Really?"

I blinked, and my face relaxed. "What?"

"You sniffed it? Ugh! I'll have you know I wash those aprons myself, so they are clean and smell free. This way." She led me to the back room full of racks and bags of clothing, and containers and shelves of stuff that people didn't want anymore.

"Here, take this rack and put the clothes in the appropriate areas in the store." She pushed the rack toward me, and I rolled it over to the clothing section.

I picked up the first skirt. "Mmm, old-fashioned. How much are they slugging for this? Five dollars!" I stared at the tag and heard a 'shh'. Guiltily, I looked up and saw Mum frowning and a couple of customers staring in amusement.

I jammed it on the rack and picked up the next. "Ooh, I like this one," I muttered under my breath. I eyed the suede skirt in my hand. Turquoise blue, zip up the back, and about knee length. "Mmm, wonder if I could keep this one for myself?"

"We don't get to keep whatever we want for

ourselves, dear."

I jumped at the voice and turned around. "Um, sorry?"

The little old lady turned around. She barely came up to my shoulder, had grey hair pulled into a bun, and a wrinkly face.

"We don't get to keep whatever we want for ourselves," she repeated with a twinkle in her eye. "We may be volunteers, but if we want something, we must buy it." She looked at the skirt and then eyed me up and down. "I don't think it would fit you anyway, dear. It's too big and belonged to someone much older than...mmm..." Her eyes studied my face. "Twelve. You're Michelle, Beth's daughter, aren't you?"

I stared from her to the skirt back to her. "Um, yeah, I am. How do you know the skirt wouldn't fit, or that it belonged to someone older? Do you know the person who donated it?" My curiosity piqued, I wondered how she knew, or could possibly know.

"Look at the size, dear. It's too big for you. And it's from someone older because children don't wear suede skirts." With another twinkle in her eye, she wandered off down the aisle.

I checked the size tag and saw she was right. A size 14 was nowhere near where I was as a twelve-year-old. Pity! I placed it on the rack and finished putting the rest of the skirts in place before moving on to the pants.

"Five dollars, black, blue, olive green, blech!" I pulled a face at the horrible colour and wondered how anyone could wear it when it was so horrible. "Ugh, these look old and worn and should we even be putting these out for sale they look horribly ugly?" I muttered, holding up a pair of worn thin black old-fashioned pants.

"We can't be picky when selling donations."

"Ah!" I jumped a second time and spun around. It was the little old lady again. "But…" I looked at the pants I was still holding. "They look worn and ugly," I whispered. "Why would you sell something so…ugly?"

"Because we can't be picky when selling donations," she repeated. "As long as the article is decent with no holes or stains, we sell it. Have to make money somehow." She wandered off, and I finished clearing the rack. When I rolled it into the back room, Mum was waiting with a box of stuffed toys.

"Go put these in the toy crate; they're ready for sale."

I carried the box to the toy section and tipped it upside down for them to all fall out into the huge wire crate.

"You need to treat them better than that; they belonged to someone, once."

I jumped for the third time. "You always sneak up on people?" I eyed the little old lady who always seemed to be following me around. This time I noticed the 'Happy Trails' apron and name tag. Her name was Winifred. God, how old-fashioned, and she clearly volunteered here.

She picked up a small teddy bear and studied it, turning it over in her hands. "Mmm, this one belonged to a little girl, about eight. But she passed away and her parents donated her things." She lovingly put it down amongst the others. "They all have stories, dear. They're little people themselves."

"How do you know who owned that bear?" I had absolutely no idea if she'd just made it up, or if she was some sort of witch.

She smiled at me with her wrinkly eyes, a sparkle going on in them. "I know the story. I sense it. I feel it. Everything has a story." She glanced away for a few seconds and then picked up a medium-sized brown bear. "This belonged to a ten-year-old boy. It's a little battered and worn now, but it was a great comfort to him when he was sick."

"Then why doesn't he still have it?" I was puzzled, and bewildered, and a few other things at this weird exchange.

"Because he died too." She gently placed it next to the other one and walked away.

I looked around the store and shivered. This place was weird. There were only three customers, but I felt like I was being watched, and Winnie wasn't helping the creep factor either. Everything seemed to be in order. The back was a bit of a mess, but for the most part, each section was clearly labelled and laid out. I saw Mum stacking the crockery at the other end of the store and glanced back to the bookshelves on my right. Maybe I should just tidy them up a bit.

I started straightening the books and tidying the

shelves, picking up stray things from the floor as I went. When I was finished, I turned to see Mum coming my way.

"That was going to be your next job, so I'm glad you took some initiative and did it yourself. Maybe you can keep that up after your break?" She glanced at her watch. "You've got ten minutes. There's a small bathroom off the back room, and I packed food in the cooler bag. Get some sun and air out back. I'll be timing you." She walked off to serve a customer.

I hurried into the bathroom to wash my hands then grabbed a sandwich and small bottle of drink from our cooler bag. I wandered out the back door to see the sun shining down and the water in the small creek whizzing by. It ran past the back of the centre, and I walked over to it while munching on my sandwich.

Ten minutes later, I turned around and walked back in to find an old man standing in the back room looking at an old pea coat on the table that was yet to be priced.

"Ooh, sorry sir, you can't be back here, volunteers only."

He looked up at me with old grizzled features and a white beard, not seeming to understand what I'd said.

"Sir, you can't be—"

"Michelle, dear."

I glanced at Winnie as she came through the door and saw her look in the direction of the old man. I turned back, but he was gone. "What the!"

"What, dear?"

I looked out the back door, but saw no one.

"What is it, dear?"

I walked into the room and shook my head. "There was an old guy here looking at that pea coat, but then he disappeared when you walked in…" I really didn't know what to think.

"You saw an old man, dear?" Winnie eyed me closely.

"Um, yeah. White hair and beard. Really wrinkly."

She nodded. "Interesting."

"What…is…?" Now I was just plain confused.

"That you saw him."

I shrugged and frowned. "Wasn't I supposed to?"

"No, dear. Unless you have an ability to see the dead."

I blinked. I stared. I blinked again. "The what?"

Winnie blinked back. "The dead, dear. That man was dead. Long gone. That was just his spirit hanging around because that was his coat."

I looked from Winnie to the coat and back again. "What?"

Her laughter tinkled through the room. "You just saw a ghost, dear. Sometimes they hang around their clothes or toys, or whatever they loved that's been donated. There's quite a few of them that come through the store."

This time my eyelids moved in rapid succession. "You mean…this place is haunted…? As in… *haunted*?" My voice squeaked out.

"Well…" She glanced away. "I'd say it's…visited."

"You see them? You saw *him*? How? Why? When?"

"I have a gift," Winnie said. "I've been visited by spirits and have seen them all my life. It looks like you have the beginnings of that gift—"

"What? I'm…no…I—"

Mum came in. "There you are, time for my break now. Sharon is manning the till; can you unload that trolley of plates and cups please." She ran into the bathroom and Winnie and I wandered into the store while I pushed the trolley.

I glanced around nervously. "Are they here now?"

"Do you see any now?"

I stopped and studied the four people in the store, landing on the one by the mirror. "Her." I gave a slight head tilt in her general direction.

"Why her?"

I shrugged. "Don't know."

The woman at the mirror turned and yelled out to the woman two rows away, and they both laughed.

Winnie laughed too. "Nope, not her."

"Mmm," I mumbled and headed for the crockery section. I couldn't find a place for the new stuff, so I moved some things around on the shelf and turned to get the plates from the trolley. "Ah!" I cried out when I saw the woman holding one of the plates.

"Mmm," she said. "Mine, mine, mine." She stared defiantly at me.

"Um, well, sorry, but it's been donated to the store, so," I shrugged, "not yours anymore."

The woman, in her white nightie type dress, and

long grey hair, held fast and clutched the plate to her chest. "Mine, mine, mine!"

"No, dear. It's no longer yours." Winnie came up beside me and held out her hand. "You're no longer here on this Earth. Your body has passed on and now must you. The plate is no longer yours." As Winnie reached for the plate, it clicked what was going on. I was talking to a spirit. This, this, woman in the old-fashioned nightie dress was a spirit.

I stared, dumbfounded, as Winnie took the plate and lay it back in the trolley, then somehow guided the woman away until she disappeared. I let out a deep breath and rubbed the chill from my arms. This place not only *smelt* like old people, but it was also *haunted* by old people. *This cannot be happening. It, just, can't, be, happening!*

"Michelle, haven't you unloaded that trolley yet?" Mum came bounding past. "I asked you twelve minutes ago."

"Huh?" I looked around. "I um, got side-tracked." I quickly unloaded the plates, and made room for the cups before taking the trolley back to the storage room. I stepped outside and took a few deep breaths hoping it would clear out the weirdness of what was going on.

"Hey kid, you all right?" Sharon popped her head out the door.

I turned. "Yeah, just needed some fresh air."

"Well, you can hang all this linen on the rack then take it out. I'm nearly done pricing it, so it can go out for sale."

I followed her back into the room and grabbed a pile of pillowcases on coat hangers then hung them on a rack. "Why are we putting linen on a clothes rack?" I thought it was a bit weird.

Sharon finished putting price tags on the last piece. "Because it's easier to hang them for people to get a better look rather than having to constantly fold them on the shelf because people have pulled them apart to get a look at them. It saves time in the long run." She snapped a hanger onto a folded sheet. "Would you like to be spending your day folding sheets and pillowcases?"

I grinned and grabbed the sheet she held out. "Nope." I finished loading the rack and took it out to the linen section. Seeing only a few things left on the rack that was there, I transferred them to the new rack and rolled the old one back out to the storage room for whatever else it was needed for.

Mum hauled a big box into the room. "Someone just dropped this off. Part of an old estate that didn't sell apparently." She put it on the table and we crowded around to see what was in it.

"Mmm, jewellery box, small box, containers, silver sequin jacket." She pulled each on out and laid them on the table.

"Ooohhh, nice jacket." I snatched it and held it up. "Wonder if it fits?" I quickly whipped it on and it fit like a glove.

"You can't have it unless you buy it," Mum said. "We don't get stuff for free here." She opened the boxes and tipped out the contents. Lots of silver sparkly jewellery and papers fell out.

"Ooohhh, jewels." I quickly spread them apart and leaned in for a closer look. Picking up an old silver watch, I turned it over to look for names and markings. Looking at the face, I noticed a small name under the twelve. "Oh, my God, it's Cartier," I gasped. I was a bit of a jewellery buff and had many books on jewellery companies and collections.

"Is that a good thing?" Mum asked, peering over my shoulder.

I glanced at her. "Are you kidding? Cartier makes it way expensive. I wonder what everything else is." Peering through the rest of the pieces I found Trifari, Tiffany & Co, and Bulgari. "All of this stuff is expensive. We can't sell these here. We should send them to auction and use the money for the charity." I laid every piece in front of me. They needed a good clean.

"Well, if they're expensive brands I better ring the head of Happy Trails and find out what to do with them." She walked off to make a phone call while I read through the papers. Most were receipts for the jewellery, but there were a few others for silverware and clothing.

"The manager wants us to bundle it up and hold it until he gets here, which won't be until five."

"I can't bundle it up like this, all dirty and in need of a clean. And I found the receipts to go with most of them, plus some things we didn't get. I'm going to take photos and give them a clean," I said.

"You don't need to," Mum said, picking up a

Trifari bracelet.

"I want to." I was adamant. There was no way I was going to be in possession of such magnificent classic pieces and not do something about it.

"Well, all right. I suppose it would be a good thing to do. There's not much else to do anyway except the odd tidy up. I'll leave you to it."

I grabbed my camera from my bag and set about taking as many photos as I could. I matched each piece to its receipt and took more pics, then pulled out the small silver polishing cloth I carried around for cleaning my jewels if they ever got dirty. I sat down, laid out each expensive, sparkling piece in order, and started cleaning.

I worked through lunchtime and into the afternoon with Mum and Sharon dropping by to see how I was going. After finishing the last piece, I stretched my neck and rubbed it, hoping to get rid of the kink in it from looking down for so long. I noticed Winnie standing by, looking at the jewellery. "Hey, look what we've got. Awesome, huh?"

She tenderly picked up a Bulgari brooch of a cheeky little monkey full of coloured crystals I knew had to be real gems. A wistful smile slid across her lips. "I had one…"

"You had one like that…wow. I need to take more pics now they're cleaner." I picked up my camera. "'I suppose the manager will take them to a jewellery store for a proper clean. It will be a better job than what I did." I snapped a few pics of the much cleaner pieces and noticed Winnie still holding the monkey. "It must have meant a lot to you, huh?"

In her dazed state, she looked at me. "What, dear?"

"The brooch you had. Like that one." I pointed to it still cradled in her hands. "The way you're staring at it, it obviously brings back memories."

The wistful smile was back. "It did. It does." She glanced at me and nodded. "Now *that* was made for you."

I looked down and realised, with surprise, I was still wearing the silver sequin evening jacket that had come in the box with the jewellery. "Yes," I murmured. "It does feel like I'm meant to have it. It fits perfectly." I spun around in the late afternoon sun that poured through the back door, sending shards of silver sparkle dancing around the room.

Sharon came into the room and saw me. "You'll have to pay for that if you want it," she reiterated what Mum had said earlier.

"How much?" I twirled in the sunlight.

"Well, let's see," she said, studying it as I moved. "Sequin, evening, looks cared for…twenty-five dollars."

I stopped. "What? Why so much? It's an op shop."

"Yes, but evening wear is priced higher than casual clothes. You want it; you buy it, otherwise, take it off and put it on the rack for pricing."

I stared down in despair, desperately wanting the jacket, but knowing I didn't have twenty-five dollars.

Mum came into the room. "Michelle, can you spend the last half hour tidying up, please."

"I want this jacket. I have to have this jacket.

Sharon says it's twenty-five dollars, but I don't have twenty-five dollars, so I need to borrow it please, please, please!"

She looked at me standing in the sun sparkling away. "Mmm, I was going to give you five dollars a day for doing this, but that means you won't get the money, you'll get the jacket instead."

"Oh, my God, please, please, please!"

She pulled the money out of her purse and handed it to Sharon. "For one silver sequin jacket."

"Woohoo!" I cheered and danced around some more.

"Put all of that jewellery away and tidy up outside. Then it's home time." She and Sharon left the room, and I quickly gathered the jewellery, along with the receipts, into the jewel box ready for pick up. I looked at Winnie still staring from me to the monkey pin. I reached out for it, and she reluctantly gave it back. "It's time for it to move on," I said.

"Just like that jacket," she replied. "Time for that to move on to you. I had a jacket like that a long, long time ago. I used to go dancing in it on Friday and Saturday nights. I was the queen of the ball."

I finished putting the jewellery away, placed it all back in the box it had been donated in, and left it next to the door for the manager.

For the last half hour, I tidied cupboards and shelves full of books and clothes, and linen on racks, plus checking on the knick-knacks. I swept the floor and waited for the manager to come, which he did at five to five.

"Apparently, we have a grand donation," he said, walking over to the counter.

"Michelle, can you…" Mum started.

I was already getting the box from the back and placed it in front of him. "Rather expensive jewels and all with receipts. I gave them a bit of a clean-up."

"Not with soap and water. You didn't ruin them did you?" he snapped and quickly opened the jewellery box.

I frowned in irritation. What did he take me for, an idiot just because I'm twelve?

"My daughter happens to know better than that, Dan. She's a jewellery buff and took very good care of them." Mum was irritated too, judging by the frown on her face.

He'd been greedily pawing through them, but at Mum's words relaxed and smoothed. "Of course she did, I see that. I'll just take them now. Thank you, girls." He took the box and bolted for the door.

I was still frowning when I said, "I have a feeling the charity won't see any of that money. I don't like him. There's something not quite right about this."

"I suppose you might be right, Mich, but it's time to go. Sharon's shutting up shop." We went into the back room for our bags and said goodbye to Sharon on the way out. We were in the car buckling up when I remembered. "Hang on, I forgot to say goodbye to Winnie. Back in a minute."

"Whoa, whoa, wait a minute. Who's Winnie?" Mum started the car.

I stopped before opening the door. "Winnie, the

old woman who volunteers. We've been talking all day. You know, Winnie."

Mum turned around in her seat to look at me. "Mich, there's no old woman named Winnie. It's only me and Sharon Monday to Thursdays. As far as I know, there's no Winnie, period. Put your belt on, we're going home."

I put my belt back on. "What do you mean there's no Winnie? Her name's Winifred, she's old with a grey bun, and had a Happy Trails apron and name tag on. We've talked off and on all day."

"I've only seen you talking to yourself, unless you were singing. I wondered what you were doing, but there is no old woman named Winifred working in the store. I've met all the volunteers; there are only six of us and no old one amongst us."

I sat back in my seat and thought about it, frowning in double time. *That's weird,* I thought. *Not possible...but then...no...she...can't...be...*

GHOSTS ON A PLANE

"Cool." My brother plastered his face against the clear glass window of the airport and stood staring at the huge *Jet Pack* plane on which we would be jetting off to Europe.

I sighed at his never-ending and exhausting energy, put my book away, and made my way over to stand beside him. Even from the lounge I could see the big white beast towered way above me, making me feel very tiny indeed.

"It's ten storeys high, has two lounges, a kids' playground, and all the seats fold down into beds." He drooled against the glass, reminding me of a dog in a car, slopping its tongue against the window.

Blech!

"Will the passengers of *Jet Pack* Flight 666 to Europe please start boarding…"

I cocked my head to listen.

"Will the passengers of *Jet Pack* Flight 666 to Europe please start boarding…"

"Kids…time to go," Mum called out, and we walked back to our seats to collect our backpacks.

"How long's our flight gonna be?" my pesky brother, who at this point, I should let you know, is called Pete, asked our parents as we trotted over to the gate.

"About twenty hours," Dad replied, handing our tickets over to the lady to check.

"Aw," Pete whined. "Can't we stay on it longer so we can have fun?"

We came to the plane and handed our tickets over.

"No, we can't," Mum said as the hostess pointed down the aisle to the business class section.

Yep, business class. Aren't we lucky? Thanks to Mum and Dad's thriving business and constant flying, they'd racked up enough frequent flyer miles to get us all seats in business class.

I stashed my bag in the overhead locker and knelt on the seat to peer out of the window.

"Aw, I wanted the window seat."

I turned to see Pete's whiny face and crossed arms, and Mum chose that moment to interrupt.

"Neither of you will have the window seat for the whole flight. You'll be sharing."

"But—" Pete started.

Mum's finger went up in warning. "No buts, Peter. The two of you will change seats every two hours so you get a chance." She handed her bag to Dad. "No arguments," she warned. "I'm not interested in getting kicked off the flight because my ten and thirteen-year-olds can't share a window."

I triumphantly sat in my window seat and started people-watching. Men in suits, women in dresses.

There were no other kids in business class, so it looked like me and Pete would have to entertain ourselves for twenty hours. Thank God I'd brought my electronics along. iPhone, iPad, iPod, MacBook. I had the whole Apple Orchard packed into an awesome fold up kit as I was planning on blogging, Instagramming, and Facebooking the whole trip. My camera was in there along with all the cords, extra batteries, and SD and Wi-Fi cards. Plus, I had a small notebook and pen on hand to take notes. You couldn't say I wasn't prepared.

"Ladies and gentleman, this is your captain speaking. We will begin our flight to London in five minutes. Please buckle up, seat up, put your trays away, and we will be underway shortly."

We heard the massive engines screech to life as we buckled up. Now *I* found myself mashing my face against the window like an excited puppy. It was our first trip to Europe, our first trip outside of Australia, and our first flight ever.

"Whoa." Pete and I grabbed our armrests at the same time as the plane shook and rattled down the runway.

"Ooohhh," I groaned. "My stomach."

"My ears." Pete yawned, trying to fix his drums.

I stuck my fingers into mine and tried to get rid of the pressure of take off.

"Don't worry, kids," Dad called from behind us. "That's normal; it's just the pressure of take off. They should pop soon."

The take off itself was smooth, but boy was it

painful getting there.

"Ladies and gentleman, this is your captain speaking. We are cruising at an altitude of thirty thousand feet. You can now remove your seatbelts and walk around. Head to one of the two lounges on board and the kids can invade their own playroom, and you won't have to worry about them getting lost. We've also got some ghosts wandering around, so if you see one, say hello for me. This is your captain signing off."

Pete and I had looked at each other at the word ghosts, and now I pulled down my backpack, rummaged around, and pulled out my camera which went around my neck, turned my phone on and shoved it in one pocket. A small torch went into the other.

Pete did the same.

"What are you two doing?" Mum raised a brow at us.

"Ghost hunting," Pete said, and off we went.

Trying to look casual, we headed down the aisle to the station between business and economy, and I quickly snapped a pic of the toilets and the hostesses' small kitchen area.

"Are you looking for the kids' play area," one attendant asked. "It's up the staircase at the back of the plane."

"Thank you." I smiled, and we wandered off. I inconspicuously took photos when people weren't looking, and we made our way to the back. Just as we were looking for the stairs, I heard a passenger talking to an attendant.

"Miss, it's awfully cold in this spot, is the air conditioner on too high?"

I stopped.

"No, ma'am," came the reply. "The air is exactly the same through the whole plane. I can get you a blanket if you like?"

"Oh, yes please."

I tugged on my brother's jacket. "Did you hear that?" I whispered excitedly as we started up the circular staircase. "That lady was in a cold spot."

"So," Pete whispered back.

"Wherever there's a cold spot there's always a ghost," I replied, and saw his eyes widen.

We made it to the top and looked around. Before us was a huge play area with games, slides, a basketball court, and cricket pitch, all within the confines of the second floor of our plane. Of course, everything was on a much smaller scale than normal, but there was still a lot to do.

Bright colours were all over the place, and at least thirty kids were already screaming, running, throwing, and bouncing their way through everything before us.

"Whoa," Pete muttered, wide-eyed and relatively speechless. "Cool!"

I sighed. Not really my type of cool. I noticed that the kids all looked around Pete's age while there seemed to be no kids my age. True, Pete and I are only three years apart, but I am *way* more mature than him for my thirteen years. I snapped a few photos and watched as Pete barged over to join in.

A cool breeze tickled the back of my neck and I turned around. Huh, no one there. Must have come up from the floor below. I moved from the stairs to see a boy I hadn't noticed before. He was standing next to a window by himself, looking out at the expansive turquoise sky, a pensive expression on his face.

Moving up behind him, I took in his appearance. Short brown hair, casual clothes, and a little taller than me. Upon reaching him, I saw eyes bluer than I'd ever seen. "Um…hi…" I have to say it. I was kinda mesmerised by those eyes. The depth of them seemed to go on forever, but the bad part was, they were tinged with sadness.

"Hi." He was soft spoken, shy even.

"Um." I glanced around. "Not playing with the other kids?"

His lips barely made it up far enough to be called a smile. "No."

Mmm, not much of a talker either. "Off to London for a holiday?" I swept my hair back and adjusted my camera. "We are. Can I take a pic?"

"No." His voice snapped to attention.

"Hey, Sarah, who you talkin' too?"

I swivelled my head to see Pete coming up behind me. "Just one of the passengers." I turned to introduce him to the boy, but he was gone. "Now where'd he go?" I ran to the stairs and peered down.

"Where'd *who* go?"

"The boy I was talking to."

"You weren't talking to a boy. You weren't talking to anyone, that's why I came over. To see what you were doing."

I watched Pete's face as he talked. "What do you *mean* I *wasn't talking to anyone?*"

"Sarah," Pete said urgently. "There was *no one* with you. You were *alone* and talking to yourself… or…"

The realisation hit me. "Get out!" I punched Pete on the arm. "Shut the front door! I was talking to a ghost."

Pete rubbed his arm. "Did you get a picture?"

"No. I asked, he said no, then you yelled out. Whoa." We looked at each other. "A ghost!"

We pounded down the stairs and stopped. I snapped pictures of everything while Pete quietly opened every door that was unlocked. We shuffled down the aisle in economy and stopped so I could take more pics, then bolted down the aisle in business to the staircase up to the lounge.

Trying to look oh so casual, we calmly walked up the stairs and found ourselves between two lounge areas. The one in front of us, toward the front of the plane, was very adult and classy. The one behind us was more casual and family friendly.

I quietly took snaps as we moved to the lounge and sat down. I pulled up the pics on my camera, and we scanned each one.

"I can't really tell if there's a ghost in them," Pete said as we sat hunched over the tiny screen. "We'll have to put them on your laptop and enlarge them."

He scanned the crowd. "Hey, there's Mum and Dad."

We wandered over to them, and the hostess brought us jello cups with jelly snakes in them.

"Cool," Pete cried. "Snakes on a Plane."

I rolled my eyes at the movie reference and chewed thoughtfully on my red one. Had I *really* just seen a ghost? On a plane?

A cool breeze wafted past me, but when I looked there was no one there. I shivered. This stuff was weird.

Finishing up, Pete and I went downstairs, and while he went to the bathroom, I went for my laptop, but stopped. The curtains between economy and business were open and all the way down the aisle I could see him. The boy I'd been talking to earlier. Leaving my bag untouched, I walked toward him, trying not to take my eyes off him in case he disappeared. I made it to the back, but he moved, walking through a door leading off the main public area.

Someone bumped into me from behind.

"Hey," I cried and turned my head.

"Sorry," Pete mumbled. "I saw you walk back here and followed. What are you doing?"

"I saw him." I pointed to the door off the attendants' space. "He went through there. The boy I saw upstairs."

"Then let's follow." Pete casually sneaked over to the door and opened it a crack. "All clear," he whispered, and I raced over to him.

We closed the door behind us and found ourselves in a small space with another staircase, this time going down into the belly of the plane.

"I don't know if we should do this," I whispered, but followed Pete down the stairs anyway. I got my camera ready and pulled up the recording app on my phone. I was going to get a sound or a photo either way.

Staying on the lookout for staff, we tiptoed down the aisle and into a kitchen storage area. Trays of stuff were piled high on trolleys, with cartons and containers, boxes, bags, and Handee towels. The lights were dim, but we found our way by the safety lights.

"There." I pointed into the belly of the big white beast and turned right into another passageway. "He's there, at the end." I shoved Pete ahead in the direction of the boy, and we found ourselves even more surrounded than before.

Something landed on my left shoulder.

"Ah," I cried, spying a hand belonging to a man.

"Ah," Pete repeated.

We spun around to see an older man in business attire.

"Hello." His voice was quiet. "What are you doing here?"

Pete and I clung to each other. "Uh, uh," we stuttered, scared we'd be in big trouble and get chucked off the plane just like Mum warned us about.

"What time is it?" he asked. "I've been on this plane for so long."

That's a strange question, I thought, and checked over the man's appearance. Old brown suit, wrinkled, with matching brown shoes. The tie around his neck was loosened and twisted to the side; his hair was unkempt and in need of brushing. His pallor was quite sickly, and his eyes were tired, red and drooping.

"Uh." Pete checked his watch. "We've only been in the air for three hours."

The man's dazed face showed confusion. "Three hours? What day is it?" He checked his watch.

"Wednesday."

"And the date?"

"The 17th of February."

His brows furrowed. "Feb the 17th? Why… I've…been flying for two weeks."

Pete and I exchanged glances. "How have you been flying for two weeks?"

The man looked at me. "Because I left on the 3rd of February." He looked around. "What year is it?"

Now I frowned. Okay, def something weird going on here. "2016."

He blinked slowly. "What?"

"2016," Pete repeated.

Blinking for a third time, the man exclaimed, "But that can't be, it must be 1995. It's 1995, isn't it?"

Pete and I took a step back. "Right," I muttered. "It's 1995. Our mistake. Bye now." I shunted Pete down the aisle and glanced back. The man was gone. I stopped. "Pete. He's gone. He must have been a ghost too."

I got an eye roll in return. "Well, duh! Did you see what vintage that get up was? He ain't from 2016, believe me."

I sighed. "Let's get out of here before a *human* from *2016* finds us."

We made our way back upstairs without being seen and meandered through economy.

I smiled at the two old ladies by the door with their knitting bags on their legs, and their needles click-clacking away.

They smiled back and one lady dropped her ball of wool.

"Would you mind getting that, dear?" she asked.

I bent down, picked it up, and offered it back, only to find there were no old ladies sitting in the seats. Both seats were now empty, but I was left holding the small ball of yarn. I straightened and rolled it around in my hand, staring at the two seats.

"Oh, you met them did you?" I heard from behind me. An attendant was standing in the passageway. "We've collected quite a few of those over the years. Always wondered where they came from until I did what you just did." She smiled. "I bent and picked it up and poof, they were gone."

I looked down at the ball. "When would they have been on?" I glanced up. "On the plane, in real life, I mean?"

The young woman's smile softened. "From what I know, in the '90s sometime."

My brows shot up. "This plane has been flying that long?"

She laughed, and I saw that her name tag read Susan. "This plane is about twenty-five years old, but sometimes, pieces of it have come from other planes. Looks like the people come with them. You can keep that if you like." She nodded at the wool in my hand. "Think of it as a souvenir."

She hurried over to help a passenger, and I wandered back to my seat thinking about the boy, the man, and the two old grey-haired ladies click-clacking their needles. For ghosts to haunt a building, or in this case a plane, wouldn't they have to die in it?

Pete rushed up to me and got my kit from my bag. "Quick, let's have a look at those photos." He pulled out my laptop and booted it up while I got the SD card ready. Five minutes of scrolling through photos later, we caught sight of white foggy things in some of the pictures. Others had people, who may not have been people, as they were there, but see-through. Yep, I could see them, but also see *through* them.

We deleted all of the pics with nothing to see and stored the rest in a folder. We chatted for a while before Mum and Dad came back and dinner was served. By now, we were way over the ocean, but still so far from London.

Munching our way through our food, we decided to head back to the play lounge after dinner. While Pete played, I booted up my laptop and started writing some blog posts about our flying experience.

I took some photos of Pete playing around, cut,

cropped, and copyrighted others for my blog posts, and checked on social media. I Instagrammed a pic of the playground letting everyone know how awesome the whole thing was. *"And you'll never believe it, but the plane's haunted. Yep, we've got ghosts!"* I sent it out to all of my followers and checked up on what my friends were doing.

"Ladies and gentleman, this is your captain speaking. It's now bedtime. So for those who wish to sleep, please do so. For those who wish to stay up in the lounges, please refrain from making too much noise as to not disturb other passengers. Have a good sleep, because when you wake up, you'll be in Europe."

Pete and I stayed upstairs until Dad came and got us. "Time for bed, kids. We have a big day planned."

I packed up my laptop, and we went downstairs to find the attendants had set up our beds with sheets, blankets and pillows. We were given a onesie jumpsuit pyjama thing to wear to bed, and I took the time to get changed. The bathrooms were bigger than normal plane toilets, so I had the room to get out of my clothes and into my onesie.

I looked in the mirror. *Oh, God, I look ridiculous.* I washed up and brushed my teeth before heading back to business class. Mum and Dad had both changed into their onesies, and Pete fell over the feet of his as he came rushing back from the bathroom.

"That is way too big for you," I said as he scored the window seat. "Hey."

"Hey, what?" He spread his hands out. "You had

it all day; now it's my turn."

I turned to Mum and Dad with my mouth open ready to protest.

Dad put his hand up to stop me. "Don't bother. You'll both be sleeping anyway."

I caved in reluctantly and snuggled down in my bed. "Hope you enjoy the window view," I muttered.

"At least I won't get foot traffic," came the reply as someone walked past me.

"Ugh." I put my sleep mask on, my ear plugs in, and shoved my pillow over my head to keep out any noise or disturbance, although I was the one doing the disturbing in the middle of the night by having to get up and pee.

I managed to make it to the bathroom without falling over. I managed to undress, pee, re-dress, and make it back to my bed without anything happening, until I looked down the end of the aisle that is.

I saw the boy, the man, and the two old ladies standing together, waving at me, waving *for* me. Like, *to go* to them. I stood there staring at them, blinking, rubbing my eyes. No. I couldn't be seeing them. An attendant came along and helped me back into bed. I snuggled down and put my mask on, turning my back on the aisle and Casper's relatives.

*****

I yawned. "Ugh."

I shifted. "Ugh."

I pulled off the mask and opened one eye. Day

was breaking in the sky, and I knew I needed to get up. Pete was already gone, and when I stood up and stretched, I saw Mum and Dad had gone too.

"Why didn't anyone wake me?" I grumbled.

Getting my toiletries and fresh clothes, I showered and dressed in the bathroom. With a grumbling stomach, I made my way back to my seat to find everything put away and a girl about my age sitting there.

"Um, *hello*," I said. "You're in *my* seat."

The girl looked up in surprise. "What?" Her eyes went wide, and her jaw dropped. "Who…who…are you…?"

"Like, I'm the passenger who's been sitting in this seat." I reached up to put my toiletries into my bag, but it was gone from the overhead locker. "Oh, God, where's my bag."

"Are you all right?" An attendant came over to us.

"No, this girl is in my seat," I managed before realising she wasn't talking to me. "Where's my stuff," I asked her, interrupting.

"Um," the girl said. "There's a girl telling me it's her seat." The young brunette moved nervously.

And so she should be nervous, she was in *my* seat, that *my* parents had worked hard to get us.

The attendant laughed. "Don't worry, that's just Sarah. You'll probably see her parents and brother Pete as well. They won't hurt you, they're just a little feisty."

"Feisty! Pete can be but not me!"

The girl sighed in relief. "Oh, that's good. I

thought I was seeing things."

"No, no." The attendant patted her shoulder. "She's just one of the ghosts the captain was talking about."

Wait, what! Ghosts!

GHOSTWRITER

"What am I going to do with that?" Sam asked his mother as he stood staring at the ancient Underwood typewriter on their kitchen table.

"Use it. Put in on the mantle and display it," his mother replied as she bustled around the kitchen.

Sam leaned over it and peered down into the keys. "Does it even work?" He punched a key.

"Don't know. But we can take it to that shop and get it cleaned up and working again. Your grandmother left it to you because you kept banging on about being a writer one day. It's a memento of her. Even if you don't use it, you still need to treasure it."

Sam remembered back to all the times he'd talked about writing with his grandma. He'd gone back and forth from wanting to be an author and write books, to being a writer for a paper or magazine. "I didn't think grandma had taken any notice," he muttered.

"Of course she did," his mum chastised. "She was old, not deaf or senile! You'll be old one day, you know, so don't mock old people."

Sam touched the old typewriter gently. "I guess I can use it."

*****

A week later, that old typewriter sat front and centre on Sam's desk. His mum had tracked down a typewriter expert who not only collected and displayed them, but cleaned them up and repaired them. It had new ink ribbons, had been oiled and polished, and looked good sitting on his desk.

"Well, Grandma," he said. "Guess I can give it a go after all." He rolled a piece of paper around the platen and started typing.

There was an old man in a shoe,
Who didn't know what to do,

"Sam, phone call," his mum yelled, and the witty ditty was all but forgotten until after dinner when he went to finish off his homework.

Preparing to move the typewriter to the side shelf so he could get his maths done, he noticed the witty ditty had three extra lines.

So he said pretty please,
And had a big sneeze,
And now he lives in Peru.

Sam frowned. "I didn't write that."

He was sure he'd only typed the first two lines before being called to the phone. He pulled the paper out and rolled in a blank one. "I'll leave you there for next time."

*****

The next day at school, he told his best friend Blake

about his grandma's typewriter and how the witty ditty had been finished.

"You sure you didn't just write it yourself and forget about it?" Blake bounced the basketball before throwing it through the net.

Sam grabbed it and threw it through the hoop. "I swear I didn't. You called before I had the chance, and then we had dinner. I didn't get back to my room until after and there it was."

Blake bounced the ball before throwing it from hand to hand. "Maybe it's haunted?" He threw the ball at Sam who missed it because he was off on another planet. "Oi! Earth to Sam, Earth to Sam. What's wrong?"

Sam frowned. "The guy that Mum took it to for fixing did a history on it and wrote it up for us. He traced it back to 1895 and said every owner ended up being a writer."

"Haven't you always said the same thing? You wanna be a writer."

"Yeah, but get this..." Sam grabbed the ball to stop Blake from bouncing it. "All of those owners who ended up being writers also died...*while writing at their typewriter.*"

Blake stared at him. "You're kidding? Really?"

"Yep!" Sam bounced the ball and threw it over his shoulder, sending it through the hoop without even trying. "I'm doomed for death."

"Aw, what!" Blake's face screwed up at the shot and threw his hands in the air in defeat. "*How dare you!*" He went back to the subject. "Or, it's all in your head and you're imagining things!"

*****

Sam wondered if Blake was right and decided to try something when he got home. He set up the typewriter on his desk and wrote one word.

Hello.

He finished his homework and had dinner, then ran back to his room to see if anything had happened.

Hello, Sam.

Whoa!" He sat down at the desk and stared at the line. *It can't be…it just can't be.*

Hello, who are you? He typed back.

I'm Thomas Freeborn… The keys typed across the page.

And who's Thomas Freeborn? Sam replied.

I'm a writer. I write for newspapers.

What year is it? Sam typed.

1895.

"Whoa." Sam sat back in his seat. "It can't be. No…" He ripped the paper out of the platen, screwed it up, and threw it into his bin.

*****

He told Blake about it the next day. "It *cannot* be haunted. That could not have been real. I must have been dreaming it."

"Were you awake?"

"Well, yeah."

"Then you weren't dreaming, numbskull!"

"Then what's happening?"

"Dude!" Blake stopped him. *"It's haunted.* Maybe you can get the ghosts to write your essays." He burst out laughing and walked toward class.

"Ugh!" Sam cried. *"It's not haunted!"*

But he began to have doubts when he got home. A whole page had been typed up. But it wasn't by Thomas Freeborn. It was by someone called Makintosh MacClusky.

Hello, Sam.

I am Makintosh MacClusky. I am a writer with the Boston Tribune, and I died at my typewriter. Do you know how I died? I died from having my head smashed into it. Do you know who did that to me?

"Whoa." Sam stood staring at the paper. "Maybe I'm imagining this? Maybe I read the report and saw the previous owners and am now imagining them writing letters to me." He ripped the paper out and threw it in the bin then put the typewriter back on the shelf. He had homework to do, and that old thing wasn't gonna cut it. He opened his laptop and got to work.

He worked until dinnertime and then worked again, typing up his essay until late, not even noticing the piece of paper in the typewriter. Packing up, he got his bag ready for school the next day and went to bed...

Tap tap tap tap tap tap tap tap tap.

Tap-tap-tap-tap-tap.

"Mmm," Sam mumbled, drifting awake. "Whuh..."

Tap-tap-tap-tap.

Sam's hand snaked out to flick his bedside light on, and he leaned up to look around the room.

Tap-tap-tap-tap.

The sound drew his gaze to the shelf beside his desk.

Tap-tap-tap-tap.

He saw the paper roll through and heard the soft ding as the line finished and moved on to the next one.

Tap-tap-tap-tap.

Sliding out of bed he inched over to the shelf and looked at the paper.

Hello Sam,

My name is William Denhold, I am a writer with the London Times. Am I dead? I don't feel dead. I feel very much alive as I tap out this letter to you, the current owner of this typewriter.

I don't know what year it is, but I bought this typewriter from a secondhand store in 1968. It feels like 1968. Is it still 1968? That's when I died, I think. I wrote myself to death, you know. I was making a measly living with writing, but could never make enough, so sat at my typewriter and wrote and wrote and wrote...

It stopped.

Sam blinked. *What was happening?* He ripped the paper out and screwed it up, but stopped at throwing it into the bin as he eyed the other two papers he'd thrown in there. Reluctantly, he pulled them out and smoothed all three out on his desk.

Thomas Freeborn, Makintosh MacClusky, and William Denhold. All previous owners of the typewriter, and all dead.

What's going on? How could this be happening? How could a typewriter, an object, so inane and boring, that had just belonged to his grandmother, be haunted?

As morning light drifted in through the curtains, Sam woke, and remembering what he'd done during the night, bounded out of bed to check the typewriter...

Nothing!

Dejected, Sam slumped against the desk. "Guess it's not haunted after all."

*****

At school, he showed Blake all three letters. "They typed themselves. This one was from last night, *in the middle of the night,*" he stressed. "I woke up, and there it was tap tapping away."

"So all three of them know they died and here they are writing you letters. Whoa." Blake stared down at the three pieces of paper in his hand. "How many other owners have there been? You might get a letter from all of them."

Sam checked the paperwork from the typewriter expert. He'd printed out photocopies the night before. "One, two, three, four...eight...twelve..."

"Was twelve your grandma?"

Same looked up "Um, yeah."

"Ooohhh," Blake teased. "That makes you unlucky number thirteen, my man."

Sam frowned. "Don't say that."

"Well, isn't it true?"

With a sigh, Sam went through the list. "Here's Thomas Freeborn, he was number one. Makintosh MacClusky was number three. William Denhold was eleven, and grandma was twelve."

"And you're unlucky number thirteen," Blake repeated.

"Stop it," Sam snapped. "It's not about me being the thirteenth owner. It's about the stupid thing being haunted and writing letters."

Blake grinned wryly. "So who are the others?"

Sam went back to the beginning. "Thomas Freeborn 1895, Benjamin Bourne 1900, Makintosh MacClusky 1908, Samuel Rightman 1913, Frederic Von Dutch 1919, Mikael Ricardo 1924, Franklin Rosco 1926, Adam Weissman 1932, Christian Donnelly 1940, Eric Richards 1955, William Denhold 1968, Martha West 1975, Samuel West 2016."

"So that's twelve male and one female owner. Mmm…interesting."

"Why's it interesting?" Sam asked.

"Well." Blake pointed to the list. "Twelve males, one female. Twelve dead, eleven maybe by their typewriter…" He shrugged. "Maybe…we don't know yet. How did your grandma die?"

"*Not* at the typewriter," Sam scoffed. "She was sick, and it was found in the attic when we cleaned out her stuff." He ran his fingers over his grandmother's name.

Blake shrugged again. "Maybe we should find out exactly *how* many of them died at their, uh, *your*," he corrected himself, "typewriter."

At lunchtime, Sam spent the hour in the library googling all of the people on the list. He couldn't find much, and clearly the typewriter had been all over the world with many owners, so, death registries were not open for inspection.

He sighed. Guess I'll just have to ask the typewriter.

✷✷✷✷✷

Hello Sam,

I miss you so much. I'm so glad you got the typewriter. I wanted you to have it.

"Crikey!"

Sam sat down with a thud. *Grandma left me a note.* "Oh, grandma, I miss you too," he muttered, wiping away a tear that found its way down his cheek. He pulled the paper out and slipped it into his drawer. He'd be keeping that one. He put another piece in and typed out a message.

I am Sam West,

I am the thirteenth owner of this typewriter. My grandma was the twelfth. What do you all want?

He sighed and got to his homework, but after dinner he checked to see if there were any messages.

Nope!

He lay awake in bed thinking about ghosts, ghouls,

and hauntings of typewriters and objects…

Tap tap tap tap.

Tap tap tap tap.

Sam's eyes opened slowly and he listened.

Tap tap tap tap.

He turned the bedside light on and turned his head toward the shelf.

Tap-tap tap tap-tap tap tappity tap.

He slid out of bed, eyes heavy with exhaustion, and watched the words appear on the page.

To live again.

To breathe again.

To write again.

To be again.

To see the world.

To write the book.

To become the author.

To become the writer.

To publish the book.

To be a literary giant.

To make millions.

To see you again, Sam.

Grandma!

All of the answers, bar Grandma's, seemed to have to do with either being alive or writing.

Sam put in another paper. *How did you all die?*

I starved to death.

I simply died.

I was told my work wasn't good enough.

I was murdered.

I had my head smashed in.

I couldn't make a living from my writing.
Nobody wanted me.
I couldn't stop writing.
I developed pneumonia.
I was shot in the back.
I was fired and died of loneliness.
Oh, Sam, you know how.

Sam frowned. Most of those, again, had to do with writing, but didn't really tell him how they died. He replaced the paper. *What do you want from me,* he tapped.

To kill you.
To live through you.
To be you.
To make you one of us.
To use you.
To take you.
To kill you.
To kill you.
To kill you.
To kill you.
To kill you.
To protect you!

Bloody hell!

Another paper. *And why do you want to kill me? I am alive, you are not, how can you kill me? Why do you want to?*

Because you are alive and I am not.
I can live through you.
I can live within you.
I will be you.

I can seep into your blood.
I can make you do what I want.
I can bash your head against the typewriter.
I will take over your life.
I will take over your soul.
I can become you.
I want to be you.
I must protect you, Sam.

This was just getting down right freaky!

He replaced the paper, but before he could type anything it started up by itself.

You will leave my grandson alone.
We want him.
You will not hurt him.
We need him.
I will not let you hurt him.
We have to have him.
You will NEVER have him.

The keys sped through each sentence and quickly roared to the end of the paper. He added another piece.

We want you.
We need you.
We must have you.
We will have you.

NO, YOU WILL NOT! You will not lay one finger on my grandson, or I will kick some afterlife butt on all of you.

Hahahahahahahahahahahahahahahahahahahaha spread across the page, row after row after row all the way to the bottom.

Sam added another page, almost mesmerised by what was happening.

We will kill you.
We will kill you.
We will kill you.
We will kill you.
We will kill you.
We will kill you.
We will kill you.
We will kill you.
We will kill you.
We will kill you.
We will kill you.

Sam stood staring as the words spread down the page and it seemed the only thing he could do, was to continually replace the paper.

Stay away from my grandson; LEAVE HIM ALONE!

We will kill you.
We will kill you.
We will kill you.
We will kill you.
We will kill you.
We will kill you.
We will kill you.
We will kill you.
We will kill you.
We will kill you.
We will kill you.

Sammy, you have to snap out of it and do something, otherwise they will take you.

We will kill you.
We will kill you.
We will kill you.
We will kill you.
We will kill you.
We will kill you.
We will kill you.
We will kill you.
We will kill you.
We will kill you.
We will kill you.
Tap tap tappity tap.
Sammy, snap out of it now, you have to do what I tell you, so they won't take you over.
He added another paper.
We will kill you.
We will kill you.
We will kill you.
We will kill you.
We will kill you.
We will kill you.
We will kill you.
We will kill you.
We will kill you.
We will kill you.
We will kill you.
Sammy, listen to me now. I'm trying to protect you. You have to do what I say, you have to—
We will kill you.
We will kill you.
We will kill you.

We will kill you.
We will kill you.
We will kill you.
We will kill you.
We will kill you.
We will kill you.
We will kill you.
We will kill you.

Sam lifted another piece of paper to add to the platen and saw the last line from his grandmother. He grabbed the typewriter and smashed it to the floor.

THE GHOSTS OF HEARTLAND HOSPITAL

"Welcome, ladies and gentleman, to the opening of the brand spanking new Heartland Hospital," the mayor of Digbyville cried into the microphone. He was standing on a podium out the front of the newly built hospital, waiting to cut the ribbon in front of him.

Wild applause filled the air, along with loud whistles of approval from the crowd who had gathered for the celebration.

He waved his hands to quieten everyone. "We are here today, to open our new hospital, a state of the art engineering feat that will serve our community for the next," he winked at the crowd, "we hope, one hundred years."

Loud cheering and clapping welcomed his words.

"Now, we waited so long for a new hospital in this town, and finally decided on this plot of land. It's been in the making for five years, and I can finally open it today, to the patients, and the people, of Digbyville." He waved his hands to egg the crowd on and accepted the large shiny scissors from the deputy mayor. Waiting for the photographers to get into place, he held the scissors over the ribbon and snipped it.

Heartland Hospital was open for business.

And open to all of the patients being transferred from nearby smaller hospitals. They were driven from far and wide to their new home at Heartland, for it contained everything a patient could possibly need. Clinics for physiotherapy, orthopaedics, maternity, gastroenterology. It even had its own psych ward.

Tommy Ward was just one patient being transferred. At ten years of age, he had been in and out of hospital all of his short life, with one ailment or another, one sprain or another, one break or another. Tommy Ward was a rambunctious kid. A kid who couldn't sit still long enough to be told not to do something, because Tommy Ward was a kid that didn't listen to what anybody ever said…

Ever…

"Tommy Ward, ten years old, broken left arm, plastered, and a busted femur," the ambulance driver told the nurse in Accident and Emergency. This was where all the patients were coming through before being registered and sent through to their specified wards.

"Right." The nurse flicked through her spreadsheet and clicked a few computer keys. "Done and done." She glanced up. "Children's Ward, third floor, take a left." She waved to an orderly. "Take him up."

"Thank you, ma'am," the driver said and relinquished

the patient. "See you next time, Tommy."

"Bye, Bob," Tommy called before being whizzed up to the third floor children's wing. After being checked in, he was taken to room 3A which had space for three beds.

"Looks like you'll be sharing, kiddo," the orderly told him, hooking up necessary wires and flicking buttons and knobs.

"Looks like," Tommy replied, looking forward to some company.

Within half an hour another boy about his age joined him.

"Hi, I'm Tommy." He peered at the boy. "What's wrong with you?"

"Busted leg," the boy replied, trying to scratch under the plaster.

"How long you in for?"

"Dunno," the kid said. "A week maybe."

"Mmm," Tommy muttered. "What's your name?" He eyed off the boy's Marvel comics case and bag.

"David."

"Cool. You into Marvel?" He pointed to the luggage.

"Yep."

"Who's your fave?"

"Iron Man."

Tommy nodded. "Yeah, he's cool."

"What about you?"

"Don't really have a favourite, but Black Widow is wicked hot."

David didn't disagree. "She is. Can't believe she hooked up with Hulk."

"Yeah, what *does* she see in him?"

Another boy was being wheeled into the room and was set up in bed 3C.

"Hey," Tommy and David said at the same time.

The boy blinked in surprise. "Um, hey…" he said slowly.

"You all right, dude? You look a bit dazed," Tommy asked. He spoke to one of the orderlies. "Is he all right?"

"Just sedated," one of them said before leaving the room.

Tommy noticed the boy's wide-eyed stare, a stare that seemed to be staring at no particular thing. He threw a glance at David. "We got a druggie here." He flicked his thumb over his shoulder at the boy.

"A druggie?" David asked with a frown. "What does that mean?"

"A kid who's on drugs for most of their stay," Tommy said, copping another look at the boy. "What's your name?"

The boy's stare was distant.

"Hey," Tommy called, waving an arm near the boy. "What's your name?"

The boy blinked and slowly turned his attention to Tommy. "What?"

"*What's your name?*" Tommy impatiently repeated. "*Your name?*"

"Michael," the boy said slowly. "Michael."

"Yeah, we get it." Tommy rolled his eyes. "I'm Tommy, this is David."

"Michael," the boy repeated.

"Yeah." Tommy sighed. *"We get it."*

For the rest of the day, David and Tommy talked all things Marvel, getting the odd and weird comment from Michael while the rest of the hospital bustled along outside their door.

Lunch came and went, as did dinner, and soon the nurse was settling the boys down for the night.

Sometime during the night, Tommy and David were woken to a semi-conscious state by screaming.

Michael was sitting up in his bed pointing to the wall in front of him. "Ah, he's going to kill me. He said he's going to kill me," Michael screamed at the top of his voice as orderlies and a nurse came rushing in, and Tommy and David covered their ears. Well, Tommy tried, but since one arm was broken and in a cast, it was a bit hard.

"Calm down, Michael, it's just a bad dream," the nurse said.

"More than a bad dream," Tommy interjected. "More like he's possessed."

"Don't be silly," the nurse snapped at him, leaving him wondering what he'd said.

The nurses quietened Michael down and waited while he drifted off to sleep before telling Tommy and David to go back to sleep themselves.

"Mmm," Tommy mumbled, "it had better be a good one."

Well, apparently it was because when Tommy whole up the next morning, Michael was gone and another kid was in his place.

"Hey." Tommy sat up and leaned back on his

good hand. "Who are you and what happened to the other kid?"

"This is Caden; you'll be sharing the ward with him," the nurse said as she entered with the breakfast trays.

"And Michael?"

She flashed Tommy a stern look. "He was taken to the mental health ward."

"You mean the nutjob ward," Tommy joked.

"It's no laughing matter," the nurse snapped, making Tommy stop dead. "Michael was a very ill boy. Ill in the head. He needed help."

Tommy's brows rose as he watched the nurse pander over the new kid with the stupid name. "If he was so ill, why was he put in here?"

She stopped at the end of his bed. "You are a *very* nosy boy," she said and left the room.

"Dude, she didn't like you," David said, gulping down some oatmeal.

Tommy turned to the new kid. "Hey."

The new kid's spoon stopped mid-air and he glanced over. "Hey."

"I'm Tommy, that's David."

"Hey."

"Hey."

The rest of the day was taken up with doctors, x-rays, scans, and general faffing about until dinnertime.

"Guess what I heard," David said over their meal of minced steak and veggies with jelly for dessert.

"What." Tommy tasted the steak. "Blech!"

"I heard some of the nurses talking about Michael,

and how he says he saw a weird dude at the end of his bed with a weird chainsaw type thing and he wanted to kill him, that's why he screamed."

Tommy frowned. "He said he saw what? Dude must have some serious issues."

"Either that or he saw a ghost," David continued.

"Ghost!" Tommy scoffed. "The hospital is too new to have ghosts."

"Well, I heard some of the nurses laugh as well, but then one mentioned that this hospital is built on the site of another hospital. An old hospital, so old it's like ancient or something, and apparently, they buried the bodies in the basement or something."

Tommy finished off his jelly. "I've never heard of a hospital being here before. But so what?" He scraped out the container. "You just said it's ancient. How old's ancient?"

"Two hundred years or something."

"All the ghosts should be gone by now, and surely they dug up the bodies, if there were any, when they did the foundation."

"I'm wondering if that's it," David said and finished off his juice. "Apparently, the old hospital was for nutjobs. It was like a psych ward."

"Mmm," Tommy muttered. "Interesting." He pushed his tray table away. "Doesn't explain what happened last night though, does it?" He turned to Caden. "As the new kid, what do you think?"

Caden looked up from his meal. "Ghosts don't exist."

Tommy's top lip curled. "Smart dude, I'm with you."

After watching TV for a few hours, it was lights out and shut eye time.

"Let's hope Jason doesn't come to get us tonight," Tommy joked.

"Who's Jason?" David asked.

"Dude! The guy with the chainsaw in all the movies. Isn't that who Michael saw standing at the end of his bed?"

David rolled his eyes. "Yeah, coz movie creeps *really* exist."

Tommy shrugged. "You never know."

Sleep drifted over them and all was peaceful, undisturbed and quiet.

"Ah, don't let him kill me. Get away, get away from me."

Tommy struggled to sit up. "Whuh, whuh's going on?"

David was sitting up in his bed pointing to the wall in front of him, screaming at the top of his lungs. "Ah, he's going to kill me. He said he's going to kill me,"

Tommy looked at the wall. There was nothing there, and no one there, except for the nurses and orderlies rushing in.

The nurses quietened David down and waited while he drifted off to sleep before telling Tommy and Caden to go back to sleep themselves.

"Mmm," Tommy mumbled, "not sure how that's gonna happen."

But sure enough, when the breakfast trays came in David was gone, and a new boy was being wheeled in.

"Where's David, and who's he?" Tommy nodded at the new kid.

"This is Mason, he'll be sharing the ward with you," the nurse said as she fixed his tubes.

"And David?"

She flashed Tommy a stern look. "He was taken to the mental health ward."

"The psych ward," Caden muttered under his breath, but the nurse heard him anyway.

"This is no laughing matter," she snapped, making Caden stop dead. "David was a very ill boy. Ill in the head. He needed help."

Tommy's brows rose and he pondered over the same thing happening to two kids in the same room.

"Didn't you mention that's what happened to the other kid?" Caden asked.

I looked over at him.

"Michael, now David," he said. "Isn't that just a *bit* suspicious?"

I sighed. "Yeah. Yeah, it is, and the *same* nurse said the *same* thing. That they were ill in the head." Tommy shook his head vehemently. "But they weren't. They just weren't."

"Um, hey," the new kid said.

"Hey," Tommy mumbled at the same time as Caden.

If something weird is going on I can't wait to see what happens tonight, Tommy thought. *Could the stories David heard be true? If the new hospital was built on an old psych ward, could the old patients be haunting the new patients? And what's with the dude and the weird chainsaw? I wonder if that's what David saw, or if he saw something different to Michael. Mmm, I wonder if there's a library or computer room here somewhere and I'll Google it.*

Tommy found out from an orderly that there was indeed a small library room for the kids with Wi-Fi and computers on hand. After being wheeled into the room, he let his fingers do the walking by checking every website and page about Heartland Hospital and its previous occupants.

Turns out, what David had overheard was true.

In 1816 the Digbyville Mental Institution was opened by the then mayor. The hospital had patients from far and wide as it had world-renowned scientific minds working there. Doctor Schivack was the highest specialist in his field with many new experiments under his belt. But it wasn't until that fateful night two hundred years ago, that the true extent of his experiments were revealed. After many years of cutting and drilling holes in their heads, some of the patients revolted. While the staff fled, Schivack did not, for he was also one of the patients.

Tommy frowned. "Hey, what? How can he be both?" He read on.

It seemed Doctor Schivack had also been experimenting on himself, and after something had gone too far, he turned mad and was committed to the hospital. Within a few days of this happening, he went crazy with a medical chainsaw that he used to decapitate and de-limb patients with. In the rampage that followed, lamps were knocked over, and the fire that destroyed the building was started. Most of the staff survived, but the patients did not.

After a one year inquest and removal and burial of the bodies, they razed the building to the ground, only to find more bodies hidden in the surrounding grounds and secret basement. The ground had been off limits and untouched until it was decided to use it for the new Heartland Hospital.

"Whoa." Tommy sat back in his chair. "It *is* true! The hospital's on the site of the old one and bodies were buried in the basement. Does that mean it's Doctor Schivack's ghost David and Michael saw?" Tommy absentmindedly scratched under his cast. "So, if they're seeing his ghost, why are they being taken to the psych ward? There's nothing wrong with them, and seeing a ghost doesn't make you a nutjob."

An orderly wheeled him back to his room where he took a nap before dinner.

"Did you find out anything," Caden asked when he woke up. "About the hospital?"

"How did you…?" Tommy started.

"You mumble in your sleep," he replied.

"I…mmm…didn't know that." Tommy frowned and hoped he hadn't given too much away. "Yep, it's all true." He waited for the orderly to leave once they were served their trays. "So if you see a madman with a weird looking chainsaw thing, it's a ghost, and they'll think you're a nutjob."

"Better not see a ghost with a weird looking

chainsaw thing then," Caden said.

They finished dinner in silence and watched TV until it was time to go to bed. But Tommy was determined to stay awake and find out what was going on, and luckily, as the clock struck midnight, the party started happening.

He appeared at the end of Tommy's bed. A man, a madman, with wild hair, and wilder eyes, red from experiments and raging inside. He wore old-fashioned clothes, with braces to hold up his pants, and he brandished, you guessed it, a weird looking chainsaw.

"God," Tommy muttered. "Doctor Schivack, I presume?"

That startled the ghost, being called by name, and the fact that Tommy was not screaming.

"I will kill you," the ghost hollered, turning the handle of the weird looking chainsaw and spinning it full throttle. "I will kill you."

"Just try," Tommy replied and waved him on. "Come on then, ghostie, give it your best shot."

Tommy Ward was not to be played with. He may have been ten years of age, but he played hard and cared even less. He wasn't scared of ghosts, and if this old geezer thought he was going to scare him, then he had another think, *and thing,* coming.

"Come on, Schivack, just try it!"

The nurses and orderlies came rushing in. "Oh no, not another one."

"Another what?" Tommy asked.

"Another poor boy in need of help," the nurse

said, sticking a needle into Tommy's arm.

"Hey, what are you doing?" Tommy cried. "I'm not even screaming."

"Oh, but you are, you poor boy, you are…"

Tommy didn't know how long he'd been out, but woke up to find himself in another room, with nurses watching through a glass window. He wiped his face. "Where am I?"

A nurse came rushing in. "It's all right, dear, you're safe now, we'll take good care of you."

"*Where am I?*" he repeated, lifting his head to view the stark white and padded room with no windows.

"You're in the mental health ward, dear. Don't worry, we'll fix you right up."

He was puzzled, and frowned as he watched her walk away. The mental health ward? *What the hell am I doing here?*

He shifted up onto his good arm. "Hey," he yelled. "What the hell am I in the nutjob ward for?"

Another nurse poked her head through the doorway. "You were seeing dead people, dear."

"Dead people?" He called back. "You mean ghosts?" That stopped her. "Yeah, bring it on." He sneered. "I ain't afraid of no ghosts." He saw the puzzled expressions on the attendees' faces before they closed the door.

Time was clearly irrelevant in the nutjob ward, and because the harsh fluoro lights were on 24/7, Tommy had no idea what the time was; not even when David and Michael walked into the room.

"Oh, my God." Tommy sat up. "You guys are

alive? I can't believe you're still here. Where's your parents? Did no one come to get you?" He stopped, for they had been silent, mouths unmoving, eyes unsearching. They rolled a wheelchair over to Tommy and motioned for him to get in.

"Um." He swung his legs over the side of the bed. "I'm not sure I should be going with you guys. Where are you taking me?"

They motioned again.

With much reluctance, Tommy hobbled off the bed and into the chair before being rolled out into the hallway.

Door after door passed by in the stark white hallway, and Tommy strained to see the boys behind him. They were silent; saying nothing, doing nothing, except for wheeling him along. They stopped at an open lift and entered.

"So, what have you boys been up to?" Tommy chatted. He noticed they were going down to some sub, sub, sub, sub-basement. "Getting better, are we? Getting your meds?"

The doors opened, and Tommy was pushed out into a dark, dank tunnel with doors along both sides; the complete opposite of the hallway four floors above.

They stopped at the end, and Michael pushed the double doors open while David wheeled him in. Turning right down another tunnel, they descended further underground turning left, then left again, to arrive at a small room with a person inside.

He turned around. He was a man, a madman,

with wild hair and wilder eyes, red from experiments and raging inside, greedily eyeing off the fresh meat he had been brought. "I've been waiting for you, Tommy Ward." He whipped his chainsaw into a frenzy and revved it hard.

"Big deal," Tommy Ward said with more bravado than he'd ever felt before.

Doctor Schivack stared hard at him. "Why are you not scared of me, Tommy Ward? Everyone else is. They scream, and yell, and run in horror."

Tommy slowly stood and removed his arm and leg casts. He rubbed his arm to get the circulation going and flexed his hand to help it along. "Why would I be scared of you great-great-great-grandfather? Now, how about we get an updated and fully powered chainsaw and see how much damage we can *really* do."

GHOSTS IN THE SHADOWS

"Hey, man, watch me bomb off the end of the dock," I yelled, running down the lake's dock, tucking myself into a ball, and landing with a thudding splash into the water. I surfaced. "Score?" I yelled.

My three friends held up score cards. 8, 8 and a 7.

"Seven, aw man." I made my way to the dock and climbed out. "What did ya give me a seven for? I coulda scored three eights." I hunkered down next to Daryl, Andrew and Toby, who'd given me the seven. "From now on, man, you're getting nothing higher than that from me." I rubbed a towel over me and lay back. "Love to see what you do."

"We have the rest of the week for that," Toby said.

"No, we don't, the week's almost over, so get up now and do it," I egged him on. "Why be a wuss? We're already on the dock, no better time." I nudged him with my foot.

Daryl and Andrew agreed, and convinced him to do it since they already had.

"What are ya? Chicken?" I cackled and squawked like a chicken.

"Nah, man, I'm not." Toby angrily climbed to his feet, stormed back down the dock, and came running. "Bombs away," he yelled and splashed into the lake.

I lifted my head and held up the number 5 paddle.

"What! Five!" Toby screeched from the water.

I shrugged. "It deserves no more."

Toby climbed out and shook water over me.

"Why you—"

The camp siren blasted out and we all gathered our things. All thirty kids in my school class had a week at Camp Shadows Lake, the most popular camp for kids in our state, organised through our school as a special end of year extracurricular activity. We were lucky to be there, and had wasted no time in partaking in all of the activities. Now, we were being called for lunch.

Piling into the dining room, we lined up to get our meal, which today consisted of fat, juicy sandwiches, small cartons of juice, and jelly with lolly snakes and frogs.

Picking a table out on the veranda, we hoed into our food like starving animals, barely coming up for air to talk.

"So what did you think of this week?"

"I loved the rock climbing."

"I loved the canoeing."

"I preferred the tennis court."

We all stopped chewing to look at Toby who kept munching.

"Don't you get enough tennis at home?" I asked.

"We've been here nearly a week, and you lived at the tennis court." I looked at the others. "Is he nuts?" They shrugged. "Seriously dude, you should have gotten into all the other cool things here and left the tennis for home."

Toby stared at me, chewing thoughtfully on his sandwich. He swallowed and said, "No," and took another bite.

I shrugged. "Well then, man, stay away from me for the rest of our time here."

We finished our food and went back to the dock, which reached out into the centre of the lake. We'd read the brochure for weeks before coming, and knew that the lake was one foot deep in the shallows and ten feet deep in the centre. It was the size of a football oval and had been man-made especially for the camp. It got a good clean out before the start of every camp season, by being drained and scrubbed. So it was kind of like a big swimming pool, but looked like a lake without all the reedy rubbish clogging it up so we didn't get caught in anything when we went swimming.

The bell went off at four-thirty, signalling the end of play, which gave us one hour to shower and rest before dinner. Toby, Andrew, Daryl and I, oh, I'm Michael by the way, were all sharing a cabin with four bunk beds, nice enough bed covers, a small table with two chairs, and a small bathroom.

Each cabin looked the same, and they were all sitting back from the lake on one side of the dock. Just around the other side of the dock was the main office and dining hall. On the other side of the lake was the boat and storage sheds where canoes and a motor boat were stored.

Yep, a motor boat…for water skiing. I *loved* water skiing.

The dinner bell rang at five-thirty, and we ran for the dining hall, starving after a hard day of play. We devoured plates of spaghetti Bolognese, and ice cream for dessert, and sat up to attention when the camp counsellors approached.

"Okay kids, guess what we have planned for tonight?" Trish, one of the young counsellors, asked. Her enthusiasm bubbled over and onto us.

"What?"

"I can't hear you," she yelled, tucking her hair behind her ear.

"What?" we yelled back. Thirty kids were mighty loud.

"We are going to roast marshmallows by a campfire and tell spooky ghost stories." She wiggled her fingers spookily.

We wiggled ours back. "Ooohhh…"

Derek, a tall brunet guy about twenty, stepped forward. "Does anyone have a good story to tell?"

"Oooh, me, me," came multiple replies as hands waved in the air.

"Great. Why don't you all go and freshen up and meet us down by the lake at the big fire pit." He waved out the window to a huge space around the side of the lake, past our cabins. "And we will have marshmallows ready to go. How does that sound?"

"Great."

"Awesome."

"Cool."

"Okay kids, go and clean up and we'll meet you there."

We all raced to our cabins, cleaned up, and made it to the fire pit by dark.

"Okay kids, gather round," Trish said. "Grab a log or blanket to sit on. Grab one of our marshmallow sticks, and we'll come around and stick some on for you." She stood talking to a group of kids while the rest of us got our sticks and waited for them to be covered in marshmallow. Once everyone had their sticks ready, the counsellors helped us hold them over the fire pit without us, or the marshmallows, getting burnt. Before long we all had blackened mallow on our sticks.

I bit into mine and a hot gooey mess dripped from my lips. "Ah, hot, hot, hot," I mumbled, rolling it around in my mouth until it was cool enough to swallow. I waved a hand at my mouth to get extra air on the burnt bit.

"You should've known after a week it would be hot," Derek said. "Blow on it before you bite."

I swallowed half a can of soda and bit off some more. Ah, that was better. "Oh, my God…so good… so good…"

"Pink ones taste better than white," Andrew said, getting his stick loaded up with more pink mallows.

"Really?" I asked and tried them. "Mmm, they do."

Derek and another guy attended to the bonfire

and then sat down.

"Okay, who's ready for ghost stories?" Trish asked as another young woman helped her put the mallows away. "Who wants to go first?"

Melanie shot her hand up. "Me, Trish, me. I have a good one."

All of us boys groaned. We all knew Melanie's ghost stories, and besides which, she loved hearing the sound of her own voice.

"It was a dark and stormy night…" Melanie started.

"Bahahahaha." The rest of us laughed, making Melanie red in the face.

"Heard it all before," I called out. "It's the same story you tell *all the time*."

"Do not," she argued.

"Do too," I shot back.

"Okay kids, how about I tell *you* one." Derek cleared his throat. "It has to do with Camp Shadows Lake…" He paused.

"Ooohhh," we all went.

"Now, apparently this is based on a true story, an event that supposedly happened, but is yet to be proven."

We were enthralled.

"For there are no records of it. No police reports. No missing files. Nothing…nothing at all…" He waved his hands in front of him. "*At all.*"

"Ooohhh," we repeated, leaning forward in our seats ready to hear a story about the very camp we were at.

Derek continued. "It happened the very first

year the camp opened. The very first time it opened and…" he paused for effect, "it was the last time it was open…until this year…"

"Ooohhh…"

"How long's it been closed then?" Ben called out. "If it was open once and then shut until recently."

"Good question." Derek pointed out and rose from his seat and began pacing. "The camp had been shut for one hundred years until recently, when new owners took over, renovated, updated it, and made it all workable again."

"One hundred years," Adrian said. "What was the point?"

"Well," Derek continued. "Apparently, it has to do with the one hundredth anniversary of the event." He stopped walking and looked at all of us. "The horrible event that shut down Camp Shadows Lake…"

"Ooohhh…"

"Get on with it," I yelled out.

Derek gave me a raised brow in return. "You can't just rush a good ghost story," he said and cleared his throat. "It all started in 1916. A man by the name of Benjamin Shadows had a big idea to build a camp just for children where they could play and swim and have fun away from school. Benjamin was a wealthy man; he owned multiple sawmills and was able to supply his own wood to build the buildings needed. Work got started early in 1916, just before winter, because Benjamin wanted it ready for the coming summer. He found the perfect plot of land." Derek spread his arms out. "You're now sitting on it. He proceeded to map and plot everything out. But the main difference was, and is, that back then, the lake itself had been real, and very, very deep…" He waited.

"Ooohhh," we gave him.

"Now the townsfolk loved that their kids would have a safe place to play during the summer months and were all for the camp being built. They even pitched in to help make it. Benjamin, being the big sawmill owner, cut all of the wood from the trees he knocked down on this very property. He thought what better way to reuse the trees that were cleared than to put them back into the buildings for the kids to stay in."

"Are we getting to the point sometime?" Adrian called out.

Derek gave him the evil eye as we all booed Adrian.

"The story of Camp Shadows Lake cannot be rushed," Derek said before continuing. "Day after day, Benjamin knocked down trees, carted them back to his mills, cut them up and stored them. Once the ground around the lake was cleared and flattened for the buildings to be built, he lugged them all back by horse and cart and built the camp buildings himself. Day after day during the cold winter months, Benjamin and the town's people hammered and nailed until a glorious two-storey building was complete. The children's rooms were on the top floor, and the office, kitchen and dining room were on the ground floor. It even had a basement where the sporting equipment was kept."

Derek paced. "On December 1st 1916, the doors to Camp Shadows Lake were opened. There was a big grand celebration with all the townsfolk and their children. Benjamin supplied food and drink and a big red ribbon that he cut to celebrate the opening of the camp he named after himself. He hired people to look after and watch over the children, like us." He waved at Trish and the other counsellors. "And bought canoes, and rackets and balls, and all sorts of fun things for the kids to do. And he had handmade all of the bunk beds himself for the kids to sleep in."

"Is this story going somewhere," Danny yelled out.

"Shhhh," the rest of us said in unison.

"For three weeks the kids came and went, everyone was happy, and the camp was a big success. As Christmas neared, it was announced that on December 23rd it was going to be closed for two days and then reopen on the 26th." He paused. "Sadly, that was not to be...

"Twenty children were staying here on December 22nd, the last night before the last day. They all had an awesome week, and had a wonderful dinner, and remember, many of the kids came from poor families, so this was their only time to get a decent meal. They all went to bed upstairs full, well fed, and happy. But..."

His eyes flicked to the shadows of the lake, and he peered out over it, *into* it. Glancing up at the full moon, he started again. "Sometime during the night, a fire broke out in the kitchen. Now, remember, back then the building was wood so definitely not fireproof, and many people used kerosene lamps for light, so it was thought that one had been left on and ended up setting the building on fire. Well, the building went up like the Hindenburg. Kids were screaming; counsellors were frantically running around trying to put the fire out. And because the bedrooms were upstairs, some of the counsellors managed to unlock the doors and get the kids out, telling them to run for the lake. Unfortunately, because of the material their nightwear was made of, some of the children were on fire. The building was on fire and raging out of control, and all anyone could do was race for the lake to cool off or put the fire out."

He stopped, with sadness on his face. "The counsellors tried to put the burning children out, and succeeded, but…because some of the children couldn't swim, and because of the clothes they were wearing, they couldn't stay afloat."

Our heads all spun towards the lake at the terrified scream of a child. It repeated, and we stood as one. It repeated, and Trish laughed. "Sorry 'bout that, just a night bird. Take your seats."

We huddled together on our logs, and the cries echoed in our ears.

"The counsellors tried to save the children, but, because it was a natural lake, full of weeds and vines and God knows what else, the burning children slipped out of their grasp and under the water."

"Oh," Melanie and the girls gasped, hands covering mouths and faces at the horror those poor children must have experienced.

"And because the counsellors kept diving and searching for the kids, they ended up perishing. By now, the townspeople had awakened to the news the camp was on fire and rushed down to put it out. Benjamin Shadows led the way, throwing bucket after bucket of water onto the blaze. Once daylight came, and the building collapsed, they searched for bodies, but found none. That's when a young woman screamed. She'd found the body of a young child floating on the lake. The townsfolk raced down and into the water. More bodies floated to the surface, but they had to drain the lake for the others. They had been caught in vines and muck on the bottom. That was the last day the camp was open. It was shut down and not reopened until this year, by, none other, a descendant of Benjamin Shadows.

"What happened to him? Benjamin?"

"Word has it he was driven out of town and rebuilt his sawmills somewhere else. He never opened a camp again. Well." Derek clapped his hand together. "Time for bed. Trish, Jan, get the kids to bed and the rest of us will put out the bonfire."

We all got to our feet; stunned by the story we'd just been told. I shivered, and glanced around, wondering if those children were watching us now from the shadows. We followed Trish back to camp and were all escorted from cabin to cabin.

"Dude, do you think that story was real?" Toby

asked, changing into his bedclothes.

I shrugged. "Derek said there was no proof, just a story."

"Doesn't mean it's not real," Andrew said, climbing into bed.

"True," I replied and hit the bathroom before bed.

Daryl locked and double-locked the door and windows, then checked and double-checked them.

"Dude, calm down," I told him, flicking off the bathroom light. "Nothing's gonna happen."

"You don't know that," he said and fearfully slid into bed.

I jumped into mine and flicked out the bedside light. "Don't think about it."

"Can't help it," Andrew said. "That story was dead set creepy."

"Yeah," Toby added. "It's going to give me nightmares for the rest of my life."

We heard other kids getting ready for bed, and the counsellors call out to each of the cabins. We were all locked up for the night.

After five minutes of darkness and complete silence, Toby turned the light back on. "Dude, I can't do this. I can't sleep without a light."

I looked over at him in the lower bunk opposite me. "It was kinda creepy without it." I tugged the covers up under my chin.

Andrew leant over the bunk above me. "I don't know if I can deal with sleeping tonight. That story's got me freaked out."

"Yep," Daryl leaned up on his elbow in the other

top bunk. "To think that we're here, on the same land, a hundred years after it happened. And," he paused for dramatic effect, "you know it's the 22nd of December? We're heading home tomorrow."

We all looked at each other as we'd forgotten about the date.

"Is it? Get out," I said. "Let's go to sleep."

Even with the light on, we all managed to drift off, as somehow, it gave us a sense of security. If we could see the cabin, we'd know we were safe. But somewhere, in the middle of the night, we were all awakened.

At first, it was a stirring, something taunting us, teasing us to wake up, then, rousing us out of our deep slumber with shouting and screaming.

"Fire, fire."

"Everybody out."

The counsellors were banging on our cabin door, dragging us out of our beds.

"Fire, everybody out."

We tumbled through the door and down the stairs, falling over each other on our way out.

"Fire, fire."

"Everybody out."

Screams, cries, searing heat, boiling flames, burning.

We saw the dining hall on fire and the camp counsellors aiming the fire hose at it, but the fire was too fast and tore through the trees around it, heading for the office beside it.

The embers floated like hellish little demons through the air, igniting grass and trees dried from the heat of an early summer. The angry little tykes spread to our cabins, setting them ablaze, chomping with the ferocity of a freight train.

"Get to the water, get into the lake," Derek yelled, waving us all toward the lake.

The girls ran screaming into the water, covering themselves so embers didn't set them alight. The rest of us followed suit.

"We've rung the fire brigade," Brock, another counsellor called out. "They're on their way and said to stay away from the fire."

We all stood waist deep in the lake, shivering despite the heat radiating from the blazing inferno around us. It was spreading fast, picking up any piece of dry leaf, grass, tree, bush, brush. It was ripping all the way around the lake, surrounding us on all sides.

I wondered if this is what hell was like.

We huddled together, continually splashing ourselves to say wet. Screams echoed through the night, making their way above the roar of the fire. I glanced around. It wasn't any of us.

"Oh, my God, look," Melanie cried out, pointing toward the building.

We turned to look at the burning dining hall which just happened to be built on the same spot the original dorm and kitchen were on. But it wasn't the burning ruins of the hall that she was pointing to. It was the children screaming down to the water's edge.

Wait, what children?

I looked around; we were in the water, so there

were no other children.

Oh, my God.

We watched the ghosts of the children from that fateful night one hundred years ago come screaming into the water. Young adults came tearing after them, trying to put out the burning ones. They came straight for us, went straight through us with a deathly cold chill, and out into the middle of the lake.

Their screams and cries had the backdrop of a raging fire and the colour of raging hell.

We watched them wet themselves down; we watched them struggle, sliding under the water, struggling to surface, slipping again and again only to fight their way back up one last time before sinking beneath the water.

The counsellors from then screamed and yelled their names, diving, ducking, trying to rescue them, only to meet the same fate. The last ones flailed, arms slapping against the choppy water trying to keep themselves up, only to fail and sink away into the deep dark depths.

They were the children who went to summer camp.

They were the children who died that night.

They were the Ghosts of Shadows Lake.

ABOUT THE AUTHOR

T.K. is a children's TV show veteran who loves watching disaster and creature/zombie movies and TV shows, but not at night.

T.K. started writing many a year ago back in primary school, but only started her author career in 2015 with the release of her first three stories and anthology. She will write and release stories until there are twelve *Bones* books and a special edition numbered 13...

T.K. lives in Australia, loves extra cheesy cheeseburgers and chocolate, and gets a kick out of watching funny dog and cat videos.

T.K. Wrathbone is the kid's/tween pen name for author Tiara King. You can find more about Tiara on her website; follow her on social media, or visit her publishing house, Royal Star Publishing.

SOCIALS

tkwrathbone.com

tiaraking.com.au

royalstarpublishing.com.au

Sign up for *Tiara's* Newsletter…

Make sure you're always in the know and never miss free exclusives, the latest news, book updates, and so much more with newsletters from…

tiaraking.com.au

HAVE YOU READ THESE?

Next Top Mannequin
Cinderfella and Princess Charming: Witch Hunters
www.badluck-youredead.com
The Bones of Wrath: Changes
One Bone: Anthology 1

The Orphanage
Hantel and Gresel: Food Critics
Mirror, Mirror On The Wall
The Bones of Wrath: Haunted
Two Bone: Anthology 2

The Howler
Shadow Walkers
Faded
The Bones of Wrath: Ghosts
Three Bone: Anthology 3

I Spy With My Little Eye
Knock, Knock…Who's Dead?
It Creeped At Midnight
The Bones of Wrath: Monsters
Four: Anthology 4

OR THESE?

Trick Or Treat
All Hallows Possession
They Rise On A Blood Moon
The Bones of Wrath: Horrors
Five Bone: Anthology 5

All Clowns Must Die!
The Demon Resides
Infestation
The Bones of Wrath: Terrors
Six Bone: Anthology 6

www.ingramcontent.com/pod-product-compliance
Lightning Source LLC
Chambersburg PA
CBHW032058180726
48284CB00002B/334